Murder of a Parish Priest

Joseph Roderick

PublishAmerica
Baltimore

ISBN: 1-4241-3224-X
PUBLISHED BY PUBLISHAMERICA, LLLP
www.publishamerica.com
Baltimore

Printed in the United States of America

To my children: Meryl, Melissa and Jason

MURDER OF A PARISH PRIEST

Joseph Roderick

CHAPTER I

The small number of Italians who came to the city in the late eighteen and early nineteen hundreds were not part of the immigration wave from the Mediterranean that swept into the big cities on the east coast of the United States. The Sicilians who peopled New York and Providence and Boston and Philadelphia were not attracted to Fall River. The Italians who came here, came as quarry workers and stone cutters. They came to quarry the granite of the ledges; the granite that would be used to build the cotton mills that rose along the Quequechan River running through the middle of the city and along the Taunton River, forming the western boundary of the city. They used brick to build the cotton mills in Pawtucket and Lowell and Lawrence, but the Italian immigrants in Fall River drilled deep into the ground to cut out the massive blocks of granite which underlay the city. These were cut into smaller blocks and made up the durable building blocks for the large factories which soared over the tenements of the city streets and still remain today.

Like most immigrants, the Italians lived close to each other in a part of the city that became known as their section, and still is today, even though their numbers have diminished as other groups moved into the area. The church and their parish became the defining point of the neighborhood, along with a small park called Magellan Park located in front of the church. Magellan Park became the focal point for activities associated with the Italian sub-culture for years to come. On Columbus Day there were fireworks and patriotic speeches and feasting, all centered in the church or the park. At night there was a dinner at the Sons of Italy Hall, cooked by the ladies of the parish and later by caterers from Federal Hill in Providence who specialized in Italian meals. The men played bocci and drank their wine in a club next door to the park and the park was never without activity except in the dead of winter when the ground was frozen over.

The church was built by the early parishioners and was to be the only Italian parish in the city. The church was built on Harold Street, and not surprisingly, close to Harold's ledge, which was a major source of granite for the city for many years. After the first immigration of Italian stone cutters and masons, there were only dribs and drabs of relatives who managed to enter the city, and after the first significant immigration, newcomers tended to be small in number. The Italians, for whatever reason, were not mill workers and adapted very poorly to working in the factories. So, whereas the Portuguese immigrants from the Azores came to make a living in the mills, the Italians were more likely to use their skillful hands to work in construction. The women joined the other immigrant women in the sewing shops, but the men needed the outdoors to survive. Oddly enough, the church was built out of brick and not of granite. The men quarried the great slabs of granite but couldn't afford to build their own church from it, but instead chose yellow brick. The church was named the Church of Saint Francis.

I am Noah Amos and I was brought up in what we called Saint Francis. My real parish was the Portuguese parish of Santa Maria, but because I liked to hear the preacher speak in Italian at the seven o'clock mass each Sunday, I chose to go to Saint Francis. My mother and father, respecting my love of the sound of the language, went along with me and we attended the Sunday mass on every Sunday of the year except on Easter Sunday when we did our Easter Duty at our duly assigned church. Masses were still in Latin then, and the priest, when they finally got an Italian pastor, gave the homily in Italian. So, in essence, we didn't understand a word that was being said in the whole mass, but I loved to hear the languages being spoken. I finally convinced the pastor to allow me to be an altar boy at the Italian mass and from that I began to understand some of the spoken word. My mother was fearful that we would someday have need of one or the other of the churches when it came time for burial, and we would, for some reason, be rejected by both. As it turned out, that wasn't the case. When my father died he was buried out of Saint Francis, since we had been three of its faithful for so many years.

When my old friend, the pastor of Saint Francis retired, I found it difficult to attend mass at the church. My mother and father had passed away and my favorite priest was gone and it seemed too painful for me to attend mass in that church that was so full of good memories for me. And the memories were good, so when I learned that the parish priest had been found murdered in the sacristy behind the main altar, it came as a shock. I knew him well and I still thought of him as the "young priest", although at the time of his murder he was in his early sixties. Patrick, my neighbor and the District Attorney of Bristol County, knew of my association with the parish and called me immediately to accompany him to the scene of the murder. I called my associate Jack Crawford who lived next door to Patrick and in no time at all we were on our way to Fall River and the Church of Saint Francis. Marge, with whom I lived, of course, went with us. Patrick knew very little about the situation that awaited us, except that the priest who was found dead had been identified as Father D'Angellini. He had been shot in the chest three times at close range.

We were living on Westport Point. Jack lived in the house his parents had used for a summer home. He, like me, was in his seventies and retired. He had inherited his parents' house and had it winterized so that he could spend his retirement years close to the ocean. He had been born in the nearby city of Fall River, but had left after finishing college to go to Manhattan where he had worked as a textile broker. He had made a substantial fortune in the stock market and although he retired from the brokerage house at which he had worked, he still kept up his interest in the stock market. He had brought his wife to the Point when she was dying of cancer and he had been widowed for two years or so when I met him.

I live across the road from Jack and Patrick. I had been left a beautiful, fully restored colonial home by a former student of mine who had died of complications due to AIDS. The inheritance came out of the blue. I had had the boy as a student in junior high school and when he died, since he had no family, he had thought of me and left me the house and his properties in Greenwich Village. Under no circumstances could I have even thought of ever owning such a house. I am a retired school teacher and I had spent most of my life trying desperately to balance my check book and to keep ahead of the bill collector. For the past five years I have lived with no worry about money. In fact, I have spent more time wondering what to do with it. My wife left me some forty-five years ago and I have never remarried. About three years ago I met a woman with whom I fell in love and we have lived together ever since. Marge is my companion now, and, I hope until I die.

The drive to the city took fifteen minutes and before I knew it I found myself in my old neighborhood. It has changed surprisingly little in the past seventy years. The streets are wider and there are more automobiles and traffic but my friends of years ago would feel right at home in the old neighborhood. Magellan Park is now a Little League park and a basketball court has replaced the volleyball court, but there are few new stores and the area has maintained its authenticity despite all the changes that have taken place in the city. The church looks exactly as it did when I was young, although it is now air conditioned and has an elevator so that older people and those that are handicapped need not brave the long flight of stairs leading to the entrance. I can remember how my father had trouble negotiating the steps at the end of his active life.

We pulled up in front of the church, but I led them to the side stairs to the entrance by one of the two side altars that led back to the sacristy. It was only a few steps from the entrance to the back of the side altar and the area was crowded with police and some of the District Attorney's men.

Patrick immediately asked the police to leave so that things would not be so confusing. There wasn't much room behind the main altar to begin with and the area in the back of the side altar was small by any measurement; certainly not big enough to hold ten or more people. The room cleared out quickly and I could see Father D'Angellini's body. He was lying on the floor almost in a sleeping position, with his arms by his side. He was lying on his side. There were dried blood spots on his black vest where he had been shot, but there was not a great deal of blood around him. He was a big man in height and girth and it seemed odd to see him lying in a sleeping position in what seemed like repose.

Before we knew it the cameraman arrived to take pictures. The sun came in the east window of the small room and cast a strong light into the small space. The cameraman was using a flash and the glare from the flash and the sunlight made my eyes smart and I almost wished I had worn sunglasses. Every time he shot a picture, I could see the light reflecting off something close to the priest's body and I asked Patrick to see what it was. He moved the body only slightly and with a plastic glove on his hand, picked up an object under Father D'Angellini's hand. It was what looked like a silver coin, but I immediately recognized it as a pocket rosary. It was a small disc, the size of a half dollar that the devout carried in their pockets as a readily accessible way to say their prayers and the rosary without the necessity of carrying beads.

"He must have known it was coming," I said. "He reached into his pocket and said his last prayers before the killer shot him."

Patrick said, "You're probably right. This wasn't the place for him to be saying prayers under normal conditions, I would guess."

"No, he was the kind of man who was always running to and fro and in a hurry. I can't imagine him praying in this place; what we would think of as a work area. He would be using this only to finish up something to prepare for tomorrow's mass. He wouldn't even use this as a place to talk to parishioners," I said.

Jack said, "Noah, can you show me the layout here? I have no idea how a church is set up."

"Before we leave here, Father D'Angellini was famous for always carrying his breviary with him everywhere he went. It was his calling card. He must have it somewhere here. Could you look for it Patrick, while I show Jack and Marge the layout of the church?" I asked.

I led them out to the front of the church where Jack could see the floor plan of the church.. There was an entry when you entered through the front doors. The doors were six feet across and the entrance was twelve feet from wall to wall. On the left rear after entering was a crying room that was glassed in and gave mothers and fathers a chance to attend mass with their little children without disturbing the proceedings. At the right rear of the church were the two confessionals which were hardly used in the present day. I can remember standing in line waiting for a confessional to be open. Confessions were held on Saturday at four o'clock in the afternoon and it was normal for most people to confess at least once a month, so that the priests were busy every Saturday. Today, no one bothers. I don't even know if confessions are even scheduled regularly any more.

The central aisle leads from the back entrance to the altar rail and is flanked on either side by rows of pews which are even in length and run to two side aisles which in turn are bordered by shorter rows of pews which run to the outside walls. There are tall stained glass windows on both sides of the building and one large circular window on the back wall of the church above the altar. For morning masses the effect of the sun coming through the east windows can be quite moving. At the top of the central aisle close to the entrance are a holy water fount and a poor box. Walking down the middle aisle one sees the altar all in white and for Sunday mass, decorated with flowers. In the middle of the altar and atop it is located a statue of Saint Francis holding the traditional lamb while a bird rests on his shoulder. On both sides of the church are the Stations of the Cross and I wondered if people still prayed at the designated areas showing the death of Christ as they did when I was young. On either side of the main altar were two side altars which, as far as I could ever determine, served only for decoration. I had never seen them used for anything but housing Christmas and Easter displays.

To Marge and me, this was all familiar territory, but to Jack it was completely new. Jack had been brought up in the minority in Fall River, which is probably ninety percent Catholic. His mother attended the Congregational Church, but his father was not a churchgoer and much to his mother's disappointment, neither was Jack. Like many non-Catholics he had many misconceptions about the Church, but I felt no need to disabuse him of them at this point. The most important thing was to get him to see where Father D'Angellini lived and worked.

Jack stood by my side as he looked at the main altar and the statues which were on pedestals in different areas of the church. I really hadn't paid much attention to them over the years. They were there but I hadn't really focused on them but I could see how a person new to the church, would be aware of them as he scanned the church interior. He asked who they represented and I spent a few minutes giving the names of Saint Anthony and St. Michael and the Virgin Mary and St. John the Baptist.

We returned to the rear of the main altar through the aisle formed by the small space between the main altar and the side altar that we had used as an entry. The photographer had just finished his work and one of the men was dusting for prints.

Patrick said, "There is no sign of a breviary, Noah."

I said, "Now, that is definitely odd. I don't think I ever saw Father without it. One of the parishioners once kidded him by saying he was the only person he knew who went swimming with a breviary in his hand."

"Well, it may have been dropped somewhere, but it isn't here. Except for those three gunshot wounds, there doesn't seem to be any signs of violence on the body. The coroner should be here any moment now, and he will take a better look at the body," Patrick said.

One of the policemen came in and whispered something to Patrick. He didn't know Marge, Jack and me and must have felt that he couldn't talk openly with strangers in the room.

Patrick smiled and said, "We have a visitor from the Bishop's staff wanting to know what happened. I had better see to him now." He turned to the young policeman and said, "Have him meet me in the church. I'll be right out. I prefer that he didn't come back here."

Patrick was dressed in a dark blue suit and he was wearing a light blue shirt and tie. He looked very professional and dapper. Jack wore his usual outfit of khakis, penny loafers without socks, and a wrinkled shirt and compared to Patrick the best thing one could say was that he was neat and clean. Women would have been taken with his handsome face and full head of blond, graying hair and tall unbent physique, but the young policeman who saw him standing next to the District Attorney would not have been impressed. I, too, did not look like I belonged in the company of the District Attorney while he was investigating a case. I'm sure he saw Marge as merely a hanger-on. But Jack and Marge and I had proven our mettle with Patrick and he used us wherever and whenever he thought we could be of use to him in solving a case. We had run into skepticism a number of times before, and we had become used to it and could actually understand how the young professionals felt about us. Jack thought it was funny and made a joke of it whenever a situation arose, but I admit that I had been offended by our treatment on more than one occasion.

The Bishop's representative met Patrick in the apse of the church while we were left to await the coroner who would give the body a cursory inspection and pronounce him officially dead. He would then most likely ask that the body be shipped to Woods Hole on Cape Cod for an autopsy if Patrick thought it was necessary. There wasn't very much to see while we waited. The room was small with a single window. It allowed some light into the back of the church. Without the overhead light the corners of the room would be dark even as the sun rose over the church itself. Father D'Angellini's body lay untouched on the floor and I was tempted to put a pillow under his head so that he could rest comfortably even in death.

Why would someone want to kill a priest? Jack always began with the assumption that most crime had to do with greed and money. In this particular case, I doubted that that would be true.

"Jack," I said, "I don't think your idea that the motive is usually money, will apply here."

14

"Why not?" Jack asked.

"Well, unless I am badly mistaken, I don't think Father had much of any money. He certainly wasn't poor, but I doubt if he accumulated very much in his position here at the church. Whether he had any money left to him by his family, I don't know. I leave the details to you, Jack. I'm sure within the week, you'll have a financial statement for us," I said jokingly.

"I am sure I will and I'll bet you dollars to donuts that money is mixed up in this somewhere," he said, and he wasn't smiling. "If there was anything I learned in Manhattan, working there all those years, it is that money is the greatest source of evil in existence and that for almost every crime, the root cause is the almighty dollar. I have seen the nicest men become vicious when it came to cheating their partners. It was as if they became different people when it came to money. But you've heard all of this before from me, Noah, so we shall see what we shall see."

Patrick returned very shortly. The Bishop's representative had no desire to see the body, but wanted to be kept abreast of any developments in the case as we went along. He asked that there be no surprises. He emphasized that the Bishop did not like surprises.

Patrick was annoyed and we knew enough about Patrick to know that it took a great deal to annoy him. "Imagine telling me that the Bishop does not like surprises. Not one word about the poor dead priest. He wasn't even curious about how the man was killed. His only concern was that the Bishop should not be embarrassed in any way. I am sure the Bishop would be more concerned about the dead man who was one of his priests than about being incommoded by his murder. At least I would hope that he would. I've never run into this priest before and I am not looking forward to working with him on this."

Jack and I both laughed because this was so unlike Patrick, who was normally very quiet and unruffled.

Jack said, "You had better be careful Patrick, if you keep showing your emotions this way, you may end up loosening the knot of your tie and unbuttoning the top button of your shirt."

"Back to the blue suit?" he asked.

He was referring to the time when we first met him and we were working on a case with Nelly, who later became his wife. He was an Assistant District Attorney then and was never to be seen without a dark blue suit, white shirt and striped tie. We called him the "blue suit". We worked on a case with him and soon learned that he was an admirable young man who deserved our affection and in Nelly's case, her love.

He gave some indication of what he was thinking about in this case and we quickly determined what our immediate roles would be. Jack was to investigate Father's finances and Marge and I were to talk to as many of the older parishioners as we could, that I knew personally, to get some feel for what was happening in the parish and what might have led to Father's brutal murder. Patrick would put his resources to work in picking up as much information as he could. The inspection of the body would be a high priority as well as a thorough search of what was presumed to be the murder area. All of the details involved in a professional investigation were not the domain of Jack and me or Marge and we were more than happy to turn them over to the professionals. From our point of view, we wanted as much help as we could get.

CHAPTER II

That evening over dinner of a hearty beef stew and freshly made corn bread, we shared what we had seen and learned. Marge was particularly interested in the case. She had been brought up in the Catholic Church and the murder of a priest went too far for her to take as a matter of course. She had always had a deep respect and almost awe for the priesthood and suddenly she was confronted by a murdered man who wore a black suit and white collar. Whereas I had become a lapsed Catholic, she had remained a churchgoer to the present day. Marge was my companion. She was a widow in her late sixties whom I had met through Patrick's mother-in-law. She had been married to a man whom she had loved for many years. We met, enjoyed each other's company and before we knew it we were living together very happily. I felt extremely fortunate to have made her a part of my life.

She had made dinner for the three of us. Let me say from the beginning that Jack has an enormous appetite and yet has no idea how to cook and has no inclination to learn. As he says so often, cooking for himself would result in eating lots of cold cereal with milk and a variety of soups out of cans. He was a man who could be described as a "meat and potatoes" guy. His idea of a good meal was a large steak, barely scorched, with a large baked potato on the side with a big chunk of Italian bread. With a glass of beer to wash it down and a big dish of Ben & Jerry's ice cream to follow, he was a happy man. As for me, I don't pretend to be a gourmet chef, but when my wife left me some forty odds years ago, I found I had no choice but to learn to cook in a hurry. Restaurants didn't serve the kind of food I felt I could live on for long periods of time and I couldn't afford them on a teacher's salary. So I took advantage of the public library to borrow some cook books to teach me the basics and to get some recipes that were within my range. From the beginning I aimed at making meals that weren't too difficult to prepare, but that gave me a minimum of two meals or even, hopefully, three. Soups and chowders became what I thought of as my specialty. The advantage to them was that they got better with age and after two days in the refrigerator, were better than the first day they were made.

The stew we were having for dinner tonight fell within my specifications for a perfect meal. Marge made it with the best quality beef cut into chunks, onions, carrot, potatoes, sweet potato, turnip and mushrooms along with a goodly portion of diced tomato. Seasoned with fresh thyme and parsley it made a meal fit for Jack's kingdom.

Now Marge and I share the cooking. It was fun having Jack to cook for since he was so appreciative of everything we made. He was never one to complain. As long as there was enough, and the food was wholesome, he was not the least bit fussy. Jack was a gentleman and although he let us prepare his food, he always showed his appreciation to both of us for the trouble he knew we went through to keep his appetite at bay.

"There isn't much that we know at this point," I said. "The only thing we know for sure is that he was shot at close range. He was shot three times in the chest. It had to have been a small caliber revolver because he was not thrown back. It looks to me like he just dropped to the floor. His hair wasn't even messed up."

"Why would someone want to kill that man? He wasn't the kind of man that made enemies, if I remember him rightly," Marge said.

Jack said, "Then you knew him too?"

"Oh, sure. I think everybody knew Father D'Angellini. I didn't know him well and I don't think I ever really had a conversation with him. He was one of those priests who was always asking for something for his church. Everyone knew that his church was Saint Francis. He tried to make friends with everybody and he was successful. He had more out-of-parish people attending his church than his own parishioners, I think."

"So, he could have had money then," Jack said.

"I have no idea," Marge said.

"Knowing him, Jack, I think you are going to find out that he had reasonable but minimal funds. He certainly didn't have the kind of money that would make him a target of a killer. But you will have to find that out for yourself," I said. "Right now I need to clear my head with a walk on the beach. Do I have any takers?"

"I would love to walk, Noah," Marge said. "Let me pull some clothes together."

The Point, as we refer to it, is a peninsula that ends in Westport Harbor where the waters of the Westport River meet before they flow into the Atlantic Ocean. The point at which they flow into the ocean marks the end of the Buzzard Bay Watershed which extends all the way from Westport to Cape Cod. Horseneck Beach, one of the hidden treasures of the coastline, runs from the channel where the waters of the harbor rush into the open sea to about three quarters of a mile to the east. The sand is white and fine and is bordered on the north by sand dunes which rise high above the beach area.

From our house high on Westport Point it was only a five minute walk to the beach as the crow flies, but we had to drive or walk north to the road leading to the highway to allow us to get over the harbor via an old bridge which seemed to be constantly under repair. From there it was only a few minutes to the beach by car. We usually drove, because walking along the busy highway was dangerous. We parked in the Westport Resident's parking lot and walked through and over the dunes to the beach.

The beach was deserted as it often was in April before the rush of sun worshippers made their appearance. Normally, in April and May, the only people who used the beach were walkers like ourselves or dog walkers who let their pets run in and out of the water or along the shore. When we cleared the dunes, we felt the wind coming off the water and I asked Marge if she was willing to walk into it. I found it cleared my brain to walk directly into the breeze. It would have been too cold in January and February, but in April it was refreshing.

On only a rare day were we able to talk on the beach in the spring. The wind pretty much made it impossible to hear the spoken word unless we were shouting. Marge took my hand and we bent into the breeze and moved slowly to the hard packed sand just above the water line. There we could walk without sinking into the soft sand. Once, Marge bent to pick up a perfect scallop shell which she showed me before slipping it into her pocket. There weren't many times when we walked that she didn't find a shell that she wanted. This one was a perfect half and I had visions of her serving a scallop nestled in the shell.

The birds overhead were making a ruckus, fighting for available food. The terns and sea gulls were being tossed in the breeze and from time to time would dive into the water to pick up some bit of flotsam they could see from above. The sandpipers were chasing the waves back into the water looking for the little animals they fed off. I marveled at how much energy they expended to get the food they needed for nourishment. Now and then a large wave broke into the shore and we found ourselves being sprayed by the droplets of water thrown into the air.

I held Marge's hand and it occurred to me how lucky I was to have her as a companion. The first sixty-five years of my life had been a struggle at times, but my latter years were a miracle that I could never have dreamt would happen. I had my health, more money than I could ever spend, and a good friend in Jack and a lovely companion with whom I spent my hours. Father D'Angellini lay dead in the morgue. What trick of fate had brought that about? That was the puzzling question to which I had to seek an answer.

I suppose that's what I meant by clearing my mind. In fact, it was not a clearing like a fire going through a hayfield that left nothing but scorched earth. It was more like a fresh breeze blowing through sheets hung on a clothesline leaving behind it a scented white flowing width of cotton cloth waving in the sun and wind.

The picture I had in my mind was of Father D'Angellini standing in that little area where he stood in preparation for every mass he ever said at the church. Someone was standing in front of him holding a gun and he knew that he was going to be shot. What went through his mind then? Was he fearful? Did he think he could persuade his assailant to hand over the weapon without using it? Did he beg? Did he pray? That was the hard part, trying to put myself in his place or at least to imagine what he had felt.

I remembered when he had first come to the church. The old priest, or at least we called him the old priest, had been the first Italian priest in the parish. Prior to him, I could remember an Irish priest who ran the church like he was in charge of a prison and was acting as the warden over a bunch of romantic, unruly Italians who were an emotional lot. Father Sperdutti was welcomed by the parishioners as if he were a savior come to free them from the prison. To have what they considered to be one of their own, was more than they could ask for.

I was disappointed when I learned that he would not allow a baseball team for the CYO League unless the team was sponsored by one of the local businesses who would supply all of the equipment and unless a manager were to come out of one of the parishioners. It was a small parish and there weren't many baseball players available for the team so that under the best of circumstances, players would have to be imported from other parishes. Fortunately, one of the parishioners was an administrator of a large construction firm out of Rhode Island and he was able to persuade his boss to come up with the necessary funds to get the team off the ground. This was in the late 1930's when money was scarce and people were not really too worried about baseball or keeping their young children off the streets. I was too young to think about playing then, but the idea of having a team close by seemed pretty wonderful. Most boys my age dreamed about playing for the Boston Red Sox or New York

Yankees, but when I saw the new uniforms and the bats and balls and gloves, I wanted nothing more than to someday play for the Saint Francis baseball team even though it wasn't long before the team was called the "SF Spaghetti Benders."

The way the pastor handled the question of a baseball team became his modus operandi. He refused the parishioners nothing as long as they could come up with the money. It was as straightforward as that. The parish was small and money was scarce. Father Sperdutti had to pay the utility bills and the many bills that came with running a large building. Fortunately he had sufficient free help so that there was never any need to pay workmen for services to the small church. But, the running of the church during the Depression was a heavy weight that he bore with humor and good will. He was a bright man who had studied in Rome and was hand-picked to serve in this small parish and to aid the Bishop in the financial affairs of the diocese.

Father D'Angellini came to the parish after Father Sperdutti became a Monsignor. Whereas Monsignor Sperdutti was thought of as a liberal priest, Father D'Angellini was a conservative priest adhering strictly to the laws of the Church as he saw them.

But, he was neither liberal nor conservative now; he was dead and now it was for us to find the murderer.

Marge and I finished our walk and I felt a great deal better for it.

CHAPTER III

The first person I wanted to talk to was Dino. Dino had been the sexton in the church for close to forty years and had retired only two years ago. If anybody knew what had been going on in the church that would lead to murder, I was sure that Dino Lagozza would know.

I called him and he invited me to his second floor tenement on the corner across the street from the church. I asked Marge to come along with me to offer a different insight into what we would be hearing in our interviews. I knew most of the people in the church and they remembered me, so it wasn't as if they would be talking to a stranger in talking to me. Marge wouldn't affect their willingness to talk so I'd no concern about her accompanying me. I admit that I was rather proud of her and wanted some of the older people who had known me as a young man to see the lovely woman I had met.

We entered the tenement by the side door and made our way up to the second floor. I could have sworn that I smelled spaghetti sauce simmering on someone's stove and Marge agreed when I mentioned it to her. One of the things I always remember about tenements is the smell of cooking.

Dino opened the door for us and I found him very old looking. I had attended his retirement dinner not so long ago and he had looked good then. He was a handsome man, a tad overweight, but a good looking sturdy man when I had last seen him. Now he walked with a cane and was having some pain. When he sat in his rocker, I could see that he sank back in relief.

"Damned sciatica drives me crazy. It runs right down my right leg. The doctors claim I have arthritis in the lower discs in my spinal chord. Whatever it is, Noah, it is enough to drive me crazy," he said.

I introduced him to Marge and he greeted her with a big smile.

"I don't know what you have to do with this guy, Marge," he said, "but he is a peach. One of the nicest kids we turned out of this place."

We both laughed at the kid remark since he could not have been too much older than I was.

I recalled that he liked to feel important around the church. I'm sure he wasn't paid much money, but he wanted to feel as close to the church as possible. He wanted to be thought of as a church official and not as custodial help. He was respected by the parishioners as a rather humble, hard working man who could always be counted on to help people out. If there was a family in dire straits, Dino could be counted on to talk to Monsignor Sperdutti. If he was a bit of a busybody, it could be overlooked considering the good he did in the church.

He sat back in his chair and said, "I know you're here about Father D'Angellini. I was shocked when I heard about it. Glad I wasn't there to find him. I'd have had a heart attack right on the spot. He never took the place of the Monsignor for me or for you either Noah, I know, but that is no way to die."

I didn't say anything but let him gather his thoughts and go on. If I remembered correctly Dino never needed any encouragement to talk. He was everyone's confidant, but at the same time there weren't many secrets that were kept secret once he had wind of them. We often said that the last person any one would want to confess to would be Dino.

"Father had a hard time being second in command here. He always wanted to run things his way. Monsignor was from a different school when it came to money. As soon as the church starting doing okay during the war, he was always giving money away for this and that. There wasn't a poor family in the parish that he didn't try to help out. Father wasn't big on giving money away. He wouldn't even give me a raise when Monsignor retired. He had me working for the same pay for the last six years I worked. He was cheap. We had some awful fights about money," he said.

"Do you think that's why someone wanted to kill him?" I asked.

"Noah, you know better than that. He was cheap, but he would never cheat anybody for money. Whatever it was, his problem wasn't money. It had to be something else. He wasn't a man you could get to know. I worked for him a long time and I really never got to know him. Take the stars, for instance. He had this weird fascination with the stars. He kept telling me he was going to learn all about them. One day he said to me, 'Dino, I am going to know the location of every constellation one of these days. I'll study the sky every night until I know all about the stars.' He never did. For an educated man, he never read a book or had any idea of beautiful things. Ever know anybody like that Miss? He couldn't see beauty in anything; music, flowers, words. Nothing was beautiful for him," he said this with a sense of mystery in his voice as if he could not believe how a man could live without appreciating beauty.

"Put a meal in front of him and you know he didn't care what you served him. Spaghetti, lasagna, chicken soup; he ate whatever he was served," he said.

I couldn't imagine the man he was describing. It didn't seem to be the man I knew and I said so to Dino.

"That's the thing about him, Noah. What's the name of that animal that changes colors?" he asked.

Marge said, "A chameleon?"

"That's it. That really is it. The man could change his personality in the flick of an eyelash. It was just the way he was. I remember one day my sister took the kids to the Science Museum in Boston and I went with them. We saw one of those chameleons on a tree in a cage and you could hardly make it out. Then it moved and it changed colors. And I thought of Father. I know that sounds silly, but that was the man. The only thing he really wouldn't budge about was evil. Evil was what he was in the priesthood about. He hated anything evil and bad. One day we saw a rat in the garbage pail in the back yard and he went out of his mind. He made me buy every rat poison in the hardware store and we chased that rat for a week. I think the rat was long gone, but every time he went by the kitchen window he would look outside for it. If you ask me he was a little crazy sometimes."

I could see that unless I asked him direct questions we were in for a very long session.

"So, Dino, as far as you are concerned you have no idea what could have caused this, is that right? I know you well enough so you can trust me, you know that. Please help me out here," I said.

"I can't think of anything, honestly. In all the years I worked with him and for him I never remember him having any enemies. He was an old ladies' priest. They loved him. The men weren't that big on him because he was not a man's man. The young women in the parish didn't get what they wanted to hear from him," he said.

"What do you mean by that?" Marge asked.

"Well, he was the Bishop's boy. He swore by whatever the Bishop said. Everybody thinks the Pope runs the show, but the local priests have to live with the Bishop and he pulls all the strings. Monsignor Sperdutti was a free thinker. He told his parishioners what he thought was good for them. Father stuck to the words of the Bishop. If the Bishop was against birth control, so was Father, no questions asked. The young mothers would come to Monsignor for advice and he would ask them, 'Do you want more children? How does your husband feel? Are you healthy enough to have more children? Can you afford them?' Then he would tell them to use their judgment. I loved it when he would say, 'Having children is a great gift from God. But, it isn't enough to have them. You have to raise them, guide and educate them.. It is one thing to have them, but another to bring them up healthy, strong and wise and good.'"

Marge said, "He sounds like the kind of priest I would love to have known."

I said, "He was."

"The question is, would I have liked Father D'Angellini?" Marge asked.

Dino rose from his chair then and stretched his arms over his head. Even in his old age he was a man of stature. "Can't sit too long before the arthritis takes over," he said. "Funny thing ma'am, you would have liked him because he would have made you like him. He would have read you in a few minutes and then given you just what you wanted to hear. That was the thing about him. He talked enough only to listen. In no time at all he would have had you talking about yourself, telling him where you lived, what mattered to you. Before you knew it he would have known all about you. A month from then he would meet you and remember everything you told him. I guarantee you would end up liking him."

"Sounds like a bit of a hypocrite to me," Marge said and I was surprised because that was not like her.

"Oh, no. He was really interested in people. He didn't like bad people or people he thought were bad. If you were a drunk or a drug addict, he wouldn't bother with you at all. But, he was no hypocrite when it came to being nice to people."

He stopped talking then and walked back to his chair with difficulty. He sat and I could see that his leg was in pain as he grimaced.

"One thing you are going to find out about if you keep talking to people is that he had trouble with young boys," he said.

"What do you mean by trouble?" I asked.

"He was attracted to them, Noah. I don't have to go into detail. You know what I am talking about," he said.

Marge asked, "How much trouble?"

"I won't talk about that. I've told you enough already. I worked in that church for a lot of years and saw things that I don't ever talk about. I'm loyal and I don't tell stories. You'll find out soon enough without hearing it from me," he said.

I could see that Dino had had enough. He suddenly looked tired and

I thought it was time to leave. Marge caught it too, so we rose, thanked him for his time and for the information he had given us, and left quite pleased with the afternoon's work.

CHAPTER IV

Jack had started nosing around among his banker friends but after sitting in the Quequechan Club and having lunch with some businessmen he had nothing to report.

"At least I had a decent lunch. However, I did find out one thing. This man is not known among the bankers and money people. His name got nothing but a blank stare. I don't think that signifies anything except that he does not do much dealing locally, if at all. The Church of Saint Francis must have a local account, so, I'll have to get some info on that, but, per usual, I'll have to have some patience," Jack said.

We told him what we were able to discover and he was as shocked as we were to hear about the possibility that Father D'Angellini was involved with young boys.

"That is one huge surprise," he said. "That opens a can of worms."

"We won't jump to conclusions on that," I said. "We'll follow through on it for sure and I trust Dino. He wouldn't have mentioned it if it wasn't based on fact."

Jack was also quite taken with the idea that the young priest was more conservative than the old one.

"Is that a general rule; the young ones being more conservative than the old ones?" Jack asked.

"I think we have to be careful of generalities when it comes to the priesthood, Jack," I said. "There were countless reasons why each man entered the priesthood and I think we have to take each priest separately. Compare the priesthood to the teaching profession. How many reasons were there why men and women entered that profession? And, like teaching, how many stayed on even when they found that they were not suited to the profession? I know that half the people I worked with would much rather have been doing something else."

"Were you one of those Noah?" Marge asked.

"Definitely not me. I was one of the lucky ones who enjoyed every minute I was in the classroom. Just as I think you enjoyed your work, Jack," I said.

"Well, I see what you mean. In my business, though, there was no room for people who didn't fit their vocation. They could sell and make money or they couldn't. Those that couldn't, were gone in no time."

Marge said, "I personally think we make too much of the priests and too little of the Church, but that's only my angle on it. When Noah says that Father D'Angellini was a woman's priest, I have to say I have seen it any number of times. The women tend to faun over their priests as if they were some sort of Hollywood idols. It becomes ludicrous and unfortunately puts them in an odd position of having to cater to the ladies."

We left it at that and I wondered what Father D'Angellini had brought to the table. When I thought of him, I had a picture in my mind of a rather portly young man dressed in his black suit which was never quite clean enough. It seemed he always had a spot on his trousers or his jacket, that one was almost inclined to wipe off for him. Or he had little bits of dandruff sprinkled on his shoulders which shone against the blackness of his jacket. I laughed thinking about that because I, in turn, always had chalk dust somewhere on my person and one of my colleagues was always joking about my "dusting." It was the mark of my trade, although dandruff shouldn't have been that of Father's.

It was easier to say what he wasn't, rather than what he was. He was not a progressive, that, we have established. He was not an athlete nor did he take any interest in the baseball or basketball teams that had been established over the years. The kids who donned their uniforms didn't particularly care as long as they had a chance to play organized ball. The last thing they needed was a priest telling them how to behave on and off the field or court. The men who played bocci never saw the priest at the bocci court. Monsignor would stop by from time to time for a glass of wine or a mug of draft beer and try his hand at bowling one or two balls. He wasn't very good at it, but gave it his best in a self-deprecating way which pleased the older men who took their game seriously. They knew he couldn't play at their level but they liked the idea that he stopped to have a drink with them. They also liked the idea that he said a mass for them every year and asked that all the players attend on the one morning when he said the mass.

Monsignor also visited the pigeon racers. The coops were a source of great pride among the flyers and many of them who raced birds every weekend were Italian. He became their priest and attended their annual meeting to say grace and also had a mass said for them once a year. All were invited to the mass regardless of faith and he always had a good turnout for his "pigeon mass" as he liked to call it. When there was a move by the Health Department to close the coops, it was the Monsignor who represented the men at the City Council and who helped defeat the resolution. Father D'Angellini did none of these things, but oddly enough the men didn't mind. They were happy to have a friend in the Monsignor, but he was not intrusive and pretty much made himself available, without being a nuisance. When one of the men swore because he made a bad bowl, Monsignor never even lifted an eyebrow. He never tried to be one of them, but he appreciated what they were and they knew it without words being spoken.

These thoughts were going through my mind and I wondered what we would find out about Father D'Angellini before we were finished. I had the feeling that we wouldn't find the killer until we found out who this priest was. The one thing we knew for sure was that he had been shot at close range and that he had been shot three times before he had fallen to the floor. The killer had been quick. He or she had used a small caliber pistol of some kind or Father D'Angellini would have been blown off his feet by the first shot. He must have been leaning against the cabinet behind him when he was shot and that must have held him up while the killer shot two more times. At this stage, everything was pure conjecture and until we had some facts to work with, there wasn't much hope that we could find out what happened.

CHAPTER V

Jack was eager about this case, but I half suspected that he was far more interested in the possibility of eating some Italian cooking rather than finding out who killed Father D'Angellini. I had been brought up among the Italians in Saint Francis parish and I had eaten the food that came out of their kitchens all my life. For Jack it was an experience that he had not had until he left home to go to Manhattan at the start of his career. It seemed that his father had decided that pasta and rice were nothing more than poor peoples' food and he refused to have them grace his table. The closest Jack came to Italian cookery was an occasional Italian bread which his mother would pick up at one of the bakeries. On the other hand, some of my most memorable culinary experiences came as a young man at the table of my next door neighbor for whom I did errands and minor chores. She would invite me into her kitchen when I had finished what she asked me to do and if I close my eyes I can still remember the special smells that came to me.

Mrs. Guaneri made her own pasta. Her pasta did not come in the shapes that you buy today in supermarkets or even in specialty Italian stores. She rolled it out in sheets in her pasta maker and then cut the sheets, when they had arrived at their desired thinness, in different widths which hung to dry on wooden pegs. She made her sauce with whatever vegetables she had on hand. Mostly, she used combinations of plum tomatoes, onions, green or red peppers, garlic, spinach, kale, broccoli, fennel, or any other green that was available or any spice that would flavor her sauce, all cooked in pungent olive oil. The pasta would be dropped into boiling water and in no time at all would be drained and put in a big soup bowl and then sauced as needed and sprinkled with freshly ground parmesan Reggiano. It was a treat for me like no other. But the coffee was another thing. As far as I could tell she put a pot on in the morning and then kept it brewing all day, adding coffee and chickory and water all day long as needed. A small cup with four or five teaspoons of sugar would give me a "buzz" that shocked my system.

Jack's idea of good Italian food began with spaghetti and meatballs and ran the gamut through lasagna and grinder sandwiches. He was easy to please. He didn't call for fancy sauces or even homemade pasta; he wanted a large plate filled with steaming pasta covered with any tomato sauce and then sprinkled with loads of parmesan cheese. With that he was a happy man. His favorite Italian restaurants were those, very simply, that served the most food. In his mind, Italian food meant that he left the table absolutely full. When I cooked pasta for him at home, I figured twice the normal amount per serving accompanied by a fresh, Italian stick bread. Sometimes that didn't quite make it and he ended up eating another portion.

On our trip to Florence, his greatest disappointment was that he felt the portions he was served were far too small. He enjoyed the food, but couldn't get past the skimpiness of his meals. On several occasions when he was served his dish, he ordered a second dish without any hesitation. He did it with grace and good humor, much to the amazement of the waiters who couldn't quite believe the crazy American with the bottomless stomach.

But for all of that, Jack Crawford was not a glutton. He enjoyed eating, but did it slowly, savoring every mouthful. Whereas his father had not allowed pasta to be served at his dinner table, Jack would have been happy to see it as often as three nights a week. It would never take the place of a thick steak, but it certainly was not far behind.

* * *

Mrs. Sousa was not Italian. Like me, she had been an import to the parish and had brought her evangelical spirit to CCD classes and the Woman's Guild so that she played a huge role in parish affairs. She lived on the first floor of a tenement two blocks from the church and had become a widow after years of tending to her sick husband at home. When I knocked on her door with Marge at my side, she answered almost immediately. She invited us into her front parlor and we found ourselves sitting on an old-fashioned couch that felt like it hadn't been used very often. I imagined it covered with sheets all week to keep the dust off the fabric and the sunshine from fading the dark colors.

She looked Marge over very carefully and was quick to say, "I understand you are living with Noah and you are unmarried. I do not approve and I make this clear from the start. You should break away from such an arrangement immediately."

"Helen," I said, "What we do or don't do is none of your business. We are not here to be lectured to, but to find out who killed Father D'Angellini and we need any information about the man and the priest that you can give us. Now, if you want to do that, fine. If not, we will leave, but I will not allow you to lecture me or Marge. Is that understood?"

"Now, Noah," she said, "Don't be so sensitive."

She was a short woman, no more than five foot tall and she was thin and almost gnarly looking. Her fingers appeared to be arthritic and added to her appearance of looking old. I knew she was younger than I was and probably close to Marge's age. But there she was dressed in mourning-black with a black shawl over her shoulders. Her skirt was old and the black cloth was shiny and her black stockings showed at the ankles. I wondered if she wore black underwear. She wore her hair pulled back with a bun in the back, holding it tight to her head. It was gray, streaked with black, and with her thick glasses made her look even older.

"Tell us about Father," I said.

"You knew him, Noah, so what can I add to what you already know?"

"I'd like to hear your view of him and let Marge hear it too," I said.

"Well, he was a great priest. I transferred from Santa Maria which was supposed to be my church to come here to Saint Francis because of him. When my dear husband was sick for so long, God rest his soul, Father came to see him at least once a week. He was like a saint. He administered the Eucharist to my beloved husband once a week and he did that to all the bed-ridden people in the area, whether they were parishioners or not," she said as she clutched her rosary beads in her hand.

She sat very still in her chair with her legs crossed at the ankles. I thought she was about to cry, but she managed to continue.

"Manuel had a stroke you know. He was paralyzed for the last six years of his life. I needed all the help I could get and the spiritual lift I got from Father was very important to me. My beloved Manuel was so pure and good that he should have been spared such misery, but, it is God's way, and he suffered the stroke. Father taught me how to accept God's will without complaint and he brought peace to my life."

Listening to her I felt like I had been taken back in time to another age. There she was, sitting in her black clothes from head to foot almost as if she were out of a Fellini movie mouthing terms like "my beloved husband" and "God rest his soul"; it was as if I were listening to my grandmother talking about the Azores when she entered one of her nostalgic moods. I felt almost like taking her by the shoulders and giving her a good shake. I had known her "blessed husband" and he was no such thing. If anything he drank far too much and spent more than he should have betting on the dogs with one of the local bookies who was constantly denying him credit. I had seen this kind of thing all too often. Living, the man was hardly a good husband or a good man, but dead, he was wonderful. Widows loved to romanticize about their husbands as if they were some kind of superhuman person to whom they had been fortunate to be wed. Mrs. Sousa in her widow's weeds, played the role to perfection.

"My Manuel, may eternal light shine upon him, was taken with Father. He used to say that he must have been born to send the world a special gift. I loved him for his purity and his desire to help everyone. One time when I had some complaints about the way I was running the First Communion class for the little ones, I was in charge of the CCD classes and communion preparation for the little ones, he stood right behind me and told the parents that complained that he thought I was doing a wonderful job," she said with pride.

Marge asked, "What were they complaining about?"

"Oh it was silly. They claimed that I was frightening the little ones talking about sin and what would happen if they didn't make their First Communions. I was only trying to impress on them how important it was for them to come to lessons each week. But, Father stuck with me without letting them take over," she said. "They love to push people around, those people of little faith."

She had the look of an aggrieved lady, but I thought it was important that we pursue this line of conversation.

"So what did he do?" I asked.

"He wouldn't meet with them. They even put a call into the Bishop's Office, those terrible people. But he wouldn't meet with them and said they should learn discipline and obedience instead of looking for trouble. A couple of the parents took their kids out of the class and they went to Immaculate Conception, but Father didn't care. I remember he said he was glad to get rid of the troublemakers," she said. "I've had the class ever since."

"Was the Monsignor still active then?" I asked.

"Of course not. I would have been out on my ear. He didn't much like me. He would never have stuck by me. He would have had a meeting with the parents and then talked to the kids, as if they knew what was good for them, and then he would have given me the heave ho. I know it," she said with finality.

Her face had taken on a bitter look as if she were about to sneer and was holding it back. "I know you were close to the old man, but he was no good for this parish. He was too soft. He wasn't a strict priest. We need a priest who deals with sin head on. Monsignor turned his face away from sin and sinners as if it didn't matter. I know for a fact that he advised women to do what they thought best about contraception. Imagine. For that he could be burning in hell," she said.

"We are here to talk about Father D'Angellini, not about Monsignor. Can you think of anybody who would want to murder him? Did he have many enemies?" I asked.

"I don't think he had enemies. He was a very strict priest and he lived his life religiously and he expected his parishioners to do the same. He didn't turn his face when he encountered a sinner, but dealt with the probem. So, did he have people who didn't like him? Yes, I'm sure he did, but I am not sure that they would hate him. There is a difference between not liking someone and hating them. And there is a big difference between not liking them, and shooting them dead. There were always the rumors, but they were made up by vicious people who were evil, workers for the devil."

"What kind of rumors?"

"I don't think I should repeat them because they are so mean and ridiculous," Mrs. Sousa said.

"This is not a matter of being discreet or polite Mrs. Sousa. We need to know everything we can if we are going to provide the district attorney with the information he needs. I'm sure you want the killer brought to justice."

She wasn't sure quite what to say or do.

Marge leaned forward and very quietly said, "Whatever the rumors were, you know we are going to hear them sooner or later. I think you should tell us so we get the story straight."

She reached out her hand and touched Mrs. Sousa's hand very lightly and then sat back in her chair as if she expected an answer. The contact seemed to settle Mrs. Sousa down and she relaxed perceptively.

"Well, it's hard for me to talk about, but you are right, you are going to hear the lies anyway so you might as well hear them from me because they are all lies. Certain people in the parish said that Father was doing bad things with some of the young boys."

"What do you mean by bad things?" I asked.

"Well, you know. God forbid, I do not talk about such things. I don't even understand what, but they said he was too close to a couple of the boys," she said with discomfort.

"You mean he was having sex with them?" I asked.

She was obviously in an area where she didn't want to be and she began to perspire.

"With all the talk about priests and boys in the newspapers and television, I think they just made it up to make Father look bad. He did have his enemies and they wanted to hurt him. I'm sure none of it was true, but you will find out for yourself, that it is all lies. But now that you know, I won't say any more about it," she said.

She was very uncomfortable now and was clutching her rosary beads in her hand. In the corner of the room in which we sat was a little kneeler before a table that had a statue of the Infant Jesus of Prague on it surrounded by candles. I knew that the minute we left she would kneel on that kneeler and begin her prayers. I could almost hear the mumbling beneath her breath as she said the decades of the rosary.

Marge gave me an anxious look which signaled me that she thought it was time to leave. Mrs. Sousa was so upset that I knew we wouldn't get much more out of her. She had told us enough. I suppose it was time to leave her in peace. She would heave a sigh of relief and pull her weary body out of her chair and then make her way to the Infant Jesus with sighs floating through the air as she prepared herself for her prayers. Would she ask forgiveness for Marge and me who she deemed to be living in sin? I doubted that, but I had no idea what she would be praying for, probably for the repose of the soul of her beloved husband. Although, on second thought, I think she knew better.

The air outside was clean and fresh and I drew some deep breaths. I, for one, was happy to get out of the tenement and into the air. Marge seemed to feel the same way but her breath was more a sigh of relief rather than for fresh air.

"Noah, that woman needs help. I get the impression of evil, not holiness, with her. Can you imagine the terrible things she told those young girls and boys? They must have been having nightmares," Marge said.

"We've always had that breed in the church here. I don't know why we attract them, but here they are," I said.

"We had them in the Irish parishes too. It is part of the way things work in the church, I think. The fanatics spring up of their own accord. My mother, in her wisdom, once told me that she thought they were empty souls who needed something to fill up their being. But, we certainly have one here in this Mrs. Sousa. You looked bemused when she was talking about her husband, any reason?" Marge asked.

I laughed and said, "The husband she was being so nostalgic about was not the man I knew. First off, he drank far too much. If I remember correctly, he was a wine drinker who spent most of his off time sitting in the Portuguese club on East St. playing cards and drinking wine in an establishment with no liquor license. I remember seeing him stumbling home on more than one occasion. He would chew on peanuts hoping to take the smell of the wine away. It didn't, of course. Then he was a gambler. A bad gambler, at that, and he was always cadging money to make bets. The local Mama and Papa stores that took book wouldn't even let him through the door and no legitimate bookie could be bothered with him. And worst of all, he was the kind of man who hated kids. He had none of his own and wouldn't hesitate to swat one if he got close enough to him. I warned him about that more than once when he went out of his way to harass some little boy," I said, and I remembered back to the time when those events were so vivid.

"Then she must know that all the sweet, nostalgic words are untruths."

"I suppose she doesn't even know it now. Like so many other widows and widowers she has made him into what she would have liked him to be. I notice you don't do that with your former husband," I said.

"Well, as you know, I did love my husband, but his imperfections were part of what I loved about him. Rather than make him into some sort of saint that he wasn't, I can enjoy thinking about him as I loved him. The years of sickness at the end, I admit, are not part of what I remember most. Those, I have pretty much put aside in thinking of him. Something kicks off my memory of little things and that is what I remember about him and our relationship. Mrs. Sousa is building a dream relationship and is rather sick, but I suspect, fairly normal," Marge said as we walked to the car.

It was a crisp day and the sun was finally climbing over the roofs of the tenement houses in that section of town. Magellan Park was open, since there were only trees on the north end of the large square and I couldn't help but think of the times when the young boys like me would drift into the park hoping for a pickup game of baseball. It was always sunny at the park from daybreak on, so it was a good place for the kids to meet even though we ourselves came from out of the darkness of the tenements. Today the sun was lighting up the diamond and already a few kids were kicking a soccer ball around what was normally the Little League infield. They had set up two big ten gallon buckets to represent their goal and were taking shots at the hapless goal tender, who couldn't have been more than four foot tall. Marge and I shared a few laughs watching them and then set out on our way.

I was thinking out loud when I said, "What did we learn from that session?"

"I think we learned one thing of paramount importance for us and that was that Father D'Angellini probably had something to do with young boys. Do you think he was a pedophile or a pederast?" she asked.

I looked at the children playing their pickup game of soccer and I tried to think back to anything I saw about Father D'Angellini that would make me believe that he had an unnatural affection for young boys and I could think of nothing. He always had some young boy or group of boys clinging to him. Usually they were altar boys and they helped with many of the little odd jobs around the parish, but I never saw or heard him do anything that would suggest improper behavior on his part. I remember that he drove the altar boy who served the daily seven o'clock mass to school after mass, but that was more a courtesy than anything else. He didn't want the young boys to be late for school after serving mass, so it was easy enough for him to drive them to school

"I draw a blank," I told Marge. "There was not even the slightest inkling of anything wrong as far as I can remember. But, I haven't been part of the parish here for close to twenty-five years probably, so who knows what went on since I left."

"Well that gives a direction to go in anyway, I think," Marge said. "Now if we were in my parish I would know just who to go to. Parish gossips are pretty well known by the women. I'm sure you weren't involved in the gossip so you wouldn't know who to see."

"I have a few ideas," I said.

CHAPTER VI

Marge and I were brought up in the parish scheme of things in the city. Fall River was primarily Roman Catholic after the years of immigration ended and the mills closed. When the textile mills shut down in the first few decades of the 1900's, most of the mill owners left town. They were mainly Protestant and the Protestant churches gradually lost their flocks over the years. The predominant religious group was Roman Catholic and within that group there was a great deal of ethnic diversity. The Church of Saint Francis was the only Italian church in the city, but there were any number of Irish churches including the Cathedral, which was the center of the diocese. The parish became the identifying agent in a person's background. If someone said that so and so was from St. Joseph's, it was understood that he or she lived in the north end of the city and that they probably went to the parish school for their elementary education and that they were Irish. Someone from St. Matthew's was French and also from the north end, while a person from Notre Dame was French and lived in the Flint or east end. It was not uncommon to hear someone say, "You know John. He played second base for St. Anne's when they won the CYO championship back in the sixties."

Marge had lived with this all her life and when we talked, we reflected our backgrounds. Jack was left out in these conversations and could never quite figure out where the talk was going. He would sit with a bemused look on his face when Marge said something like "she was lace-curtain Irish from St. Louis Parish. She wasn't sure if she should allow her son to go to the parish school or send him to St. Mary's to the Sisters of Mercy." What she said to me had a whole world of meaning in it that poor Jack could never divine. She was saying in fact that the woman lived on "top of the hill" on Bradford Avenue or Middle Street by South Park where the south end professional Irish lived as opposed to "below the hill" where the Irish poor still lived, mixed in with the French immigrants from Canada. St. Louis Church was run by the Franciscans who were dedicated to the poor and the school was run by an ethnic mix of nuns. St. Mary's was run by the Sisters of Mercy who were almost exclusively Irish. The moment Marge said what she did I knew exactly what she meant while Jack could make none of the connections.

Jack had difficulty trying to understand why there were ethnic parishes. "You are all Roman Catholics so why not go to the same churches? I don't get the business of each ethnic group having its own church."

Marge understood how Jack felt because her husband had not been a Catholic and had felt the same way. She had explained it to him and the same logic applied now.

"There were waves of immigrations of Roman Catholics into the country. They didn't all come at once. The Irish came first and they built their churches in different parts of the city. There was St. Joseph's and Holy Name in the North end of the city, Immaculate Conception in the east end, Sacred Heart in the center along with St Mary's which was the Cathedral and St. Peter and Paul; then St. Louis, St. William and St. Patrick in the south end rounded out the Irish Catholic churches. When the French Canadians came to the city they wanted nothing to do with the English-speaking Irish churches. They looked to build their own churches where French would be spoken exclusively. They built six churches and two of those were mammoth structures to challenge the cathedral. There followed two Polish churches, one Italian, and a total of seven Portuguese churches. Only in recent times have the closings that were threatened for years been undertaken. This ended up in breaking up the ethnic churches in some parts of the city where the population is older and English has finally become the universal language in the churches."

"Wow, that tells the story doesn't it?" Jack said laughing.

"I'm sorry if I went on too long. But, it is a subject I know well and it is hard to understand what made things the way they are in the local church. This doesn't happen in the suburbs to any great extent. It is a city thing and where Fall River had such a big ethnic mix, it is more pronounced here. It led to a great many problems including a definite prejudice which exists to this day, but that is enough from me," Marge said.

"Saint Francis became popular with parishioners from other parishes because people saw it as a small and intimate church. Father D'Angellini used his skills to charm people and he became well-liked. It was the parish with the greatest number of people moving into it from other parishes. My family is a good example and so is Mrs. Sousa. He also ran a shorter mass and set up a convenient parking lot so that people didn't have to worry about parking for mass. Before he knew it, he had as many non-Italians for parishioners as Italians and that was unique in this city," I said. "He gave the people exactly what they wanted. He wasn't a priest who tried to solve problems. In fact, he avoided dealing with personal problems outside of health and sickness. Marital problems were not his forte and he ran from those without looking back. Drugs and alcohol were also not in play as far as he was concerned, but that wasn't what the type of person he was attracting to the parish was concerned about. Those with personal problems found other places to go to for solace and advice."

"Okay, I think I get a pretty good picture of the church and this man, Father D'Angellini. The question becomes where do we go from here? I haven't found anything of any significance in terms of money, so I don't know if that is a dead end or not. I've only been on it one day, so I'll give it at least a week before I call it quits," Jack said.

We were sitting in my kitchen after having had lunch. Jack got out of his chair to go to the freezer for another helping of ice cream and Marge and I were relaxing after taking a walk on the beach when the telephone rang.

It was a man who identified himself as Father D'Angellini's brother and who demanded that I meet him immediately to discuss his brother's murder. He had a rough manner and I felt he was either trying to play the tough guy or was uncomfortable and was showing his discomfort by being aggressive. He said that he had heard that we were asking questions about his brother and that that was not acceptable to him or the family. He demanded a meeting immediately.

We work with and for the District Attorney as unpaid advisors and I certainly was not going to have a meeting with anyone without advising Patrick as to what we were doing. In this case I thought it best to meet at the Fall River office so there would be no chance for anything approaching what I would call "rough stuff". My years of teaching had taught me how to handle people who were overly aggressive, both parents and students, but I still thought it best to meet officially with this man.

He wanted to meet post haste, but I would have nothing to do with that, and he finally realized that I was not going to give in to his demands.

"My colleagues and I will meet you in the District Attorney's Fall River Office at ten tomorrow morning. It will be an informal meeting and the District Attorney may or may not be there depending on his schedule," I said.

When he agreed, I gave him directions to the office from Providence and a phone number to call if he happened to get lost coming into the city. He hung up abruptly and I was left wondering what I would be dealing with the next morning. I explained the call to Jack and Marge and picked up the phone to call Patrick to let him know what was going on and to tell him that the meeting would be in his office in Fall River or in one of the rooms available within the general office space. He agreed that it was a good idea to meet him in an official setting, although he said that he couldn't make the meeting which he thought was just as well, so that Father's brother would feel freer to talk.

We met the next morning as we had planned to. Jack insisted that we stop at Dunkin Donuts on Quarry St. on his way in for his coffee and more importantly his coconut jelly stick and coffee roll and a few extras for the office. He waited in line for ten minutes and I thought that would make us late and I began to get a bit anxious. Fortunately, Mr. D'Angellini hadn't arrived when we parked our car and made our way into the offices. The secretary at the front desk suggested that we use the room that we had always used as a temporary office and Jack made a hit by placing a dozen donuts and muffins on her desk with the words, "Whatever isn't eaten, why don't you take home for the kids? There's a bag of donut holes in there too, which I think they'd like."

We waited for a half hour and began to think that our visitor would not show. Jack finished what he considered to be a snack and became restless. "Well I suspect that our man will not show. Maybe the idea of the District Attorney's Office scared him off. Who knows?"

He had no sooner said that when the phone rang and the secretary in the outer office announced to me that Mr. D'Angellini was waiting to enter our office. I went to the door to meet him and in a few moments we were seated in a circle in the small office.

After the introductions were made, he started right in with what was bothering him. "I hear you're going around asking questions about my brother. Why are you doing that?"

I explained that we needed to know as much as we could about him, as a starting point, if we were going to get some clue as to why someone would have wanted to see him dead.

He was very unlike his brother in appearance. He was a tall man, in what I would guess to be very good shape, unlike his brother who I thought to be on the portly side. There was a hardness about him that was more than his stubble of beard or his heavily wrinkled face. His hair was gray and sparse, but the back of his hands were thick with graying hair. His hands were big with long fingers that looked arthritic with heavily gnarled fingers and joints. He struck me as a man who had suffered a great deal and was still in considerable pain.

"So, if you are interested in finding out who killed your brother, fill us in on what we need to know. We want to learn as much about him as possible. You're his brother and I am sure you know more about him than anyone," Marge said. "It would certainly be a big help to Jack and me. Noah knew him personally. I met him only once and Jack never met him."

"I didn't come here for that. I came hoping to stop you from digging around. He's dead and he should lie in peace. What's the use of letting the jerks and haters smear his name for nothing? My mother is worried they will dirty his memory with a bunch of lies. So I came here to tell you to stop it now," he said and there was just a hint of a threat in his voice.

Jack said, "Either that or you want to hide the truth."

Frank D'Angellini almost jumped out of his seat to approach Jack angrily. I wasn't sure what was going to happen next, but Jack had anticipated the reaction and without backing down said in a steady voice, "You can say whatever you want to, but we are going to investigate this murder regardless of where it leads until we find out who murdered your brother. So scream, yell, throw a tantrum, it makes no difference. We will follow this wherever it leads. Now I would suggest that you sit down and give us your side of the story. Tell us as much as you can about your brother and do it now, then we'll have something to go on. I know you'd like nothing better than to smash me in the face, but that takes us nowhere. So, Frank, sit down and think of things that would be helpful to us now if we are going to get to the bottom of this without upsetting everyone in the process."

That seemed to register with Frank D'Angellini and he sat down in his chair again. He leaned back a bit in the captain's chair and seemed to be trying to think through what Jack had just said to him. My first thought was that he would never make a poker player, all his emotions showed in his face. Now he sat quietly and looked at the wall behind me as if to avoid eye contact while he thought. Finally he stood and walked to the water cooler and poured himself a paper cup half full of water. Then he drank the water, threw the cup into the trash receptacle and came back ready to talk to us.

"Well what do you want to know?" he asked looking from one to the other of us.

"First off, tell us if your brother ever told you that he was frightened for his life or if he had ever been threatened by anyone," I said.

"No, not a chance. If he was worried about someone hurting him, he would have come right to me. I'm older and I always protected him from wise guys. Growing up he always knew I would take care of him. In school or outside playing, anybody who hurt him or picked on him knew they had me to deal with. The kid would never have let someone threaten him without telling me. We got too many friends to let anybody get away with that," he said. "No, whoever shot him, didn't let him know in advance. You can bet your ass on that," he said.

Jack said, "Watch your language, please."

"Okay, I'm sorry. It just slips out. We were brought up on the Hill and you had to be tough there just to survive. The kid was never tough and they would have torn him apart if it wasn't for the family. We took care of him," he said.

Marge asked, "What do you mean by the Hill?"

"Federal Hill lady. Federal Hill in Providence. It's the Italian section of Providence. You must have heard of it," he said.

"Yes, I have. I've been any number of times shopping and to the restaurants there. I just wasn't sure how many people lived there," Marge said.

"Well you probably just been to Atwell's Ave., the main street, but there are houses all over the hill. It's a busy section. A lot of the people have moved out into the suburbs, but still, it's a big section. My family is still there."

"What kind of a child was your brother?" Jack asked.

"He was a good kid. Nothing like me. Right from the beginning we knew he wasn't like the rest of us. Mama was very proud of him. You know my father did time and I've done time too. Nothing much to be proud about in either of us. But Marco, he was different. I don't know where he came from, but he wasn't anything like the rest of us. Even Mama is a tough lady. She puts me to shame. Papa always said that he felt sorry for the man who crossed her," he said with obvious pride.

"And did anyone cross her in terms of your brother?" Jack asked.

"Yeah. But she took care of that with no trouble," he stopped then as if he thought he had said too much.

"What did that involve?" I asked.

"No way, I'm not going to give you that one to chew on. You're on your own. I'll just say she handled the problems that came up with no trouble at all. She is like iron. Nothing rattles her, that's for sure. You'll meet her and you'll find out for yourself. One thing I have to ask you. She is hurting real bad right now, so wait 'til after the funeral before you bother her with a lot of questions," he said and I gave him credit for changing the subject.

"Did you get along with your brother?" Jack asked.

"You mean because I served time? No I didn't. He didn't want much to do with me. He didn't even bother with my wife and kids. I always figured that was his problem. Papa wasn't his favorite either. It wasn't because he thought he was better than we were. I think it was because he didn't want to dirty his name with us," he said.

Marge said, "Did that bother you?"

He sat up in his chair and stretched his legs. There was no light coming in through the windows at that time of day and only the electric lights lit the room. There were shadows cast by the overhead light and the floor lamp behind me gave everything an eerie look. The deep furrows in Mr. D'Angellini's face were even more pronounced in the muted light and he looked almost menacing as he moved his long legs and then crossed them in an attempt to get comfortable.

"Maybe, maybe not. It bothered me to think that he thought I was not good enough for him to associate with. I used to think to myself, 'Who does he think he is?' But I knew why he did it. It wasn't because he thought he was better than us. He didn't want anything to do with us because he was ambitious and wanted to be 'a somebody' in the Church. He didn't want it known that his brother and father were cons. It didn't do him any good because he didn't go anywhere but to a parish. The truth is, he wasn't smart enough. Believe it or not, I was smarter than he was. He had a way about him but he wasn't what the higher-ups were looking for. He was just a nice kid who grew into a nice man who happened to be a priest," he said.

"And you. What happened to you?" Marge asked.

"A bad boy who turned into a bad man and a lousy crook," he said with disdain.

Marge continued, "Why?"

"This isn't about me, is it? Who knows why? I can tell you why, though, if you really want to know. I think I got into crime when the kind of crime I learned wasn't good any more. The State took over the numbers with the lottery and scratch tickets. My father did a big business in numbers. Then they opened the casinos next door in Connecticut and that took away our gambling business. The blacks and South Americans took over drugs and we were out of business. Even the prostitutes staked out their own territory. The strip clubs made women available to the players and that left us out of the woman business. So what was left? Petty crime, chop shops, warehouse raids and that kind of thing. Tough to make a living on the odds and ends that nobody else wants," he said.

He had lost all of his tension and actually seemed to be enjoying the attention. The cloud left his face and I suspected that he would have liked to be sitting at a bar having a draft beer and talking about the new face of crime.

"It's all in what they call white collar crime now. Halliburton and those guys clean up and they are supposed to be clean and they get away with murder. You know Papa started in prohibition and the money was in bootlegging. They used the ocean to ship booze in from Canada and they made a killing. The average guy wanted booze so that was all right for the Kennedys and their crew. There was a big demand for booze among the rich people so it was all right. Drugs are frowned upon by most people, so that is out. Anyway to make a long story short, the crime business isn't what it used to be," he said with a frown.

"We still hear stories about the Mafia on Federal Hill. Raymond Patriarca, even in jail, was one of the most recognizable names in Rhode Island for years," I said. "Is the Mafia still at work on the Hill?"

"There are more FBI men on the Hill than there are Mafiosa. Take my word for it. People are still scared of mixing with the Italians on Atwell's Avenue or Broadway, but the power is all gone now. You got a bunch of petty thieves like me there now," he said. "The power, whatever is left, is in South Boston and even that is getting thinner and thinner."

"So your brother wanted no part of any of your background, right?" Jack asked.

"No, he wasn't like us from the beginning. In a lot of ways he was what we used to call a 'sissy'. He was the kind of kid that was an altar boy and spent a lot of time with Mama and the other women. He took a liking to one of the priests in the parish we belonged to and he followed him around like a little puppy dog. He was like his pet. Mama thought it was wonderful to have a son who was so holy and good."

"How did your father feel about it?" I asked.

"Papa didn't know what to make of it. Papa was from the old school. He wanted his sons to be men the way he thought of men. Macho, and all that stuff. But he shook it off. Marco was Mama's boy and he didn't worry about it. The only thing he ever worried about as far as Marco was concerned was that Marco would look down on him for going to jail. And the worst thing for him was that Marco did. He never got over that. There is a lot of pride in Italian families and the idea that a kid did not respect his father was tough to take," he said.

"How did you take it?" I asked.

"Hey, it's part of our business. You don't steal for years and not get caught. It's the price you pay. Half the men on the Hill have served time including the big guys like Raymond Patriarca. It's a fact of life. Marco was a jerk for making Papa feel bad. But, Papa got over it, like he did with most things having to do with Marco. I was his son and Marco belonged to Mama."

52

He stretched again and said, 'Hey, this is enough. I'm tired and I want to get out of here. Got things to steal; right? Didn't do what I wanted to here, but that's nothing new to me. I never do what I set out to do. Okay, I'm out of here," he said and got out of his chair. He reached out to shake my hand and Jack's and nodded at Marge, and before we could say anything, he was gone.

"Well," Marge said, "He has certainly given us enough to think about, hasn't he?"

"To say the least. It will take me two days to put things together in my mind. I was interested in what he said about the narrowing crime market," Jack said. "I've never really considered that. I still think of crime as if we were in the 1930's in Chicago with Al Capone and all the movies we've seen. Frank had me almost feeling sorry for him. The way he talked about the shrinking market, almost made me think of him as a businessman," Jack said.

"I got the impression that he really didn't think much of his brother. He may have been a priest, but Frank didn't like him much and didn't really respect him. Usually, or at least in my limited experience, the priest in the family was highly respected by members of the family. He was the one every one looked up to. I suspect that that wasn't the case here, at least, with Frank. I don't get the sense that he was jealous. That doesn't seem to be the case. Actually it is more like disdain than jealousy. He admits that he thought he was smarter than his brother Marco and he feels that Marco treated his father badly. I get the sense that Frank didn't think his brother was very savvy. He didn't understand or appreciate what his family was. That makes me wonder what the mother thought about her spouse and one of her children being involved in crime. That we will find out sooner or later, I think," I said.

Marge was very quiet and seemed to be thinking things through. My experience with her had taught me that she was not a person who thought out loud, but one who pondered things very thoroughly before voicing an opinion. Jack and I had also learned that when she did voice an opinion, she was rarely wrong.

"Well, I don't know about you guys, but I am starved," Jack said. "Donuts are like Chinese food as far as I am concerned. An hour after I eat them I am hungry again."

Marge and I both laughed. Marge said, "Jack, you eat a steak and are hungry in an hour. You have a bottomless pit for a stomach."

"Maybe so, but I am in the mood for some good old comfort food. A meat loaf with plenty of mashed potatoes and gravy and a big chunk of Portuguese Vienna bread. Sound good?" he asked.

"The only place I can think of that will have that for you at lunch would be a diner and that means AlMacs Diner, right?" I said.

"How did you guess?" Jack asked with a smile.

So, we found ourselves sitting in one of the booths at the diner which was located about an eighth of a mile from the school I had taught in for my whole teaching career. The ownership had changed many times over the years, but the diner still maintained a lively business. Its main business came mornings when it served its famous breakfasts and the short order cook held sway. When I did go for breakfast I would always make sure I had a stool at the counter so that I could see the short order cook make his many dishes on the grill. The grill was large, at least five foot wide and three feet deep, and always spotlessly clean. He worked alone and turned out every breakfast in a smooth rhythm of work that seemed effortless. He was perfection in action.

The orders were given to him on slips of paper which were hung over the grill and he prepared each so that all the dishes on a single slip were plated at the same time. He made the full array of diner breakfast dishes including omelets, eggs of all kinds, waffles in different flavors, pancakes, and even odd dishes like steaks and eggs. On one part of the grill was the partially cooked bacon and sausage and a mound of home fries which were added to every plate. The eight slice toaster was working every second and the various toasted varieties were constantly popping up and being buttered quickly and sliced to fit on the plate.

The short order cook talked to no one. His job was to turn out the breakfast or lunch dishes without any unnecessary delays and he did the job to perfection. He was a marvel to watch as he worked in his small area with his back to the counter. From the diner counter sitting on a stool, I marveled at how he kept things in precise order and yet managed to have as many as ten items working on the grill at the same time. Directly in front of him might be the makings of an omelet and directly behind that, two fried eggsand pancakes to the right, all cooking and needing attention and all being prepared one right after another.

Lunch was another matter. The short order cook was gone for the day and the regular cooks took over, supplying their prepared foods like meat loaf and chicken pot pie with prepared side dishes. Without hesitation, Jack ordered the meat loaf he had obviously been pining for with an extra helping of mashed potatoes and no vegetables, and the whole thing covered with gravy. He asked for an extra order of Vienna bread and he was hardly able to contain himself while the order was being prepared. Marge settled for an egg salad sandwich on whole wheat bread while I had a cup of fish chowder. We all ordered tea and while we were waiting for our main dishes to arrive we were entertained by three young men in the next booth discussing the pros and cons of marriage. It seemed that one of the men was about to get married and the others were heckling him about the fact that life would end as he knew it, once he put on the ring, and said "I do." Before much time passed, diners in the other booths were chiming in and the comments were getting more outrageous by the moment. It was what a diner was and what it would always be, I hoped. It was not a dining place, it was a restaurant that was more a village meeting place, where everyone either knew everyone else or felt they could say whatever they felt.

One of the older men who was sitting in a booth with his family, finally said, "All this talk about marriage is baloney. I've been married for forty years, no fifty, no I think forty-five, or something like that, and I remember every wonderful moment of it." That made the whole place laugh and our meals arrived and we settled back to eat and to watch Jack enjoying his meat loaf and mashed potatoes.

CHAPTER VII

There have been great changes in the city in the past twenty years. As the big cities like Boston and Springfield in Massachusetts and New Haven and Hartford in Connecticut became more fashionable and the market in condos increased, the poor were forced out of their homes and driven to cities like New Bedford and Fall River. The big cities became gentrified and the smaller, poor cities became poorer. The cycle continues. Fall River, in particular, was a unique city in that the poor it was populated with for years were the working poor. Large numbers of immigrants, in latter years, Portuguese immigrants from the Azores came to the city to break away from the poverty they suffered in their homeland. The women worked in the sewing shops and the men in construction. They came from the poverty of the islands to a new chance. It was the American dream repeated as it had been so many times for immigrant groups before. But the Portuguese immigrants had an advantage over the current newcomers. They were white and their extended families were here before them. They were met at the airport by their uncles and aunts and cousins. They were new to the country, but they were met by relatives and friends, many of whom were second generation immigrants. Theirs was a hard, but, easier road than the needy who were driven out of American cities. The new group was made up of mostly people of color or of Latin American ancestry and they stood out in a city that had had few people of color in its whole history. The new group was made up of the dispossessed poor; the urban detritus who had little hope of fulfilling anything resembling the American dream. They came to the cities like Fall River and New Bedford because those cities were depressed areas where everything was cheaper and they had a chance to survive.

They had no chance to settle in the suburbs, so they chose the small, failed cities in places like Massachusetts. The cities of Brockton, Lowell, Lawrence, New Bedford and Fall River were perfect for their needs. And they came in large numbers to communities that were not ready for them and could not adapt quickly enough to the changes they brought with them. The primarily white population of Fall River, in particular, had a difficult time adjusting to the sudden appearance of black people walking the streets. The parochial schools found themselves overburdened with applicants. Parents feared for their children going to school with blacks, Cambodians and Latinos and in their bigoted mindset, paid too much money for too little education in the private schools. At one time the parochial schools were staffed by the nuns, but the new staffing was mainly made up of unqualified teachers, many not even college graduates, working for less than adequate salaries and no fringe benefits but who needed to meet no standards in the private area. Nevertheless, there are approximately 16,000 students in the schools in Fall River with more than 5,000 enrolled in private schools. As a result, the public schools have been drained of the middle class children who so enrich a school population. Go to one of these parochial schools and one will see a school population that is 99% white, while on the other hand the closest public school nearby will be seventy percent Latino, black or Asian. Oddly enough, we are depriving the private school student of good teachers and the chance at a top-notch education by building a wall around them to protect them from people of color.

Not only are the schools not ready to deal with the problem of the poor, the police fail completely in the cities. A city like Fall River that was relatively crime free, suddenly becomes a center of a drug culture that the police have no idea how to attack. Gangs begin to appear and a community that had never known more than illegal gambling and underage drinking with a sprinkling of prostitution is overwhelmed by street crime, housebreaks, gang turf wars and uncontrolled violence, especially in the poorer sections of town.

Two streets north of The Church of Saint Francis there is a housing project which houses many of the newly arrived poor. Father D'Angellini hated that project with all of his being. His was not a devotion to the poor and he showed it in his disdain for the Catholic poor that came out of that project and who would normally be members of his parish. He was particularly upset by the Salvation Army and its attempt to recruit converts. Not only the Salvation Army but the Seventh Day Adventists, the Mormons and some small Evangelical sects became very active in setting up recruiting programs to involve the housing project's tenants in their activities. He wanted no part of the inhabitants of the project, but he would not allow himself to think that the people would leave his church for another. I thought it was a laughable situation.

"You can't have it both ways, you know, Father," I said to him the only time the subject came up. "You have to meet those people on their own ground or give up any hope of having them remain part of your church."

"I know. It's just that when I go into that project I see all the evil I hate. One day I went to a woman's house and found her son playing Nintendo while her boyfriend or whoever he was, was shooting heroin in the kitchen. I didn't even know what the device was until I described it to one of the men in Marcucci's and he told me what it was. I can't deal with that. It is too upsetting. I can't face it," he said. "It seems like every time I go into that project I run into something like that and it scares me off."

"Well, that's your problem. They are all God's children, Father. Just like some of the kids I have in school aren't easy. But I don't get paid to turn my back on them. I get paid to do as much as I can to help them. Granted, many times I accomplish nothing, but then again, I have helped some of the kids and that makes all of the failures worthwhile."

He looked at me for a second and then said, "I'm the preacher, not you."

He could never make the transition from working with working class parishioners to those who were needy and hopeless. Having worked with the same clientele myself, I knew what he was facing. Children coming from homes with parents who have terrible problems bring their problems to school with them. Many are overweight from eating fast foods and snack foods and are in reality undernourished or at least poorly nourished. They come to school with a chip on their shoulders and exhibit all of the antisocial behavior that sets them apart from children brought up in normal surroundings. The best part of their day should be the time they spend in school, but that is often spoiled by their anger and hatred for anything that resembles discipline and order and school many times becomes a place for resentment as they see what other children are born to as compared to their lot in life. But, the rewards, when that rare success came, were worth all of the difficulties. There were successes which he never experienced. I remember one boy who was living alone in an old-broken down house after his parents deserted him for a life of alcohol. I took him under my wing out of a sense of pity for him, but as it turned out he was quite bright and did very well in school. With the proper guidance and lots of free lunches he was able to do well in high school and go to college where he trained to be a teacher. He taught in a neighboring suburb for years and one day when I met him he thanked me for my help and told me that he was going to Chicago for his daughter's graduation from medical school. Granted, such successes were rare, but they carried a long way. Father D'Angellini never felt that sense of accomplishment that came from knowing you had helped someone who probably would never have had a chance in life. Unfortunately, I had learned that the American dream was a lie. The successes are few and far between and it takes a lot more than the hard work that we seem to think does the job. Bill Gates did not come from poverty and although Bill Clinton did, he had the brilliance to get him out of the mire. That is extremely rare and is becoming rarer as the gulf between the rich and the poor widens.

CHAPTER VIII

The funeral mass was held at Saint Francis and all the church dignitaries were there, led by the Bishop of the Fall River Diocese. He said the mass with all the ceremony it called for. Mrs. D'Angellini was there with Frank and what we assumed to be his wife and children. It was a long service and the Bishop gave the eulogy in vague enough terms to suggest that he knew Father but at the same time saw him as a faithful pastor doing the bidding of the Church and not following the whims of change and liberal fashion within the Church. I thought it caught the ministry of Father D'Angellini as he had lived it and I was surprised that the Bishop was that familiar with this insignificant parish priest. At best he had to be considered insignificant in the large scheme of things. He had run a small parish that was losing ground against the revival of the Envangelicals and the spread of the influence of the Seventh Day Adventists among the poor in the city. Storefront churches were springing up all over the city especially among the immigrants from Brazil and Latin America. The Catholic Church in New England, not too long ago the dominant power, spiritually and politically, was fast being diminished. So, a little church like Saint Francis would seem to be a minor player in a bigger picture. This diocese that ran from Fall River east to include New Bedford and Cape

Cod and north to the Attleboros and Taunton was huge in area and had a mixed population of poor, working poor, middle class and included families as rich as the Kennedys. So, I was surprised to think that with all of his problems, the Bishop would know Father as well as he seemed to. I had to wonder why.

I stood in the rear of the church for the entire mass hoping to see something that would give me a clue to the killer. I saw nothing. I knew a great many of the parishioners who came to pay their last respects to Father D'Angellini, but in the years I had been away from the church it would seem from the numbers of people I didn't know, that he had expanded the parish substantially by involving outsiders for whom he had an appeal. It was a question I would need answered if what I was seeing made any sense at all.

The church was filled to capacity and the Bishop conducted a High Mass for the Dead which was a long ceremony. Mrs. D'Angellini wore black from head to foot as did her daughter-in-law or what I supposed to be her daughter-in-law and surprisingly so did what I presumed to be her grandsons who looked to be boys of no more than ten years old. Rarely did boys as young as they were dress in black for a funeral. Marge was quite surprised and whispered to me that she had never seen that before. Nothing could be considered more traditional than black at a funeral, although, like most traditional things, that was fading fast. Among the Portuguese in Fall River, the women who were widowed or lost a close family member like a father or son, wore black for the rest of their lives, although that was becoming less common as well. But, Mrs. Sousa wore black from head to foot like a beacon of traditionalism and I suspected that Father's mother would do the same. The same would not hold true for her son's wife and the children, of course, but for this one day, they were dressed in black. Had Father's mother worn black for her husband who had died? I made a mental note to check on that as well.

The front pews were taken up by the priests and church dignitaries except for the first two rows which were given over to designated family members. The offerings were brought up to the altar by Father's mother and brother and no eulogy was offered by any member of the family. The readings, which were more often than not read by family members in the modern Church, were read by a priest who was an assistant to the Bishop. If anything struck me about the mass, it was that it was as traditional and old-fashioned as it could be. The only difference between this mass and the ones I remembered as a child, was that this one was conducted in English rather than Latin. Had it been in Latin, most of the older priests would have been right at home, I'm sure, and probably would have wished that they could go back to what they considered happier times when their flocks were docile and before the "windows" were opened to let in fresh air and all the turmoil that went with it.

I looked the crowd over as carefully as I was able, but I saw nothing suspicious in any way. There was no one acting in any peculiar or exceptional manner, which is what I had anticipated I'd find, but it was worth a look. The mass moved along slowly and then finally came to an end and we went out to our cars to await the funeral procession to the cemetery in Providence on Federal Hill in which Father would be buried. We had asked permission of Frank to attend the burial itself and he had agreed if we promised to keep out of the way and just observe and not upset his mother. We took our place at the end of the funeral cortege and in no time at all we found ourselves on the tag end of the line of cars making its way on Route 195 west to Providence. It was only twenty minutes from the church in Fall River to the cemetery on Federal Hill in Providence and since many of the people who had attended the mass would not be attending the burial, there weren't many people at the grave. The Bishop and his entourage had left and only the priest in the Italian parish in Providence, Father's home parish, was there to carry out the burial rites. Only about forty people remained and it was obvious that they were members of the immediate and extended family who had come to pay their respects. I looked over the area quickly and then decided that we had nothing to gain by staying and signaled to Marge and Jack that we should leave. They agreed and we went to our car and pulled away from the area.

Jack said, "I hate to be here and not stop to eat lunch somewhere. What do you think?"

"Personally," Marge said, "I would prefer to go somewhere away from here. The idea of stopping for lunch right now doesn't appeal to me, especially with the burial still going on. Let's go downtown Jack, okay?"

I agreed and Jack quickly acquiesced.

We decided though, that an Italian restaurant would be appropriate and I suggested Raphael's, which was my favorite of all the Italian restaurants in Providence. This one was located behind the old train station in the center of the city and was a short distance from Federal Hill. The city of Providence had made great strides in the past ten years or so, even though its mayor had been put in jail on a variety of charges. But that same mayor, Mayor Vincent Cianci, had made the city hum and Providence was now an exciting city to visit. The old train station was a good example of what had happened seemingly overnight. The building had lain dormant for years with no apparent use in sight. Then a hotel was built out of what was the middle of the station and restaurants suddenly emerged on either side of the hotel and they were good, successful ones. The Capital Grille was much to Jack's liking and specialized in meat; huge steaks and chops and everything the traditional businessman was known to enjoy and appreciate. Raphael's is more of an upscale Italian restaurant serving dishes which probably wouldn't be found in most Italian homes on Federal Hill, but which I find exciting and different enough to tickle my palate.

We arrived just as they were beginning to seat customers for lunch and in no time at all we found ourselves dipping freshly served bread in seasoned olive oil as has become the fashion in Italian restaurants nowadays.

I spoke first on the subject of the funeral mass we had attended and the burial ceremony which we had left early.

"That was the most old-fashioned mass I have been to in a long time. It reminded me of the masses I attended as a little boy," I said. "It was like going back into the past."

Marge said, "Jack, I know you are not familiar with the Catholic Church, but Noah is right. That mass could have come directly from Sicily. Believe me, the diocese has not seen the likes of it for some time. Even the music was from another time. We have to find out who arranged this whole thing. I am curious to know if the mass was set by Father's mother or by the Bishop. What did you think of the selections played by the organ, Noah?"

"One was a famous Requiem but I don't know the name of it. It definitely was never heard in this church before. The organist must have been brought in especially for this service. For some reason Verdi's Requiem Mass keeps popping into my head but that's probably the only one I know the name of. Church music isn't my special area," I said.

"At any rate," Marge said, "It was heavy and I found it oddly moving in a negative kind of way. I found it depressing rather than uplifting, but I don't know why."

"What we witnessed was what I would have to call a conservative mass from another time. That is what keeps going through my head. Who arranged it, is the question I keep asking myself? Was it the Bishop and his staff? Or was it Father's mother and family? And why would they want that kind of funeral mass?"

"We should know that when we interview Mrs. D'Angellini," Marge said. "The whole thing struck me as odd, too."

We settled down to what I thought was an excellent lunch and as was Jack's normal practice, he didn't talk much when he ate. Jack loved to eat but was not by any means anything but a polite, careful eater. He enjoyed food, and in his mind, the time to talk was after a meal, not during it. When he had finished eating and had had a monstrous dessert that looked to me like a double portion of a thick chocolate torte with whipped cream or cr me freche piled over it, he said, "I feel left out of this case. I have nothing to fall back on when it comes to this religious business. What do I know about requiem organ pieces or traditional or old-fashioned services? The only thing I know anything about is money, and, so far this doesn't seem to have anything to do with money as far as I can see."

"I think we are making too much of what we know, actually, Jack. What we have talked about probably has nothing to do with the murder," I said. "It just seems odd to the two of us."

"There has to be money in here somewhere, I can feel it. I'm not whining. I just feel frustrated. I'll get to it sooner or later, I know it. When you interview the mother, make sure I am in on it. I watched her during the mass as well as I could even though she was down front and I think she will be an interesting interview. You know, she is very stoic. She didn't break down, crying or weeping; there was none of that. Even at the grave in the short time we were there. She is a lady who knows how to keep her feelings knotted up inside herself. She wasn't about to show anyone that she couldn't control her emotions. That was surprising to me," Jack said.

Marge said, "I missed that Jack. I was so taken with the mass, I didn't pay attention to her."

"I expected her to throw herself on the coffin and wail and scream, but there was none of that. There was some tear shedding among the family guests, but even that was subdued. It was as if she set the tone for behavior. It was quite surprising to me," Jack said.

"You're right. It was subdued. I've been to quite a few of these funerals and the Italians aren't especially noted for being subdued, nor are the other Mediterranean immigrants. The old-fashioned Portuguese are quite capable of throwing themselves into the graves as well," I said. "And, you are right about setting the tone. Mrs. D'Angellini, it would appear, did set the tone. Having the Bishop officiate at the mass may have made a difference too, but there is no question that is was a restrained mass."

The check came and we paid the bill and we went outside into the fresh air. I had eaten more than I normally do and I felt bloated. I was in no mood to sit in the car while Jack drove to Fall River and then to Westport Point. I suggested walking along the river which was a few minutes from the parking lot in which we were standing. Marge and Jack agreed that a walk would be nice and we walked to the river and then east toward College Hill using the causeway which had been built in recent years with the express purpose of serving as a walkway for people just like us to enjoy. It had been a hard morning in many ways, certainly an uncomfortable one for all of us. We were in no mood to discuss the case at that point. We walked slowly along the waterfront and discussed the changes that had happened in the city in our time. Providence, like many of the cities on the east coast had been deserted by the industry that had made it an important city at one time, and was now relying on Brown University and Rhode Island School of Design and most recently Johnson and Wales Culinary Institute to reinvigorate the city and the downtown. From our standpoint walking along the river walk we could see the results. New hotels were in evidence and a new mall in the center replacing the old shopping district all of us had known as children. The east end was wonderful with its old Federal buildings perched on the upwardly sloping hill leading from the RISD campus to the Brown quadrangle, if one had the strength and energy to walk up the steep slopes.

I remember as a child the trips to the Outlet Store, which was the major department store in the city at the time and seeing the Christmas displays in the windows and what seemed like miles of toys inside with a real live Santa Claus to tell our wishes to. Fall River had its McWhirr's, but it was nothing in comparison to the Outlet Store which to me during the Great Depression was like walking into Santa's workshop. Like most of the stores in the center city it was gone. A huge mall had been built at the western end of the open river which had an indoor parking lot and myriads of stores and restaurants. Nothing in the downtown area could compete with it as a draw. The combination of newness, volume, easy access and ample parking was enough to make the mall work in the middle of the city where things had been going downhill for thirty or forty years. In a few short years, Providence was a great place to visit with good restaurants, outstanding theater, great architecture, a wonderful museum at RISD and enough shopping to make any woman happy.

We finished our walk and, I, for one, felt much better working off part of the big meal I had just eaten. We walked back the way we had come and had a different view of the city. By the time we reached the car we all felt it had been a busy day and we would take the rest of the day off. We were silent most of the way back to the Point. When we arrived we were surprised to see Patrick waiting for us.

CHAPTER IX

"I've decided to take the afternoon off," he said, "but we had a call from a man in the parish who claims he has a good idea who was involved in Father D'Angellini's murder. He will meet with you in the office at five on his way home after he drops his son off at work. He says he knows you, Noah, and that is why he is coming forth with information," Patrick said. "I thought it best that you meet with him."

"Did you get a name?" I asked.

Patrick opened the notebook he had in his hand and said, "DeMarco. He said you would know him as Sheikie. He said you were old friends."

"We grew up together. I haven't seen him in quite a while. I had his son in school and I remember seeing him at the boy's graduation. I thought he was living out of town. I'll be happy to see him again even in these circumstances."

Patrick had made the appointment for us and since we had to be in the city at five we decided to rest up for the rest of the afternoon. Old age has its drawbacks. Rest is a necessary ingredient before any action and we had had an emotionally tiring morning. I know I needed a nap just to replenish my energy level. I sat in my comfortable chair just off the kitchen, put on a Beethoven violin sonata and before I knew it I was in a deep sleep. I couldn't have slept more than an hour when I was wakened by Marge telling me it was time to get ready to go into town. I looked up to see Jack coming through the kitchen door in his usual uniform of a pair of khakis, a button-down shirt and his boat shoes without socks. He had the look of being refreshed in the shower and his hair was still a bit moist. I ran upstairs to change out of my dressy clothes and to put on something more casual and in a few minutes we were driving down 88 heading for I95W toward Fall River and our appointment. Jack was driving and he couldn't resist stopping at the Dunkin Donuts on Quarry St. for his usual snack of a coconut jelly stick and a coffee roll.

"This could be a long session and I know I'll be starved if we cut into dinner time," he said.

My old friend was there when we arrived at the office and I was surprised to see that the years had not been good to him. I would not have recognized him if I had met him on the street. It hadn't been that long since I had seen him last, maybe twenty years, but he had gained at least one hundred pounds in that time and could barely walk. He used a walker and he was enormous. The man we met was a far cry from the boy I had known and even the father I had seen at his son's graduation from junior high school. He was always heavy but if I remember correctly he had wanted to be a boxer and had kept himself in what he called "fighting shape." At seventy-four, my exact age, he was more like a man in dying condition.

"Not the man you knew, huh Noah?" he said. "Been through a lot over the past twenty years. My knees and hips let go, then I had a stroke, and diabetes showed itself along with high blood pressure and another blood clot. What you see is what the doctor's managed to save and about a hundred extra pounds besides. But, damn, you look good."

"I'm sorry for your troubles, Izzy," I said.

"I haven't had anyone call me Izzy for years," he said. He turned to Jack and Marge and said, "My real name is Isadore and not many people even know that."

I introduced him to Marge and Jack and then we went into the room we used as an office and settled down to work.

I said, "Izzy, the District Attorney told us that you had contacted him and that you might have information about who killed Father D'Angellini. Is that right?"

"Not exactly. I don't know who killed him really, although, I have a few ideas, but I think I know why he got it. But that is an involved story if you've got the time," he said.

"Time we have," Jack said.

"Well as you know Noah, Saint Francis was my parish all my life. We were both brought up in the parish, received our First Communion and Confirmation there and were regular churchgoers. We even played basketball and baseball in the CYO for them. And, like you, I was a good parishioner for most of my life. Then things went sour," he said.

He sat in the chair and it seemed to sag under his weight. I have said he was a big man, but sitting in a chair that was made for a normal person, he looked even bigger. His bottom literary spilled over the seat of the chair and his thighs completely engulfed the chair bottom so it was invisible to the eye. I would not have been surprised to see the chair suddenly collapse and my old friend find himself sitting on the floor. He held his walker directly in front of him and seemed to be leaning on it as if to take some of his weight off the chair seat.

"The problems started for me with my grandson. The kid is twenty-one. He is gay and he makes no bones about it. You remember my middle son, Noah? He's the one you had in school. Well, it's his son. The kid is sharp as a tack. He's a junior at Harvard and he won't back down for nobody. Hell of a great kid. Well, our friend Father D'Angellini, the jerk, refuses to give the kid communion because he admits to being gay and according to Father that is against the teachings of the Church. Now, you and I know that this guy doesn't have the guts to do this on his own, so you know it comes from that clown, the Bishop," he said. "The Bishop decides to use Saint Francis as a test parish. I figure he thinks it's small, so even if people raise hell there won't be much of a ruckus. Problem is he doesn't think about the cuckoos out there who are active against gays. What do they call them, homophobes?"

"They are out there," Jack said. "I think it is a shame, but there it is. Hate never seems to go away."

"This hate backfired on them, though. It didn't take too long before Father D'Angellini got the reputation as the priest who was fighting gays in the Church in the Fall River Diocese. The reps talk about 'unanticipated consequences' when they pass a bill. Here there was a load of unanticipated consequences. The church filled up with haters. They came to celebrate their hatred of gays with Father D'Angellini. The odd thing about that was that my grandson says he knows that the guy was gay himself; an active gay, not a celibate gay. Doesn't that top all?" he asked with a glint in his eyes.

Marge said, "If he were gay himself why would he make an issue of the gay thing?"

"Well I think he was forced into it. He was one of those young conservative priests who seem to be coming along more and more now. But when he got started, there weren't so many of them. He came up through the sixties and he got tighter and tighter as the years went by. I don't think he could stand the freedom. Then when Pope John opened the windows, he froze into his style that most of us didn't much care for. I know you stopped coming to the church, Noah, but I still hung in, even though he was not my idea of much of a priest. But the old ladies loved him and he was Italian and I hung in," he said, "even though some of us complained about him."

He sat back again and said, "Told you this would take some telling. You guys okay or are you getting sick of listening to me? Noah, I could use a drink of water out of that bubbler, if you could get it for me?"

Jack was closest to it and he poured him a small cup of water and gave it to him and waited for the empty cup. Sheikie drank it down in one swallow and asked for another. He was perspiring profusely at that point and I gave him a few paper towels so that he could wipe his forehead and face.

"Well, at the beginning he drew the conservatives from some of the Irish parishes who were not happy with the 'new Church' and the big guys must have picked that up. I think they started urging him to go farther and farther. There was even talk that he would be made a monsignor. My own feeling is that he got caught up in it until he was their boy and he didn't have the guts to get out. Then the gay marriage thing came up and all the bad feelings about gays. It was the 'in' thing. The Republicans were using it to get their base moving. The President wanted an amendment to the Constitution to prevent gay marriages and one of the local representatives to the State Legislature got on the band wagon. In my view it was strictly a political issue. The pols didn't care who they stepped on or hurt. Kids like my grandson who are decent and good got trampled all over. They got used. To make a long, long story shorter, Saint Francis drew the cuckoos and then the bigwigs decided to use the church as a place to deny gays the Eucharist."

"How did you feel about all this?" Jack asked.

"Mad enough to kill the guys who did it to kids like my grandson, if that's what you are trying to find out. Yes I was mad enough, but not crazy enough to shoot Father D'Angellini. He was only a pawn and I knew that. I was close to smacking him once,"

"When was that?" I asked.

Jack interrupted then and said, "Guys, this has been going on for quite a while and since it is informal, I say let's go to a more comfortable place and maybe have dinner. It isn't as if you two don't know each other. So what's the harm unless you can't spare the time Mr. DeMarco. I'm starved."

"Hey, it's okay by me. This is very uncomfortable. This chair was made for a dwarf. Let's go, I'm dying to get out of here," he said. He rose from the chair slowly, gripping the walker with both hands and struggled to his feet. I wondered if he would make it, but he finally did, with a great deal of effort. "Where are we going? I'll meet you there. My van is equipped to handle me, but let's make it somewhere nearby. I'm tired and hungry."

We decided on Magoni's which was across the river but not very far in terms of mileage and Sheikie agreed to meet us there.

We waited in the parking lot about five minutes until he arrived and then waited five minutes longer while he got himself out of his van. I wondered what I would feel like if our positions were reversed and once again felt lucky to be able to lead a good active life.

We entered the restaurant by way of a ramp on the side of the main entrance and when we were given a table, Sheikie sank heavily into the captain's chair that was provided for him. He was soaking wet with perspiration, but he seemed to be comfortable in the chair.

Marge and I ordered a glass of Chianti which we intended to nurse until our main dish arrived. Jack and Izzy each had a beer and after our orders were placed, Jack reminded Izzy of where he had left his story. The restaurant was unusually quiet and there was nobody sitting close to us, so we had no concern about being heard.

"Well," Sheikie said, "It was the day my grandson, Mark, planned the ribbon showing. He quietly put out the word that Catholic gays in the area should show up for 10:30 mass on a Sunday at Saint Francis. They would bring their families and friends and everyone would wear a white ribbon somewhere visible on their person. When it was time for communion, each person would walk up to the altar to take the Eucharist."

He knew he had our full attention, so he wanted to make the most of it.

"So picture it. Here we have a church full of ultra-conservative gay haters and a standing-room only group of gays and their friends and relatives. You can figure that there was plenty of hate in that church."

"It's funny we didn't hear much about it. You would have thought that the news would have been full of it," I said.

"The Bishop managed to squelch the whole story, per usual," Sheikie said, "but not among the parishioners. They all know what happened. The funny thing was that between the group that Father D'Angellini had coming to the church and Mark's group, there weren't that many parishioners there on that Sunday morning. The church was dead quiet as Father said the mass. People were looking at each other but nothing was said. Then when it was time for communion, Mark led the way to the altar. You could have cut the tension with a knife. My son and his wife were behind him and then my wife and me. My grandson was refused the wafer and so was my son and his wife. I expected that. But to tell you the truth I just about blew up when he refused my wife. He refused my wife. I could have knocked him down and he knew it. He turned as pale as a ghost. I was close to smacking him, let me tell you. Think about it. In that church, cheats and crooks, prostitutes, adulterers and all the rest had been given the Eucharist and he was refusing my wife. Compared to even the people in that church, she was a saint. But there is one thing more you have to understand."

"And, what is that?" I asked.

"Well, my grandson swears up and down, that this guy was as gay as he is, believe it or not."

"Are you pulling our leg?" Jack asked, "I can't believe it? How could he have done what he did then?"

"I think he was forced into it. I told you that. The hierarchy was looking for a parish to test out their feelings about gays and this one was small enough to use as a starting point. When he showed an inclination to bow to his superiors and he was easy to handle, they chose his parish and him. It began, I think, with abortion. He raised quite a stink about abortion and how evil it was. I think he really believed that, but it didn't take him long to get a following. He was a natural, a true believer. But, I think he had real problems with kids, especially altar boys. The word is that his mother took care of the biggest problem. One family accused him of molesting their son," he said.

He had a captive audience and Izzy was making the most of it. He sat back and then when the waitress brought a plate of gynocchis he stopped talking completely. The restaurant served gynocchis with every meal and I admit that even with my diabetes, I had a difficult time not tearing into a few. These were small pieces of fried dough which were rolled in sugar and cinnamon, enough sugar to cause me problems, but I ate a half of one while Marge ate the other half. Jack and Izzy demolished the plate of fried dough.

Izzy took time out from his eating to continue, "The word is that his

74

mother took care of that problem. She's a tough lady, old school Sicilian lady. She protected her baby. Wait until you meet her. She's what we call a tough broad, hard as nails that lady." He said this and laughed. "She reminds me of my own mother. Say what you want about her or her husband and she wouldn't say a word. But, say something about her kids or do something to them and you had a war on your hands. It didn't make any difference whether you were right or wrong; she didn't care. Just keep away from her kids, that was the message. Mrs. D'Angellini is the same way. She would defend her kids with her own life. You can be sure someone from the Hill is out there right now investigating this murder."

"This idea that he was gay; what do you base that on?" I asked.

"My grandson. He swears that he was gay. And, then there was talk in the parish that he liked young boys. There was one particular kid, who was with him all the time. He was like his shadow. His name was Gino Alberto. He isn't in town any more. I don't know where he is, but his mother still lives on Arthur St. Her husband passed away, I think, but she might be worth a visit, Noah. Anyway, there were all kinds of rumors about that kid and Father. But, you don't need gossip from me. Check her out for yourself, Noah."

Our salads came then and we set about eating our meal. Jack rarely said anything when he ate and Marge seemed to be in a contemplative mood. Izzy wanted to talk, however, and he felt nostalgic for our childhoods when I suspected things were better than they had ever been since for him. We attended the same elementary school and then we had separated as he went to a grammar school which was near to his home, while I went to the junior high where I was to spend my teaching career. He left school at age 16. By that time World War II had ended and there were plenty of good jobs available in the manufacturing sector as the country returned to peacetime production. He worked at the Firestone plant in Fall River and worked there until the plant closed in the 1970's. From then on in, he worked in any number of jobs until he qualified for retirement under Social Security. He looked back with some joy at his early years in school and the period after he had left school and made a good pay at Firestone in the adult world of work. I saw something of him then because he had wanted to be a prizefighter and he spent his non-working time in a gym, training. I had seen a few of his fights. Those were the days when every city had a fight night and boxing was a very big, local sport. He was a big, likable guy and was a crowd favorite, but his lack of speed afoot betrayed him and he failed to make much of a mark above the local level. He had earned the sobriquet of "Sheikie" because he wore a sheik's headpiece when he entered the ring. Those were the days when wrestlers and prizefighters thought to separate themselves from the crowd by wearing something distinctive or tried to present themselves to the audience in some unique way. Izzy had chosen to be a sheik and the name stuck with him for the rest of his life. He had been too young to serve in WWII. He had enlisted for the Korean conflict and had spent three years in the navy. He considered himself lucky to have missed combat action although he was a Korean veteran even though he was one sailor who had not left port in Virginia on too many occasions.

We talked quietly, remembering people that we knew from our early years and we managed to maintain a genial conversation while we ate our dinner. Both Jack and Izzy ate heartily and seemed to be enjoying themselves, while Marge and I ate a light, but satisfying meal. We were all a bit tired after our session in the office followed by another in the restaurant. We had absorbed a great deal of information in a short period of time. I, for one, had had enough. We had learned a great deal in that period and I felt that Izzy had opened quite a few doors for us. I couldn't believe that I had not heard about the mass in which the Eucharist had been refused to the gay communicants and their supporters. It had been some time since I had been to church, but that was not the kind of thing that was kept quiet. Later, Marge expressed her surprise again, as well.

We waited for Izzy to get his body loaded in his vehicle and then we thanked him for his help. He thought it might be useful if we met with his grandson if the boy could get free to come to Fall River. We said that we would be willing to go to Cambridge if need be, to talk to him rather than make him come to see us. We wanted to talk to him to see how he felt about Father D'Angellini and to explore why he felt the priest was gay. I gave him my telephone number and he said that either he or the young man would contact me as soon as he talked to his grandson. We thanked him for the information he had given us again, and we watched him drive out of the parking lot and onto the road that leads to the bridge leaving Somerset for Fall River. I suddenly was hit with the premonition that I would not be seeing him again. I suppose because of that feeling, I didn't say much on the way back home. It had been a long day.

Marge finally said, "Can you imagine how much those people were hurt that day at the mass? I felt so badly for that poor man and I felt as badly for his grandson."

My thoughts were on the man I had known as a boy. He had been a big boy then, as compared to the rest of us who had shared his grade in school. We grew up in an era when Joe Louis reigned as the heavyweight champion of the world and Ted Williams, Joe DiMaggio and Stan Musial were our heroes. Izzy loved Joe Louis. He was never much of a student, but he was not the kind of a boy who was a troublemaker in class. In fact, I was a tad jealous of him at the time because he was the teacher's errand boy in every grade. He was also the boy who was chosen to clean the blackboard and the erasers and the one who was chosen to hand out straws at milk time. Once, the custodian even took him up on the flat roof of the building to retrieve the rubber balls that managed to get over the façade of the roof when we played stick ball in the school yard after school was out for the day.

The one thing about him that stands out the most in my mind is that he was what we called "tough." The older boys in the school did not try to test his strength or his courage. I saw him fight only once in the school yard. Unlike most of the school boys who fought by grasping each other and tumbling over each other on the ground, he fought differently. He stood up straight and pounded the boy he was fighting against with his fists. He hit his poor opponent several times until the boy turned and ran, rather than stand there and be pummeled.

I lost track of him after we left elementary school, until I saw him entering the ring as Sheikie. I didn't see him again until his son graduated from junior high school.

Looking back, I suppose that Izzy did as well with his life as we could have expected. His talent was in his big, oversized physical being. He did not have the mental tools to become a student, so he used the one gift he possessed, his body. He spent most of his working life in a factory doing heavy, wearying work. Then his body betrayed him by becoming worn out and he became almost crippled, as I saw him today. Who would have thought that the big scrapping boy of nine years old would be using a walker to allow him to move his body? Looking at him now, I realized that it was almost inevitable that such bulk would be impossible to support for so many years. I had a picture of him trying to get into his vehicle and I realized that his body had broken down under his shear weight and size, both of which had not given him very much of value after his early years. The cards had been dealt and he had been given a poor hand. That body of his had been good over the short run, but it had taken its toll over the seventy-four years he had lived in it. I could only hope that it didn't get worse.

We arrived at the Point and Jack decided to take the time to give Patrick a rundown on what we had learned from our discussion with Sheikie and what we hoped to learn from his grandson in the near future. Marge and I passed on that one. We were exhausted. Before Jack left we told him that we would have a late, light snack and that he would have to settle for leftovers. In our case that would be sufficient, but we knew that Jack would be "starving" in an hour or so, so we decided to prepare him ahead of time for the smallest of bites.

For my part, I decided to take a rest and from the look of Marge, I knew she needed the same. She decided to shower and change her clothes while I sat in my favorite chair, leaned back and listened to a Mozart piano concerto. In no time at all, I fell asleep and managed to have a very restful nap.

CHAPTER X

Patrick called us to his office to deal with Father Sousa who was the Bishop's right hand man in the Fall River Diocese. I had never met him, but I knew him by reputation. He was known to be a difficult man. On this occasion he was not the least bit happy about meeting with us in the District Attorney's Office. I had the impression that he was normally the host at meetings of any kind and he did not appreciate leaving his home base to discuss the Bishop's business with underlings. He represented the Bishop now in the Bishop's desire to set the parameters for the investigation of the murder of one of his priests. The last thing he needed was three old people in the persons of Marge, Jack and me present while he wanted to have a private discussion with the District Attorney.

"I really don't understand how these people are involved in this case. I find it objectionable that I should have to discuss private and delicate matters in their presence," he said.

He was a small man, almost diminutive, but he held his body upright as if he had a ramrod down his spine. He was dressed in his official black suit with a white collar. Looking at him standing stiffly before us as we were introduced after his little complaint about our meeting, he struck me as rather pompous, but I forced myself to withhold judgment until I knew him better.

Patrick said, "I have taken Noah and Jack as unpaid assistants in the office in special cases. They have proven their value to this office in a number of cases over the past few years and I have great faith in them. Marge joined them recently and they all have been very important to this office. I chose Noah in this particular case because he grew up in this parish and he knows many of the parishioners personally. Our sole interest in this case is to discover who murdered the pastor and to see that he or she is punished."

"Are you a practicing Catholic, sir?" he asked Patrick.

Patrick seemed to be taken aback by the question. I was waiting for the explosion. But, per usual, Patrick kept his composure and said, "My religious beliefs are irrelevant. I was elected to the office of District Attorney as a professional dedicated to serving the people and that I have sworn to do to the best of my ability."

"I mention it only because with all the adverse publicity the priesthood has received in the past three years or so, we hardly need more at this time in this diocese," he said without hesitation. "The Bishop asks that you consider the impact of anything you might say about the case to the media or the press. At least, he asks that you be aware of the damage that can be done by careless talk."

"Father Sousa, I have no intention of hurting the Church, but, at the same time, I insist on being able to do my job as I see it. I repeat again, that I was not elected to serve the Bishop or to put the best face on anything. I will not go out of my way to hurt anyone, but I insist on the freedom to take this wherever it leads and to do justice," he said and I could feel the undertow of anger in his voice.

Sensing the tension, Jack said, "And, Father, be assured that Noah, Marge and I never talk to the press under any circumstances. We stay out of the public eye. We have never done so and we will not do it now. There will be no loose cannons on this case. There will be one spokesman for the District Attorney and that will be the District Attorney. Personally, I think the voters were wise in choosing such a level-headed, honest man to represent them."

"Nevertheless, I cannot say that I am totally satisfied with your attitude, sir," he said. "You know that the Bishop has a great deal of influence at election time, should he wish to use it."

"Frankly, Father Sousa, I don't like the way this is going. I think your coming here and threatening me is outrageous. I think it is arrogant and it has strained my patience. If you represented anyone else, I would throw you out of here on your ear," Patrick said. He was fuming and could barely contain himself. He could not control the blood flowing to his face at that point and he looked like he would explode.

"Now I am going to repeat my position for the last time. I will serve my constituency by pursuing the murderer of this man, who happens to be a priest. We will go wherever our investigation takes us. I will do nothing less, even if it costs me my job. I do not think you represent the Bishop. I cannot imagine a man with his experience taking the position you have just taken. If we come across anything hurtful to the Church, I will, out of courtesy to the Bishop, inform him of what we find, but I will not change my judgment under any circumstances. Now I think the subject is closed. Have I made myself clear?"

That was a long speech for Patrick who was not normally very loquacious. He had said his piece and as far as he was concerned Father Sousa was dismissed.

"I understand fully. I just hope you realize the consequences for your sake," he said. "The Bishop is going to take a great deal of interest in this affair."

He stood up then and without a word, turned slightly and nodded to Marge, Jack and me and then staring at Patrick with what was supposed to be a withering look, said, "I hope you find a way to accommodate all of us in this unfortunate business."

With that he turned quickly on his heel, walked to the door and was gone.

Patrick came out from behind his desk and walked to the water cooler, chose a paper cup, and opened the spigot to pour himself a drink of the ice cold water and then drank it down in one gulp. We stood by without saying a word knowing that he would have himself under control. He was visibly attempting to control his anger.

Finally, he said, "I can't believe what I just heard."

He returned to his chair and sat quietly while he moved things around on his desktop as he continued to quiet his nerves and blood pressure.

Jack broke the silence and the tension by saying, "God, he was a little pompous ass. I felt like giving him a good boot in the bottom."

Marge said, "I could almost have done it myself. I hate to say this, but did you notice that he had a wart on the side of his neck with bristly hair growing out of it? I felt like grabbing the hair and pulling it out. I feel stupid saying that, but I really did have the urge."

We all laughed at the foolishness of it. Even Patrick laughed. There was nothing we could say to top that, so we didn't try.

Patrick said, "We will go forward. You guys will have to solve this crime so we can put it behind us. So, let's get to it and do everything else we have to do.'"

We left, then, without any concern about watching our backs or having to please the Bishop.

* * *

Jack pursued the money angle and within the next few days came up with some interesting information. Father D'Angellini, although, not poverty stricken, had no money to speak of, certainly nothing more than could be expected for a man of his income and his age. As far as Jack could determine, he had roughly $10,000 invested with a broker in a non-taxable bond account. He also had a personal account holding some $14,000. How Jack managed to find these facts, I don't know, and I suspected the District Attorney would not want to know.

"He may have dribs and drabs here or there, but the important thing is that we are not talking about a fortune and certainly not enough money as a motive for murder. He had no more nor less, than a person in a moderate paying profession, who is careful with his money would be expected to have. Not much for a lifetime's work, is it?" Jack said. "If he is typical, that dispels my Protestant notion of priests as people in black suits who get rich on their parishioners."

"So do you think that closes the door on finances?" I asked.

"Not really. Mom has a good bit of money. She has it in trust for the grandchildren. There are two of them, Frank's kids. Where the money came from, I have no clue yet. The one thing I have heard is that it is a big amount. It is going to take a while to dig all this out. If it is a trust in the name of the kids, I don't think it would be our victim's money. The gossip among my sources is that the money came from a big job that Father's father pulled off before he went to jail. That is only talk. I'm going to get off the phone for now and do some personal stuff in Providence. Hopefully, I can dig a little deeper than I can over the phone, but who knows? Rumors about wealth are easy to come by, but facts are a bit more difficult to get at."

"Well, if anyone can get the facts about money, I'm sure you can, Jack," Marge said. "You're like a hunter stalking his prey."

"I don't know if I should thank you or not for that comment, but, at any rate, we should be able to pin this down in the next couple of weeks," Jack said. "In the meantime what have you guys turned up?"

"Nothing of any importance so far that you don't know about, but I certainly would like to interview Mrs. D'Angellini as soon as we can. I think you should be in on that one, Jack. Then I would like to meet with Sheikie's grandson to get to the bottom of how he felt about Father D'Angellini. I'd like to determine how much resentment there was to the priest by him and the gay community. I wonder if the resentment, if any, was deep enough to be called hatred."

"And, we can't overlook what your old friend said about the possibility that his grandson thought that the victim was gay. If that is, in fact, the case, then that should color our perception of how he conducted himself in the church. With all the charges of pedophilia made in so many parishes against so many priests now, we have to consider his possible gayness in that light even though we recognize that gayness and pedophilia are not one and the same," Marge said.

"If something like that shows up we can expect the Bishop to go out of his mind," I added. "That was my first thought listening to Father Sousa. I couldn't help but think that he was here anticipating the ricochets that could come out of this case and trying to fend them off before they came up. Why else would he be so direct and threatening? I personally think that there is pedophilia involved here and that the Bishop is worried about how the homophobes will react. Can you imagine the reaction if this case is linked with homosexuality or pedophilia in any form?"

Marge said, "No, I can't. It would be earth shattering for the haters to find out that their leader, their symbol, one of their own was a homosexual, much less, a pedophile."

Jack said, "Let's not jump to conclusions. Let's hope we get some facts first."

* * *

The report came through on the pistol which was used in the murder of Father D'Angellini. It was a thirty-eight caliber revolver and there was no question that he was shot at close range, no more than four feet. Three shots were fired in quick succession and they appeared to be no more than six inches apart. One bullet had penetrated the man's heart and two had entered his lungs. Death was immediate. The three shots were fired while he was standing with his back to the cabinet and that, according to the coroner, would have held him up at impact. There were bruises on his back that showed where he had been thrown back against the shelving at his lower back level. Since death was instantaneous, the doctor felt that he had undergone no suffering at all from the impact of the bullets striking his chest.

There wasn't much to be learned from the report except as a means of eliminating any conjecture that might arise in the absence of the precise report. It was my experience that the danger in an investigation of a crime of this kind, was that we would grow tired and begin reaching for straws. This report would help to keep us on our feet by knowing exactly how

Father had been killed. It has been my brief experience that solving a crime isn't a matter of great revelations, but rather the gradual collection of facts that, when amassed and looked at correctly, lead us to the truth.

Patrick called a meeting of the detectives who had been at the scene of the crime on that fatal day when Father D'Angellini had been shot and killed. He had received the coroner's report and he felt it was a good time to review everything that had been garnered by everyone concerned with the case. The detectives were still not very receptive to Jack and me, and, certainly not to Marge. They saw her as my companion and of little value in the business at hand. They were professionals who looked down on us as old-timers who were amateurs and who were sticking our noses in where they didn't belong.

Patrick read the summary of the coroner's report without going into too much detail.

"First of all, Father D'Angellini was killed by shots in the chest. One of those entered the heart and the other two penetrated the lung. The coroner feels that death was instantaneous and came as a direct result of the shots. The victim's heart wasn't in great shape, but he died directly because of damage to the heart by the wounds and not because of heart failure. The pistol was a 38 revolver. The coroner feels the shots were fired from a distance of about two feet, no more than four. The priest was facing the assailant and the force of the shots drove him backward into the counter. There are bruises on his lower back which indicate that he was thrown back with some force and then he slid to the floor where we found him. He estimates the time of the murder between one and three in the afternoon. The report is here for anyone to see. I've summarized it only to save time."

We were meeting in the room next to his office and he was standing on a raised platform that stood about six inches off the floor. We were sitting in metal folding chairs that were normally stacked against the wall until needed.

There were six professionals in the room along with Marge, Jack and me.

"Any questions, so far?" Patrick asked.

No one had a question so he turned to one of the older detectives and said, "Michael, give us a rundown on prints and anything you were able to find in the room."

"There were prints everywhere. But there is nothing that means anything. Most of them are smudges belonging to the victim. It would be impossible to isolate the prints of the assailant if there are any. It could be that if we find a suspect we can check back and find his or her prints among those I've collected, but even that is iffy. I don't think that counter was ever wiped clean. And as you would expect, there is nothing on the door handles that is clean. I'm afraid what I have isn't very useful. The same thing can be said for the floor. It is tiled and nothing clings to it. There are a few scuff marks but no real prints of any value. There was nothing of any significance on the victim's shoes, either. He wore black leather shoes with a hard sole and that shows nothing at all. I'm afraid we have nothing of any value there," he said. There was a finality in his voice that didn't seem to leave much room for questions.

He was a trusted professional who knew his job and not one who could perform miracles.

"Any questions?" Patrick asked. "Michael, I know you'll save everything you have. You never know if something there might be useful."

"Jack, how about the money end?" he asked.

"Nothing much there either; certainly nothing that would constitute a motive. So far, I would say Father had about $14,000 in liquid assets and about $10,000 in non-taxable bonds. I don't think there is much more unless he put it in someone else's name. His mother has a sizeable account and I am looking into that now. The rumor is that it came from a big job her husband pulled off before he went to prison. I should have that pinned down in the next week or so," Jack said. "I don't know how this affects Father D'Angellini, but I'll just follow the money trail and see where it leads."

"Marge and Noah," Patrick said.

"Well," Marge said, "We have been interviewing parishioners and we have some interesting leads to follow, including the possibility that Father was gay. Nothing substantiated yet, but we'll be working on that all week. There was some talk about a conservative movement in Saint Francis that was quite controversial and that has to be followed up too."

I said, "The important thing is that we keep pursuing whatever leads we get. We hope to meet with Father's mother this week and to get as much information as possible from her. But, who knows?"

Marge said, "I would like to know what they were doing in the sacristy."

One of the detectives said, "What's that got to do with anything? Why would that be important? I don't get it."

Marge quietly said, "I think it is very important. It was a weekday and that means that there was a morning mass. I have checked the church schedule and there was nothing else scheduled in the church that day. There was no funeral mass or services of any kind. There were no classes scheduled and for all intents and purposes the church was empty that day. Then why would the priest be in the sacristy? It isn't exactly a place where meetings are held."

Patrick said, "I see your point Marge. She's right. That is an important question. Normally any business is done in the rectory and even if it was informal, it is unlikely that Father D'Angellini would be meeting someone in the sacristy. There had to be a specific reason for them being in that place at that time. Good thinking, Marge. Anything else?"

A young detective whom I hadn't seen in the past, said, "I hear talk that this priest, what's his name, was having a war with some of the drug dealers who live outside the project. I mean they live one street behind the church and one street away from the project. They sell drugs to the people in the project. The word is that this priest was trying to get the police department to shut them down and getting nowhere. Maybe there is an outside chance that one of the dealers decided to put him out of the way. It's probably a long shot, but who knows?

"There just may be something in that," Patrick said. "Why don't you follow through on that angle detective? Keep these people informed. You guys can follow your instincts," he said, nodding at the three of us.

The young man seemed to be waiting for the others to leave and we sensed that he wanted to talk to us so we lingered for a few moments.

He said, "My name is Peter, Peter Madeiro and I thought I'd like to meet you personally and to introduce myself to you since we'll be working on this case together. This is my first case and I have heard lots of talk about you."

Jack said, "I hope it has been good."

"To be honest, it has been mixed. A lot of the men feel resentment toward you because they think you're amateurs, sticking your nose in where it doesn't belong. But the District Attorney thinks a great deal of you, so I trust his judgment. I'm working toward a law degree nights, and I'd like to work in this office as a lawyer some day, so I want to learn as much as I can. I hope you will take me under your wing as we work together on this case."

He was so honest and forthcoming, it was refreshing.

"I'm not sure how much you can learn from us young man. We sort of play it by ear and sometime we flounder around a bit, so you may be disappointed in our methods," I said. "More often than not we chase leads that end in nothing. The advantage we have is that we are all retired and can afford to waste the time since we have nothing else to do. The professionals you work with don't have that luxury."

He was a black man of medium height and almost frail body. He wore a navy jacket with light gray trousers and highly polished black shoes. His shirt was white and he wore a dark blue patterned tie. He was a dapper man who looked very good in clothes. I detected a Cape Cod accent so I asked, "Where are you from Peter? You sound like you come from the Cape."

"Buzzards Bay is where I was brought up. You spotted my accent, I see. My parents are Cape Verdeans and I am the third generation," he said.

Marge said, "Noah was wrong you see. You couldn't be closer to the Cape, but you are not a Cape Codder, right?"

"I feel like a Cape Codder and I talk like a Cape Codder, but the people across the Cape Cod Canal tell me that I am not a Cape Codder. I am a pretender," he said laughing. "But I know in my heart that simple geography, doesn't make a cultural difference. A bridge across a manmade canal doesn't separate very much, does it?"

I sensed that all three of us liked him almost immediately, but it was Marge who said, "I couldn't imagine two better guides than these gentlemen, in more ways than just the investigation of crime. Welcome."

Marge put his cell phone number in the little book that she carried for her scheduling and we invited him to dinner that night so that we could talk to him about the case and what we had discovered. He was familiar with Patrick's house so he said he would have no problem finding us because I lived across the road from Patrick and Jack lived next door on Westport Point. Clarissa was home from Brown University for a few days and we thought it might be nice for her to have a young person with us at dinner for a change. So, we left him then and firmed up dinner at 7:00 at our place.

So, we had dinner for five planned at 7:00 and I thought immediately of lobsters. At the end of the Point, a finger of land reaching into the Westport River is a fishing pier which the professional fishermen use for wholesaling their daily catch. With luck we can find a lobsterman who has just unloaded his traps and has some fresh lobsters that he will retail. As soon as I pulled into our driveway, I walked the half mile or so to the end of the pier hoping to find one of our many friends and, hopefully, some freshly caught lobsters. Jack tagged along with me hoping that we would come across one or two of the Portuguese fishermen so that he could try his brand of Portuguese in a conversation.

We were lucky to find one of my favorite lobstermen just bringing his boat into the pier. Jack jumped on board and helped our man secure the old beaten up tug that was his lobster boat. Then, I asked him for lobsters and he said, "I've got some beauties for you guys. Mr. Amos, I would buy a couple of extra, cook them and freeze the meat before we start running short. These run between 1 ½ and 2 pounds, just the right size. How many people you got?"

I said we were having five for dinner so I wanted four for us and two more for Jack and another three extra. I thought I would take his advice and cook the lobsters while I had a fire on and then open them, take out the meat and freeze it for another day and another meal of maybe a lobster salad or a casserole of lobster.

I had learned from experience that I needed a few bags to carry the lobsters in. The first time I had bought two of them I made quite a sight walking from the pier to my house clutching a lobster in each hand. I had found what I called my "lobster bags" in France; the netted bags that the housewives use for their daily shopping and I had picked up three of them which took up little room in my suitcase. Now we filled them with the nine lobsters and carried the wriggling mass back to the house and the refrigerator.

Marge and I worked together to put the meal on the table. It couldn't have been easier. A nice fresh salad, freshly baked rolls and baked potatoes and the freshly boiled lobster with melted butter was perfect. It was easy to prepare and easy to serve. Breaking the lobster open might be messy, but the sweet lobster meat was worth the effort and the mess.

Peter was at the house at about ten minutes to seven and he looked as dapper as he had earlier in the day. He was a handsome man who enjoyed dressing and looking good. We had asked him to dress casually and he came wearing a pair of khakis and a long sleeved sport shirt. Even dressed casually, he looked like he had just stepped out of the shower and put on the perfect ensemble.

Marge tried to make him feel comfortable and showed him the house. Even though I had inherited the house I felt there was something of me in it. It was a restored summer home and could not have been nicer. Peter was impressed. It came as no surprise since the house was a beauty. The view from the kitchen windows alone, looking down the grassy slope to the water's edge was worth a visit in itself. The view from on high of the harbor below with the sailboats and yachts was something to behold. I found the bright blue water invigorating even to look at from a distance.

Clarissa and Jack came through the kitchen door in a few minutes. I had never known Jack to be late for a meal. Clarissa was quite surprised to see Peter with Marge. Jack had obviously not told her that we were having company. Peter was quite stunned at the beauty of the young woman being introduced to him.

Clarissa is a beautiful woman. Tall for a woman, with chocolate skin, she comes from the Carribean Islands where she was an outstanding student. We first met her when she was working in a local store and Jack was struck by her ability to work with the store's books. Childless himself, Jack took an immediate liking to this youngish woman and decided after working with her on a case and getting to know her, that he would become her benefactor. We discovered that she was exceptionally bright and Jack arranged to have her interviewed at Brown University where she was sponsored by the dean of the English Department and enrolled as a student.

School was agreeing with her. She was back home with Jack for a few days and we were all thrilled to see her. On this night she wore a lemon colored dress with broad straps at the shoulders and a ruffled bottom. She had crossed the road wearing a beige shawl around her shoulders to protect her from the sea breeze and now she took that off as she greeted us with a hug and kiss on our cheeks. Marge bubbled in her company.

The young people relaxed once they realized that we were not conducting a dating service and they had come together as our guests, not by design, but by happenstance. As far as I was concerned, I felt they could not have dressed nicer or looked better than they did if they had prepared for a special date. At one point, while we were preparing the meal, Marge remarked what a beautiful couple they were.

Lobster isn't the easiest meal to eat when one is dressed. Marge had had the foresight, on a previous occasion, to buy a supply of lobster bibs which could be worn to protect the diner's clothing from splashing when the claws are cracked. We gave one to each of the young people and Marge donned one to make them feel more comfortable. Jack and I were willing to bypass them, but we were not wearing anything that could not be thrown into the washing machine.

The lobsters were fresh and full of meat and we had a wonderful meal. I boiled them and drained most of the water out of them and split the tails and placed an empty bowl on the table to collect the shells. We dug into them like true New Englanders.

After the initial reserve, the young people got along swimmingly and seemed to enjoy each other's company. I could see that Jack was pleased that Clarissa had someone to share her experiences with and it wasn't too long before Marge, Jack and I sat back and let them get to know each other. We certainly had no intention of playing matchmakers, but from the response the young people had to each other, it was almost as if we had done just that. I even had the feeling that when the night came to an end, they were reluctant to separate.

CHAPTER XI

I contacted Mrs. Alberto, whose name was given to us by Izzy when he had talked about her son Gino as a protégé of Father D'Angellini. She was reluctant to talk to me, but I finally convinced her that she would be doing some good.

She lived in a single family house about a quarter mile from the church. She was expecting us but it took her some time to open the door but after much delay she invited us in and we found ourselves entering a room that could have come out of the nineteen hundreds. There were portraits on the walls that must have been taken in Italy; stiffly posed couples that must have been her great grandmother and grandfather on both sides. I would like to have taken the time to look at them all, but I didn't want to be diverted from my main purpose which was to find out about the relationship between Father and the boy.

I began as soon as we were seated and I introduced Marge to Mrs. Alberto.

"Mrs. Alberto," I said, "We've heard that your boy was very close to Father. We would like you to tell us about it, if you can."

The poor woman sat stiffly in her rocking chair thinking. She was a tiny, plump woman and her feet barely touched the floor as she rocked slowly back and forth. She rested her hands on the arms of the rocking chair and I could sense the tension in her hands.

"Everybody knows about it. Why do I have to go through it?" she asked almost plaintively.

Marge leaned forward to touch her hand and said, "Mrs. Alberto, a man has been murdered and we are trying to find out who did it. It is important that we hear from the people who know most about the man. We are not interested in gossip. We want to get to the truth and we think you can help us. I know it is hard for you, but we ask you for your help."

The poor woman sighed and seemed to become resigned to the fact that we truly needed her help.

"Gino was a good boy. When he was small, he looked like an angel, and he was as an angel. He was different even when he was small. He was, how do you call it, sympathico. One time we were downtown when he was about seven years old and we saw a man who had no hands. Poor Gino, he felt so bad, he started crying. Imagine a little boy crying because he felt so sad for the man," she said this and continued to rock in her chair.

Marge said, "He sounds very sensitive."

"He was and still is. He began with Father D'Angellini when he was an altar boy. He was Father's favorite. The boy loved him and he was with him as often as he could be. He used to do the early mass every day and then Father would take him to school. Then after school first thing he did was head for the rectory to see if he could help Father do anything. He was about twelve then and he wanted to be a priest," she said.

She said this with pride and I understood how she felt. I was brought up at a time when the greatest honor that could come to a Catholic family was to have one of their children enter the priesthood or become a nun. Mrs. Alberto would have been honored to have a son who was a priest.

"Father came to talk to me about it. He said that Gino would be a wonderful priest, if he could make it. I took him out of public school and sent him to a parochial school to get a good start. He went to Holy Name and Father paid for the tuition every month. Father was good to him. He was always helping Father and was with him all the time. He was a good boy. He never raised his voice to me or disobeyed me. He did what he was told and he was good in school too. He always had good marks," she said almost in tears now.

Marge gave her a tissue and that opened a floodgate of tears and she began to tremble and the tears flowed down her cheeks. Gradually, she came back to herself, and asked for another tissue which Marge gave her from her pocketbook.

"Somehow things never turn out the way we think they will. I began to see changes in him when he went to high school. Most boys change in their teens, but there was more than that with Gino. He became very quiet. Like he drew into himself and was hiding away from everything around him. He didn't go to church then or go near Father. And Father didn't come here. Then one day, February 25, it was, he didn't come to breakfast. He was 18 and when I went to his room to wake him up, he was gone. My husband was very bitter about his leaving. He blamed Father, but I don't know why. He would never talk about it. I was so upset. February 25 is the worse day of the year. That's the same date when my husband had his heart attack and died. Like my son. One minute he was here and the next minute gone. It isn't fair," she said this and she started weeping uncontrollably.

My heart went out to her but there was nothing I could say or do except sit and weep inside for her. Marge felt the same emotions, I knew, and we were both very uncomfortable.

"So you never found out why your son left," I asked.

"I always had a feeling it was something Father did to him. My husband once called the priest a 'filthy bastard.' I think I know what that means but I don't want to think about it," she said, between her sobs and tears. "Priests are holy. If this one was not, I don't want to know what he did to my boy."

"Where is your son, now, Mrs. Alberto?" Marge asked.

"He's in California. He works in the post office in San Francisco. He sends me a card for my birthday, Mother's Day and Christmas. I have never seen him since he left, my beautiful boy. I will see him only when

I die; from the coffin. He didn't even come to his father's funeral. My lovely boy is not mine any more. Do you have children, lady?" she asked Marge.

"No, I don't," Marge answered.

"Then you don't know how it feels to lose one. It rips my insides out. I sit here every day saying the rosary, praying that he will come back. The worse thing is that I don't think I believe any more. I think God is not nice to hurt people the way He hurt me. Why? I didn't do anything bad. I was a good mother," she said, still weeping. "I go to church now and all I see is that priest on the altar and my boy dressed in a white altar boy's gown serving mass. That's all I can see and I don't know if I can believe anymore. I am blind except for that."

"When he left did he give you any clue that he was going?" I asked.

"Nothing," she said.

"Before he left was he depressed, acting different in any way?"

"I have thought back over and over again. I can't remember anything. The only thing I can remember was the night before he left, I made lasagna and he said, 'I'll never have as good a lasagna again.' I didn't know what he meant then, but I do now."

"So it sounds to me like you blame the priest. Do you?" I asked.

"Of course. He took advantage of the goodness of my son and turned him into something different than he was. You understand that? I know that. How he did it, I don't know and I don't want to know, but you know what I think? I'm glad he is dead. He deserves to burn in Hell," she said. "The only thing that bothers me is that I won't get to see it. I would give my life to see my son again," she said.

She rose from the rocking chair with difficulty and taking Marge by the hand, said, "I have talked enough. You know how I feel now about that man who stole my son from me. I want that boy back. He is a man now, but I want to see him before I die."

"You know he was shot to death, don't you?" I asked.

"Yes, I do and when I heard it I was happy. But, it didn't bring my Gino back to me."

She said this and began shaking visibly. Marge stepped forward and took the woman's hands in hers and helped her go back to her chair to sit down. She was short in stature, but now she seemed to crumble in on herself. It was almost as if her bones had turned to sand. My heart went out to her.

We couldn't leave until she recovered her composure and settled down. Marge went to the kitchen to get her a glass of water and came back with it in a minute or so. Then she knelt on the floor next to her and held the glass to her lips.

She began talking in a half whisper then.

"What did he do to my boy? What did he do?" she kept saying over and over again. Sometimes, I could hear her, but at other times she was barely audible. Marge held the glass to her lips and she began rocking so that the water spilled over the lip of the glass and onto her chest. She continued murmuring and I thought I heard her say San Francisco a few times.

After about fifteen minutes she seemed to come back to her senses but she continued to rock. I could see the indentations in the rug that showed that she had done that for many years.

Marge took her hand in hers and felt her pulse. She held it for several minutes and then said to me, "I think she is back to normal now. Mrs. Alberto are you okay now? How do you feel?"

"Fine," she said. "I'm okay now. I just felt a little dizzy. I'll be okay. You can go."

Marge looked at me as if to tell me to leave and she remained kneeling by the woman's legs. I left the house then and waited for Marge outside.

In ten minutes, Marge came out of the house and came to the car where I was waiting for her.

"How is she?" I asked.

"She'll be fine," Marge said.

"Why did you stay with her?" I asked.

"She was lying. That whole thing was a performance. I'll bet anything she was acting," Marge said.

"Really," I said in disbelief.

"I'm sure of it. What is that Shakespeare line? 'Thou dost protest too much.' I could smell a rat right away. I would guess she was trying to protect her son, Gino, with the whole cock and bull story about never seeing him. I would bet any money he came back home to see her in the last few weeks and he was here when Father was murdered. She was trying to throw us off the scent. We'll have to ask Patrick to have his men track down whether her son came here or not. Maybe Peter could do it for us."

"Well, if you are right, she had me completely taken in. She has to be quite an actress."

"Maybe I'm wrong, but I don't think so. She may feel that her son did kill Father D'Angellini, I don't know. I couldn't get anything out of her after you left," Marge said.

It was an interesting morning. I found myself being thrown from one extreme to another. On the one hand I could have sworn that the woman was sincere and I felt sorry for her pain. I had been deeply moved to the point that when Marge nodded to me to tell me to leave, I had been relieved to leave the house. Then when Marge said that she thought she had been acting, I was angry at myself for being taken in. I felt foolish to think that I could be duped so easily by a woman's tears. It wasn't the first time, and, I am sure it won't be the last.

I was speechless on the way back to the Point. What were the repercussions of what Marge was suggesting? Had Mrs. Alberto's son flown in from the west coast with the intent of killing Father D'Angellini? Was theirs a sexual relationship which had forced the young man to leave home out of fear of being discovered? Or was their some other reason, just as credible, for making the drastic move of leaving his city and going to the other coast of the country? The only way we would find out would be to meet with the man and determine what his motivation was for leaving. Had he been in the city, as Marge suggested, on the day of the murder? And, if so, had he done it?

Those were the questions I was trying to deal with as we drove out of Fall River and onto the highway leading to Rte. 88 to the cutoff to Westport Point. We were halfway there when I turned to Marge and said,

"You may have hit on the solution to this case, Marge. The more I think about it, the more I think that what you said is the best lead we have. Supposing Gino came back to town, met Father and decided to kill him in revenge for what he did to him. I'm assuming they had some sexual relationship and that is why the boy left town. Who knows, you may be right. You may have hit on it with Mrs. Alberto. She certainly gave a good performance. She had me fooled."

"I'm not sure who killed Father, but I do know she was lying to us Noah. I'm sure of that," Marge said. "So the question becomes, how do we pursue this?"

"First we have to find out if Gino was in town the day Father was killed. Then we can go from there. One step at a time, I guess. Let's talk to Patrick first and see if he can put Peter on the case," I said, just as we were pulling into our driveway.

Marge was in the mood for tea and biscotti and while she put the water on, I sat at the kitchen window looking out at the birds. I turned once and the light shone on her face in such a way that her skin looked translucent; like the porcelain dolls I remember seeing in the antique shops. She was so beautiful, she made me shiver. And right at that moment I tried to think back to what my first wife looked like some 44 years ago, before she left me. Her face eluded me. I had not a clue.

The telephone rang. It was Izzy with the telephone number of his grandson. He had talked to him and the young man had said that he could give me his number and that I should call when I had the chance. He did want to talk to me. I thanked Izzy and called Jack to find out if he had a date when he couldn't meet with the young man and he said his schedule was wide open and that I should try to arrange a meeting as soon as possible.

I called the number that Izzy gave me and the phone was answered immediately. I asked for Mark and was told that I had him. I introduced myself and he said that he would be happy to talk but it was impossible for him to come to Fall River since he was in the middle of some serious study. I offered to come to Cambridge and he immediately agreed to that.

We set the time for the next morning at ten o'clock at the newsstand in Harvard Square. I told him that Marge and Jack would be accompanying me as well and he had no objection to that, so we had a time and a place to meet.

Jack was excited at the prospect of going back to Boston and Cambridge. The last time we had gone, we had eaten at Durgin Park and he had regaled me with his stories about eating in that old establishment with his father.

Oddly enough, Marge was not overly familiar with Boston. Her husband had avoided the city, as many people do, because he dreaded the Boston traffic. I had gone to school at BU and I knew the city fairly well so maneuvering had never been a problem for me. In addition, I made regular trips to the Museum of Fine Arts on Huntington and the Boston Symphony when I could afford it. More often I ended up at Jordan Hall for the free student concerts and special free events that made an evening in Boston something to look forward to. My teacher's pay took me only so far and aside from joining the MFA every year, I couldn't afford many concerts at Symphony Hall. But now I found myself in a position where I could show my new partner the town and I enjoyed the prospect. People love to think that 'people who can't do, teach,' but I feel that 'teachers who can teach, have to teach.' Teachers love to teach and almost have to teach and I certainly fall into that category. So, with Marge I knew I wouldn't be teaching, but I would be acting as a guide to a city that I love and that would be a thrill for me and hopefully be fulfilling for her.

The next morning we left at about eight to drive to Boston. At that time the traffic was the lightest it would be all day. The morning rush was over by the time we turned off Rte. 24 onto Rte. 128 through Braintree and on to 93 N to Boston. From Fall River, the trip took about an hour although I had made it many times in fifty minutes if there was no traffic slowing me down.

I took the Massachusetts Avenue exit when I reached Boston rather than the new route under the "Big Dig" which was an unknown to me. We traveled along Mass. Ave. to the Harvard Bridge where we crossed the

Charles River into Cambridge and along Mass. Ave. to Harvard Square. It was 9:20 when I parked my car in the garage off Harvard Square and we made our way through the square to the vicinity of the newsstand.

Mark described himself as about 5' 11" tall with blond tipped brown hair. He had said, "They tell me I resemble my grandfather, but I'll be looking for you, two older men and a woman."

We were a little early and I amused myself looking at the headlines of the foreign newspapers. I had always dreamed of visiting all of the countries I saw represented here, but I had never had the wherewithal. Now I did, and the only places I had seen were the UK and Florence. I thought now that I was in love again would be a good time to visit France and I determined to do that after this case ended.

It was while I was looking at Le Monde that I felt a tap on my shoulder and I turned to see a young man standing next to me. I knew it was Mark the moment I turned.

He smiled and said, "Maybe I should have worn a white ribbon so you would recognize me."

I signaled to Marge and Jack and they came to where we were standing to be introduced. After the introductions were made, Mark suggested that we go to a coffee shop off the square where we could talk and have dessert and coffee.

"I love the place and I can't afford it too often, so I figure to take advantage of you to give me a treat if you don't mind," he said, with a charming smile.

"It's okay by me," Jack said. "I could use something to eat about now. The more the merrier if you ask me."

Mark led the way across the busy street and we walked by the Harvard Coop to the coffee shop behind it off Brattle Street. This was all familiar territory to me and I felt I was back home even though I didn't get to Cambridge that often of late.

As it turned out we were able to get a corner table out of the way of the "to go" traffic and we settled down to an excellent cup of coffee. Mark introduced Marge and Jack to the pastry display case and I listened to the "oohs and ahs" as I set my mind to having a bit of a taste of whatever Marge selected and just feasting my eyes on those things my diabetes would not allow.

Jack was delighted with the variety and managed to get two different breakfast rolls for a starter.

Mark said, "I won't waste your time so I think we should get to the bottom of this right away. I am sure my grandfather filled you in on the white ribbon fiasco and how Father D'Angellini reacted to it. I probably should never have set it up, but it was just a show of the way we, as gays, felt at the way the Church was treating us. I don't know what I hoped to accomplish or what came out of it, but it seemed like a good idea at the time."

Marge said, "I think it was a very brave and courageous thing to do and I think your grandfather was very proud of you."

"Oh, he has always been proud of me. I couldn't have asked for more from that man my whole life long. I love him very much," he said. "You have no idea, I'm sure, how we can feel the estrangement among people who are not comfortable with us. We develop a set of antennae that detect the least discomfort. Never have I felt that in the presence of my grandfather. Here he is, a big ex-boxer with a flattened nose and cauliflower ears and he is not the least put out by what I am that is so different from what he is. He is remarkable," he said.

"We were impressed with him," Jack said. "I liked him."

"But we are here to talk about Father D'Angellini and Saint Francis, aren't we? I'm sure grandfather told you how I felt about Father D'Angellini," he said.

"To be blunt," I said, "Izzy suggested that you thought he was gay. Is that right?"

"I know he was. I can't tell you of specific incidents because he never did or tried anything with me. But I could feel it. He was attracted to me. There was one kid who was with him all the time, they tell me. Gino his name was. I was too young to know anything then. Gino left when I was still small but from what I heard, I'm sure they had something going that was more than just friendship. They tell me Father was very discreet and did not do anything overtly, but my dad tells me that everyone in the parish felt there was something between them," he said.

"Were there any other boys or men that you know of?" Jack asked.

"Well, during my time there was a group of young priests who hung out together. Father D'Angellini was one of them. There were about four of them. They would dress in civilian clothes and go out to dinner together. People would see them here and there and one of them owned a cottage on the Cape where they spent quite a bit of time. I know that right after mass on Sunday, Father D'Angellini would take off for the day and I thought that's where he went. I never heard of any other kids but Gino. It was a tough time for those guys then. They were all in the closet and in a strange position. It was a time when there weren't many recruits for the priesthood and a lot of the seminarians were gay. The vocation as we had known it was gone. There were a lot more cafeteria Catholics then, the pick and choose type. Since the sixties and seventies, the Church has become more and more conservative and people are being driven out by the rigidity of the system. The anti-gay movement is part of that retrenchment and exclusion," he said. "But we are not alone. There are a lot more people being pushed out, but I won't go into that now."

"What are the implications in this particular case, do you think, if Father was gay?" Marge asked.

"I think it is very tricky for the Bishop. You see, I think he used Saint Francis for a test parish. It all started with the abortion question. Father really, sincerely wanted to lead a crusade against abortions, and he began to get a following. He was a very simple guy, without too many smarts. Everything was black and white for him; no shades of gray. The parish is really small, you know. Last year they did fourteen baptisms. Actually it should have been closed years ago, but it kept going because so many people from outside the parish attended mass there even before this whole anti-abortion, anti-gay business started," he said.

Marge asked, "Why was that?"

"Father got into the short mass thing. All of his masses were short and there was parking near the church. None of his masses lasted more than a half hour and were actually closer to twenty-five minutes. Masses at the churches in that end of town lasted forty-five minutes. So, people began coming to Saint Francis for what we used to call 'the quickie.' One other thing, he had a way with the older women. He charmed them. They loved him. He wasn't a man's man like some of the priests. He could never tell a joke or kid around. He was strictly for the ladies, who really did like him."

He stopped to eat some of his pastry. He had ordered a chocolate almond croissant and he was obviously enjoying it. He didn't bite into it, but picked it apart with his fingers and savored every bite. Jack had eaten a sticky bun which had enough sugar on it to throw me into a diabetic coma and he was eyeing the display case for more.

"Before we leave," he said, "I'll have to get some of those delicious pastries to take home to Clarissa."

"Then the abortion issue became really big and he drew a following there. He wasn't much of a preacher, but on that issue he brought passion to what he said, which was rare for him. He became obsessed with it. He became a 'one-note Johnny' and that drove away some of his visiting parishioners, but it also attracted people from all over the area who wanted to hear the message. And, that's where he got caught in a trap, I think. He was caught between delivering his new message and keeping his old flock. His quickie mass people were not the zealots. They were just quiet, not too enthusiastic people doing their duty as easily as they could. They didn't come to church to be whipped up into a frenzy. They came to do their weekly duty as quickly as they could, with as little trouble as was necessary. It didn't take long before they were seeking other churches with short masses and friendly priests. So he was caught in a bind. If he stopped the ranting and raving he would lose his new flock. The old one was not coming back for sure and the new one wasn't big enough to carry the show. You get the picture?" he asked.

"I think we do," I said. "So he couldn't remain a 'Johnny one-note' as you put it. He needed other issues, is that what you are getting at?"

"Yes, I think that is exactly what happened. The abortion issue had only so much mileage and it has been kicked around forever. But the pro-lifers are limited in number especially here in the northeast, so as the regulars slipped away, the church began to suffer. He needed an issue badly and I think the Bishop, through his emissaries, provided it. I can't prove it but I think they needed a test parish to see how things would go. The average Catholic thinks that many of the controversial issues are decided on the basis of their ethical values alone. But, if I have learned anything about the American church, it is that feelers are put out all of the time to see which way the wind is blowing. The issue became gay marriage," he said.

We sat and listened. This young man had spent a great deal of time dealing with the fact that he was a gay man in a society that hadn't fully accepted the gay community as part of theirs and he was dealing with it intellectually as well as viscerally. I could see that Jack liked the boy almost immediately and he was listening very intently to what he was saying.

"You see, when gays began to come out of the closet, a lot of people became very upset. You certainly know that. When you were young I am sure that gays were few and far between and that was all right with the average Joe and his wife. We were thought of as rare aberrations. But now things have changed, I don't have to tell you that, since you have lived through the whole thing. People want us to disappear. The Christian Right people would like to see us destroyed; maybe put in gas chambers a la the Jews in Nazi Germany, but that is not going to happen. But, we are not going to disappear now. We are part of the landscape. Now they are trying to hold back the flood before they find themselves washed away. What they don't understand is that there is no danger of being hurt by us and the sooner they integrate us into society, the better for everyone involved," he said. "I'm afraid I am speechifying here, but I don't know how else to get to it. My biggest problem in life is not that I am gay, but that I talk too much."

"Not at all," I said. "It is very important that we get the picture you are giving us so that we can put the whole thing together. Go right ahead, you have a rapt audience."

"Well I think they used him. Before I left for college there was some talk about closing the parish down. There weren't enough parishioners to make much of a fuss and a lot of them had started drifting to other churches where there was less controversy and they felt more comfortable. Saint Francis, Mr. Amos knows, was a comfortable parish. The women had their church parties and did their thing and the men left the church up to the women. Certainly there was never any controversy in that church. So I think the hierarchy had him in a bind. Increase your congregation or close; that was the subtle word they were sending him. I think that is what happened anyway," he said.

He sat thinking for several minutes while he finished his croissant. Jack suggested that he pick out some desserts for himself or his friends for later in the day while Jack picked out some sweets for Clarissa. I had to laugh at the idea of Jack selecting things for Clarissa because in the many times we had served her dinner or tea, she rarely took more than the slightest taste of what we had for dessert, no matter how good it was. So, Marge and I knew in our hearts that he would end up eating all of the sweets he was buying for Clarissa, even though he had the best of intentions of truly giving her a treat. Mark said he would take advantage of Jack's kind offer when he finished his little "dissertation" as he put it.

"How did he get into the anti-gay thing, then?" Marge asked.

"I think it came from inside his rabid crew," he said. "I've thought about that and I think that is the best answer. You see these people are never satisfied without a cause. I'm sure they feel that they are sincere, but I also think that what we call 'true believers' are the 'true haters'. They thrive on attacking anything that isn't a mirror image of themselves. I have met some of them who actually hate me. They know nothing about me, but hate me with their whole being. But I don't feel special because I am only one of the many hates they have. I could be black or Muslim or Indian or French or a movie director or an opera star or an artist, and they would hate me just as much. They are not too particular about whom they hate, so I realize I am only one of a long list. They are sad, but dangerous people, because they really believe they have God on their side. They are exclusionary. It's as if they want to exclude every one who doesn't agree with them. From my point of view, and the reason I care, is that from where I sit, Christ's message was inclusive. His message was to bring every one into the fold, sinners or not. So, in brief, I see this as just the opposite of what Christ preached, which causes me a problem and I see them and their leaders as stealing my Church from me."

We could see that these things had weighed on his mind and he was unloading. Could he have been moved to violence by Father D'Angellini? I wondered as I sat there listening to this passionate young man. He was not handsome, but there was a boyish charm about him that belied his enthusiasm about his religious conviction. It was a foolish thought on my part, but I didn't think the two went together. Like Jack, his hands seemed to have a life of their own, and as he spoke he moved them so they were as much a part of his verbal expression as his words. The combination of his words and actions actually kept our attention and even though he was prone to long speeches, my mind didn't wander from what he was saying.

"Let me wrap this up and get off the soap box," he said laughing, "When I went to Fall River that day and brought many of my friends with me, I had no idea what to expect. I figured we'd be attacked as we approached the altar, but not one of them stepped forward to stop us. There were a few words of derision, but not much else. I think Father had prepped them thoroughly before we arrived; they knew we were coming and they were told to control themselves. Of course, you know the rest. Father refused to allow us to partake of the Eucharist and that was that. He lost a lot of support that day in the parish and I don't think he ever recovered from it."

"Why was that?" I asked.

"Well, it's one thing to talk about gays in general. If you ask most people who are straight, what they think about gays, their reaction is negative. But, when you ask how they feel about their neighbor or friends or family members being gay, the question has a different meaning. It comes home. Because, believe it or not, most families have a gay member as part of their family and the question is different when you're asking how they feel about their brother or son or sister. I think that is what happened here. People were very proud of me here. I was a good athlete in high school and an honors student. I was top ten in high school, all county baseball and basketball, got a scholarship to Harvard and these people were acting the way they did to hurt me in the eyes of many of the parishioners. Father D'Angellini hurt a lot of people with his refusal to give us communion. Up until then, all his talk about gays had nothing to do with anything in their lives. When he refused my grandfather, grandmother, mom and dad and me, it became personal and they were very upset about it. He lost a lot that day and like I said, I don't think he ever recovered."

"Do you think that led to his murder?" Jack asked.

"I can't tell you. I can't imagine any of the parishioners getting that upset to be honest with you. Hurt they might have been, but enough to kill, is probably stretching it far too much. My grandfather is a big softie and I know Dad would never do anything of the sort. In my wildest dreams, I can't imagine it. So, to answer your question, I have not the slightest idea."

He had talked himself out and I could see him groping for words now. It was an emotional subject for him and he had given us a good idea of what he thought had gone on with Father D'Angellini and Saint Francis.

Marge said, "Your grandfather was very upset by all of this? How did you feel personally?"

He looked at Marge and smiled and sat back in his chair, pushing it slightly away from the café table at which we were sitting. He didn't answer immediately, but was obviously thinking how best to phrase his feelings. He drank the rest of his coffee and began picking up the loose ends of napkins and crumbs to put them in the trash container near the exit to the small café.

Then he said, "I had such a mixture of emotions it is hard to describe. Of course, I felt hurt, but I had expected that. Then, I became angry at the idea that this buffoon of a priest who was hardly my idea of a holy man or a fitting shepherd of his flock, should be in a position to reject what I was.

Then I felt terribly proud of all of the people who had stood behind us. I can't tell you how proud I was of my grandfather and grandmother on that day. Until I came along, I am sure Grandpa wanted nothing to do with gays. His generation and yours, I am sure, felt very uncomfortable with us. And here he was standing tall at that altar and I was afraid that he was going to smash that man. By the way, Father turned absolutely white standing there facing him as if he thought it was coming. But most of all, I felt terribly disappointed. I was brought up a Catholic and I am actually quite religious and I knew I was being rejected, excommunicated in a sense. It wasn't official, but I knew that I was excommunicated and I knew at that moment that I would never step into the church again. I felt very sad; not only for me, but for the Church that it should reject so many of us out of hand over something as ridiculous as sexual preference," he said. "You'll have to excuse me but this is very emotionally upsetting for me and I think I have said enough on the subject."

With that he rose from the table and threw the things he had picked up off the table into the trash bin. Jack rose then and reminded him that he should pick out some things for himself and his roommate or roommates. He took Jack at his word and went to the display case and picked out several things that appealed to him. He thanked Jack and waited until Jack had done the same and paid the bill before he shook my hand and Marge's. Marge leaned forward and gave him a kiss on the cheek and thanked him for his time with us and before we knew it, he was gone.

It was my first trip to Boston and Cambridge with Marge, but, we were accompanied by Jack, so whatever thoughts I had of taking her to a restaurant for a light lunch which would have been to our liking, were put on the back burner because I knew that Jack would want a "real man's meal" on his rare trip to the big city. I quietly suggested to Marge that until we could make the trip alone in the near future that it would be considerate of us to allow Jack his day in the sun. I immediately thought of Redbones, a restaurant that specializes in barbecued spare ribs and other southwestern delicacies. I knew that would delight Jack and I have to admit that I enjoyed seeing him happy.

But first we strolled across Harvard Yard by the Wagoner Library to the Fogg Museum which contains one of my favorite paintings; Picasso's Blue Period painting which he named simply "Mother and Child". I hoped Marge would share the beauty of the painting with me. I thought she would feel the emotion Picasso managed to get with his colorful simplicity. The museum proved to be a perfect interlude for us after the emotional talk with Izzy's grandson. Jack was taken with the architecture of the building and wandered off by himself while Marge and I spent two hours or so enjoying the treasures of the museum. And, there were many sculptures and paintings shown under ideal conditions in perfect light. I was in my glory and unless I was wrong, Marge was deeply moved by the experience as well.

For some reason I was drawn to the Renaissance paintings on the first floor. There were a number of paintings by Italian artists depicting the special relationship between the Mother of Christ and the young Christ Child that had at one time adorned the altars of the churches of Italy and which were the subjects of veneration of the peasants in the small towns in Tuscany; those untutored peasants who felt the Church through the depictions of the great artists rather than in the books that they could never hope to read. Looking at paintings by Boticelli or Fra Angelico I was struck by the simplicity of the subject. Hardly the sort of thing we were seeing in the Church of Saint Francis. What was depicted in those simple paintings and in their simple message was not one of exclusion, but one of love and charity. Looking at the paintings one didn't get the feeling of hate and disgust that came from the conservative element of the Church that I saw as exclusionary. It could very well be that those paintings did not represent the true Church at the time of their painting and maybe they were meant to take advantage of an innocent population, but they were representations of the best the Church had to offer, not the worst.

Marge loved the museum as a whole, but there were several paintings that I think moved her. At first she trailed after me following my lead, but then she slowly began to look at the paintings in terms of her own interests. As she began to feel the power and beauty of the paintings, I could see her appreciation quicken and her spirit come to life. I couldn't believe that she had had very little experience with art, but she admitted that for whatever reason she had seldom been to Boston or New York, and then, only to see a stage play. She was glowing by the time we decided that our afternoon at the Fogg was played out, but I promised her that we would be returning as soon as possible. By then, too, Jack was in an eating mood, so we walked back to the garage and the car and drove to Redbones for an early dinner.

Marge was thrilled at what she considered a new and worthwhile discovery and made me promise again to bring her back as soon as it was feasible. I loved the feeling of being able to offer something as exciting to her as this afternoon had turned out to be.

Redbones was everything Jack could have asked for and more. Barbecue wasn't my favorite meal but I found it passable while I know that Marge did her best to eat what she could so as not to ruin Jack's delight at finding a restaurant in the Boston area aside from Durgin Park that served what he considered to be a worthwhile dinner.

So, for me it was a successful day. I thought we had learned a great deal from young Mark. Jack had been made happy with the sweet morning pastries in the pastry shop and an enormous helping of barbecued ribs at Redbones. But my day with Marge pleased me most. It had been a long time since I could share something important to me with a woman. She had loved it and I felt it was something special between us. It was part of my nature as a teacher to want people to grow and to see things that they hadn't seen before. I couldn't believe that at her age, it was still possible for Marge to become enthusiastic about something completely new to her. In my own case the great moment of revelation came in the recognition of the power of literature. I was a student in seventh grade when our English teacher had read "The Rime of the Ancient Mariner" to us in class. I remember sitting shocked at the beauty of the language and was so overwhelmed that tears actually ran down my cheeks as she read. I had never had such an epiphany and have never felt the likes of it since. That reading opened a life to me that I have always appreciated. The odd thing was that when I came back to teach in the same school nine years later, my English teacher had retired and I never had the opportunity to thank her for the miracle she had performed with that one reading.

After a full day in Cambridge, the drive back to the Point seemed endless. I drove and Jack stretched out on the back seat as well as he could at his height. He normally didn't nap when we drove anywhere, but he knew that Marge would keep an eye on me as I drove. It didn't take long before he fell fast asleep. Luckily, traffic was light leaving Boston and we took only an hour and a half to make it to the Point and home.

We said nothing about the case on the way back home, which was a rarity for us. We were usually so obsessed by our cases that we could think of nothing else with our tunnel vision, but on this occasion, the day had been so full that fatigue took over and our minds stopped working.

* * *

Marge felt she needed a quiet day the next day and I agreed with her that we were working at quite a pace. It was a pleasure to be back in our quiet little town of Westport. We woke early, had a quiet breakfast with Jack and a few of the goodies he had picked up in the bakery shop the day before and spent a leisurely hour listening to music and watching the birds at our feeders. Marge invited me to go shopping at a few of the stores on Main Road which I had never visited.

"You're introducing me to art and I'll introduce you to woman's clothing," she said. "That will be quite a switch."

Our first stop was A.S. Deams which turned out to be a charming store located in a former, single family cottage. Marge loved it and did a great deal of her clothes shopping there.

"Can't beat the place. They have a great selection of things that I like and the service is marvelous. It's like going into someone's home and being treated like a person; not like the large mall stores that treat you like a number," she said as we entered the store.

We were greeted with, "Marge, great to see you. We've got a jacket in, that I think you'd like for walking the beach. It will look great on you."

Marge introduced me to everyone on hand and although I felt rather awkward, I found enough to keep me busy. I was particularly taken with a number of books having to do with the Westport area which I hadn't seen before and quite a few maps of the waterfront and the Point, mounted on hanging plaques that I thought were very interesting.

One of the women, knowing I was feeling uncomfortable, went out of her way to speak to me and to talk about the town as she knew it and loved it. As it turned out several more women came in, two with their husbands, so I had sufficient company to keep me busy.

Marge disappeared into the back room where I assumed she was trying on some clothes. I fiddled with a chess set and one of the men I had been talking to told me a story about his time in the Merchant Marine and how he had learned to play chess then. He claimed he spent hours on end playing, and when he came back to life as a fisherman, had found a few of his friends to play with. I told him I loved to play and we exchanged phone numbers. I sincerely hoped that he would contact me so that we could play a few games. I missed the occasional game of chess that I was used to playing when I lived in the city.

Marge appeared shortly, sporting her new jacket; this one with a hood with fur around the outside that, indeed, looked like she could use it for walking the beach and also for filling the bird feeders. She looked delightful in it and I couldn't help but reach for my wallet to get it for her as a gift. I didn't often buy her gifts, mainly because we rarely were to be found in places where I could buy her anything, but this was the perfect opportunity and I didn't want to pass it up.

We said our goodbyes and Marge, when we were on the road going toward the Point, said, "I'm sorry if you were embarrassed."

"Actually I wasn't embarrassed at all. It was a different experience. I think you should take Jack to the store to get something for Clarissa. That would be fun for him, I think," I said. "The one thing I know is that I wasn't thinking about the case and that is a great plus."

We drove past Lee's Market where we did a great deal of our shopping. Out of habit I almost pulled into the parking lot, but Marge wanted to go to Partners to get something to read. We drove through the central business area where the big problem of sidewalks had emerged. There were no sidewalks along Main Road. However, a number of housing units had been springing up in the area, mostly for the elderly, and there was some concern about the safety of pedestrians walking along the road with no designated places for them to walk. From the articles that had been appearing in the local newspapers, it was apparent to me that Westport was not ready for change. There were enough old-time Westport residents left whose major concern about their town was the tax rate and not the safety of either school children or the elderly newcomers. On the few occasions when I had stopped into one of the local restaurants for breakfast, I had heard the comments from the locals who met there every morning and discussed the hot news in their little town. Margarite's was the local meeting place and the talk was pretty open and sometimes heated in its small confines. There were some native Westporters about, but the most vociferous were the relative newcomers who had moved in from places like Fall River and New Bedford, and who were determined to keep the pastoral flavor of Westport alive. They were like the little Dutch boy who put his finger in the dike to stop the flood. Unlike him, they would be unsuccessful as the properties around them continued to be developed and a "new breed" moved into town. Sidewalks would be built to accommodate the elderly whether they liked it or not because the elderly would attend the town meetings and vote them out of power.

The only reminder of the case we were on was when we drove by St. John the Baptist Church on the Main Road going to Partners which was the church that Marge attended. I had been living in Westport for about three years and I was a regular visitor to Partners. Jack was a big fan of the food area of the store where they served great lunches and desserts. Jack enjoyed their muffins and scones as well as their sandwiches which were always unique. On those occasions when I dropped in for food, I enjoyed their soups which were almost perfect on cold, wintry days. On this day

I picked up some lemon scones for Jack while Marge was browsing in the book section. I joined her and decided to try an audio book that I had missed reading in hard cover. The audio books were new to me but Partners had a good selection and I enjoyed listening to them from time to time, although I still enjoyed sitting quietly with a book in my hand. Time was short for us, so I wondered if I would have time to listen to it, but I rented it anyway.

Marge picked up a book of short stories which she hoped to squeeze into some sort of reading schedule in the few minutes we seemed to have to ourselves. Marge also picked up a book that she thought Clarissa might enjoy. The shopping in a pleasant atmosphere in both shops was very nice and we drifted along in no special hurry which was perfect for us. As much as I am not a shopper, there is a quality about the local stores that makes shopping pleasant. In both stores we had visited, the women taking care of us were very personal, not pushy certainly, and earnestly interested in helping us buy what we needed. I had been to too many stores where the clerks made you feel that they were doing you a favor in taking your money. For a few hours anyway we were able to get our minds off the business of murder and it was just what we needed. I managed to listen to part of my audio book and Marge read a couple of her short stories to fill out the rest of the day and when Jack came to the house to insist that he take us out to dinner, our lazy day was just about perfect.

CHAPTER XII

The meeting with Mrs. D'Angellini took place in her house on Federal Hill with her lawyer in attendance. Jack, Marge and I met with her and it was understood that we would not tape our talk or make records of any kind of the proceedings.

Everything about Mrs. D'Angellini spoke of hard times. Dressed in mourning black, she met us at the door and ushered us into her parlor. She had the first floor of a two-family home off Broadway on Federal Hill. As she preceded us into the room I noticed that her skin was olive brown and only her gray hair broke the look of darkness about her. She was a tiny woman. She couldn't have been more than 5' 2" tall, but she appeared to have very little excess weight on her body. Her hair was pulled back and I could see her neck muscles which were drawn tight. Everyone we had talked to described her as "hard" and "tough" and I could see that in her up close, but I would describe her as tautly strung. Her voice was crisp and she spoke with a sharpness that gave me the feeling that she would be tart or acerbic if she were crossed.

We were introduced to the attorney and we introduced ourselves in turn. The tension was pervasive, and it was Jack sensing this, who broke the silence.

"Unfortunately, Mrs. DeAngellini, we have no news about your son's murderer. We also have no credible motive for his murder. We hope you can help us by giving us an insight into your son to help us try to solve this terrible crime," Jack said.

She settled herself into a wooden chair with a spindle back and a cushion on the seat and then looked over the three of us very carefully and said, "Is the city of Fall River so poor that they give a crime like this to three old people like you to solve? They have to be pretty hard up."

The attorney broke his silence by saying, "They are legitimate, believe it or not. The two gentlemen here have solved a number of crimes for the District Attorney and everyone tells me they are very good. Age doesn't seem to have anything to do with it."

He was a handsome man. He had curly gray hair growing close to his skull. I couldn't tell whether it was natural or set, but I suspected the latter. He was impeccably dressed in a blue pin-striped suit with what looked like a custom made white shirt with a diamond stick pin in his silk tie. A good tan would have done his looks some good. Too much office work or too much food gave him a look of a man who didn't use his body as much as he should have.

"Harry," she said, "I'll handle this. I don't need you stepping in to apologize for me."

He took what I would have considered an insult without any outward response and sat resolutely in his chair.

"So, nobody answered me. Cat got your tongues?" she said.

It was Jack who said, "If you are attempting to intimidate us ma'am, we have long since passed the point of intimidation. We're here to bring closure to you; not to threaten you. If you want our help in finding the killer, fine, if not, I am not going to sit here playing power games with you. As far as I can see, you are the least likely person to be involved in this murder but you are probably in the best position to tell us why someone would do it. So please decide what you want to do. While we are on the Hill I'd like to pick up some fresh ravioli and manicotti before we go back home, so if we are here on serious business, let's get to it and stop the game playing."

Her attorney started to say something, but Mrs. DeAngellini lifted her hand to stop him and said, "Good for you. I think I underestimated you guys. I get away with that kind of thing all the time, mister. Okay, now that we understand each other let's get down to business. What do you want to know?"

Jack said, "Let's start with money. Your son had very little in his name; maybe $25,000 in cash and investments. I can't establish money as a motive if that is the kind of money we are talking about."

"You're right," she said. "He had chicken feed. The Church doesn't pay much. He was always short of money; never had much and nothing to spare."

I noticed that her eyes were sensitive to the light. The room we were sitting in was furnished with old, but good furniture. The settee and side board that I could see from where I was sitting were made of a dark walnut and were highly polished. The grain in the wood shone clearly and was quite impressive. The room was lit by a few dim lights augmented by the sunlight coming through the east window. That light made her squint noticeably when the sun broke through the clouds. When the sun rose a little higher and was too high in the sky to shine through the windows directly, she relaxed and was able to look at us straight on without blinking. As she rested her eyes her appearance softened considerably.

"Now," Jack continued, "I know you have a sizeable nest egg in a trust fund for your grandchildren. We haven't seen the exact numbers, but we've heard some big ones. The one question I have to ask is whether your son had anything to do with putting together a good amount of that money?"

Harry popped up with, "How do you know how much money she has or doesn't have? What right have you got to go poking around in her finances?"

Mrs. D'Angellini retorted sharply, "Harry, shut up. You are good, aren't you mister? Before we go any further though, the money I have, had nothing to do with my boys. So, you can put that one away."

"Is there any way that the trust can be broken?" Jack asked.

She said, "No, unless the lawyers screwed up. Why?"

"I am trying to determine motive. Let's say for instance, that a suit was brought against your son, could someone get money out of your trust?" Jack asked.

"That's exactly why I have the trust. My other son is always in trouble and I didn't want anyone suing him for my money. The other was a priest and you never know what the crazies can do today, so I tied the money up to keep it safe and I want the kids to profit from it. They're both great kids and smart as hell. I want them to be somebody. What would you do smart guy?" she asked and I could see that she was as much as asking Jack for advice.

"I have no idea until I see what you've done with it and how wisely the money is invested. Your motivation sounds great to me, but you should be sure that the trust can't be broken. I'd hate to tell you how often people put their money in 'unbreakable' trusts only to see them dissolve in the courts."

"I have no idea why, but I trust you. Would you be willing to look at mine and tell me what you think?" she asked.

"I don't invest money for people and I am not in the business. So, outside of telling you whether I think your trust holds water, I wouldn't go a step further. If you want a judgment on the value and strength of your trust, I'll do that but no more. I have a young woman who is a student at Brown across town who has been working with me on financial matters and if you are interested I'd like her to look things over with me, if that's okay with you. I'd ask that you pay her a decent fee if you thought that her results were worth it," he said.

Harry said, "You come on strong mister. How do we know you have any idea about what you are talking about and that you are not some kind of a con man?"

It was then that Mrs. D'Angellini spoke curtly to her distinguished looking lawyer and said, "Harry, you can leave the house right now, I think your work is done here for today. Thank you."

"Well, before I go, just don't let this guy hustle you. I don't like his looks or his style. Does he look like a financial wizard?" he said.

He left then, unceremoniously, after giving Jack a look that could kill.

Mrs. D'Angellini said, "Leave me your telephone number and your full name before you leave and I'll have the people handling the trust contact you. Now, anything else you people want to know?"

"Lots," Marge said. "I never knew your son, but the more I hear about him the more confused I get. It seems to me that he was a many-sided man. Everybody we talk to sees him in a different light. How did you see him as a mother?" she asked.

"I'm not sure what you're getting at," Mrs. D'Angellini said.

"Sorry. We've interviewed a number of people now and it seems to me that each one has seen your son in a different light; a catechism teacher, a gay young man and his grandfather, a former sexton, the mother of a child who was close to Father and your own son; all of whom see him differently. How do you see him as his mother? I feel it is important that we get an insight into him if we are going to get anywhere in this," Marge said.

"Well, what can I say?" she said. "My whole family came from Italy. There were not many decent men in my history. His father was a thief and spent ten years in jail. That's where the money came from that we were talking about a few minutes ago. His history isn't a pretty one and I don't talk about it. Besides he was a brute to me and a drinker who loved nothing better than to beat me up whenever he had a few drinks in him. His brother has already served a stretch and is lucky if he doesn't go back in again. Now along comes Marco and he is an angel. In my whole family or my husband's we never had anyone like him. There were times when I wondered if he was my own son; if the nuns didn't switch him in the hospital when he was born, but as he grew up he looked a lot like his father so I never worried about that. When all that DNA stuff came out, I even thought of having his blood tested."

She said all of this and I could see that she was beginning to relax a little. She was never going to be a woman who let down her guard, but the hard edge had gone from her voice.

"From the beginning he was a pleaser. I think that was why he was good at being a priest. The only person he could never really please was his father. They didn't get along at all. He could never forgive his father for being what he was, a crook. He never was as bad with his brother, but he didn't like his father and that was hard on all of us. I remember the time his father gave him a television set and Marco wouldn't use it because he said he knew his father stole it. The worst part was that the kid was right. They stole a whole warehouse full of them," she said with a laugh.

"He never understood that we are what we are and we can't change people and make them into what we want them to be. All I did was worry. Worry about my husband and my son and what was going to happen to us. Marco never gave me one second of worry. What good is the worry? Now it is the son who is left alive that I will worry about. But I can't do a thing to stop him from doing something stupid and going back to jail or worse. I never thought in a thousand years that Marco would be the one to go. But, your question. He was a fine, good boy and I couldn't have had a better son," she said finally.

The room had darkened considerably and I could see that Mrs. D'Angellini was feeling less and less tense without the eye strain that I had seen when the sunlight was hitting her eyes and she was squinting so badly. I couldn't help but wonder what was wrong with her eyes and why she couldn't get the problem tended to.

"Did he confide in you, Mrs. D'Angellini? Did he give you any indication that someone was trying to hurt him? Did he have any enemies that you knew about?" I asked.

"No, never," she answered brusquely. "The only time he ever 'confided in me' to use your words, was when he was short of money and that was most of the time when he came to see me. He never told me anything personal. He played a little game of making me talk about myself and he never talked about himself. I'm getting tired now. I think I've had enough for today."

"Well then, I have to ask you one more question before we leave and it is a hard one for me to ask," I said. "We have been told that you bailed your son out of a pedophilia case and suit? Is there any truth to that?"

She sighed, moved in her chair as if to settle in, and seemed to be thinking of what she was going to say.

Finally, she said, "It is true that I handled the situation. But there was no truth in the charge. It was a story that was meant to extort money from us. There were cases all over the place and these bastards were trying to rip off the family. They made up a whole story that didn't hold water and then tried to blackmail us. I taught them a lesson though."

"How?" I asked.

"Well, I scared them. The Mafia. I'm from the Hill and the Hill has a reputation. Everybody believes that the Mafia is on every corner up here. So, I let them believe it. I let them believe that I had connections and if anything happened to my son to hurt him, the price would be their lives. They were scared stiff. I hired a guy to follow them around and let them know they were being followed. They were shaking in their boots and they dropped the whole thing in a hurry," she said with a semi-smile on her face. It was the first time I had seen her smile.

"So," I said, "You felt there was no basis for the charge, is that right?"

"What do you expect me to say? Are you crazy?" she said, "Of course there was no basis for the charge. It was all made up and a lot of lies."

She stood up then and said to Jack, "Write down your telephone number and I'll have my lawyers get in touch with you. I want to be sure that trust is solid. I don't trust lawyers."

She was finished and we knew it. So we said our goodbyes and took our leave. We drove to the shopping area on the Hill and went shopping. We went to Vendi's which is my favorite store and bought some of the delicacies that we loved so much. There was fresh ravioli and manicotti and fresh pasta. I preferred my sauces to theirs but I enjoyed their pastas and cheeses and we loaded up before heading for the city and the office. Marge picked out an eggplant salad that she enjoyed and Jack picked out one of the breads that he enjoyed so much. There was a chocolate shop that Marge couldn't pass up under any condition and Jack bought a number of chocolate goodies for Clarissa, Nelly and Peggy. He laughed after paying for Marge's order as well and said, "With one fell swoop I've taken care of my four favorite ladies."

In no time at all we were on I95 back to Fall River and home to Westport.

Jack said, "Don't underestimate that lady. She is bright as can be and very hard. That is a tough combination to beat. They'll be no giving in there. I can just imagine her dealing with those people who were charging her son with sexual abuse. I would love to have been there to see it. Imagine her threatening them with a non-existent Mafia? Now that takes a bit of doing."

Marge said, "Are you sure the Mafia is non-existent?"

"That's the word as far as Providence is concerned. After Patriarca went down, the FBI pretty much cleaned up what was left. There is still thievery, the chop shops continue to thrive, and the whole place has an unsavory reputation, but the big crime has settled on the Irish Mafia in Southie in Boston and even that isn't the same as it once was," Jack said.

"Do you think you'll find anything wrong with the trust?" she asked.

"I have no idea. But, take that as an indication of how thorough she is. She trusts no one and takes nothing for granted. You can bet your life she has hired someone to find out who killed her son. I'm sure we'll run into him or her sooner or later."

Marge said, "I can see you were impressed by her."

"I'm not sure what you mean by impressed. I am impressed by the fact that this is a woman you don't meet very often. For instance, why the interest in the trust? Two reasons; one to make sure it is solid, but there is a second reason. The second reason is that she wants to keep contact with us. Since you are obviously a couple, she chose me. Why? Because she is determined to find out who killed her son. And when she finds out, that person will never come to trial. So, if I am right, would you say that she is impressive?" he said. "I have no doubt that I am right. She is cool and calculating. She will take anybody apart who steps in her way. You saw how she treated her lawyer. That was to send us a message. He reacted very coolly and without anger because he knew exactly what she was doing. So to answer your question, I am impressed, but in a negative way," he said.

I was impressed once again by Jack's ability to see below the surface. This quiet man continued to surprise me with his insights into the character of the people we met.

CHAPTER XIII

The Opera Society of Southeastern Massachusetts had its beginning in Saint Francis where a few opera lovers decided that their best hope of getting to see one opera a year at the Metropolitan in New York was to buy tickets as a group and to hire a bus to take them to the big city and return the same day. I was one of those. On my salary as a teacher, even taking into account the discount price we paid for the package, I was stretching my budget to the breaking point, but a day at the opera was a great treat. Roger Cormier, who knew more about opera than any of the rest of us, organized the club that made opera available to all of us.

Father D'Angellini tolerated the group holding monthly meetings in the church basement recreation area at no fee, but he was not thrilled at the idea. The group needed a minimum of 36 tickets to satisfy the bus company and the Metropolitan Opera, and we sometimes had difficulty raising that number, so Roger began our monthly meetings in the hope that we could raise some interest. We would invite speakers who were knowledgeable about the opera or classical music and on a couple of occasions we invited performers. The group managed to survive for about ten years before membership waned and we found ourselves unable to continue.

The AA group didn't fare as well. Most of the Alcoholic Anonymous groups were hosted by Protestant Churches in the city and one of our parishioners who was a member of AA wanted to establish an AA meeting in Saint Francis and an Al Anon group as well to meet the same night. They were never given an outright refusal, but they were never given a night when they could meet on a regular basis. After months of trying, the group leaders gave up the attempt and did manage to get a nearby parish to sponsor the meetings.

The Woman's Guild held sway in terms of the recreation hall usage and at one time the Boy Scouts and Girl Scouts had an afternoon a week. A soup kitchen was rejected out of hand as was a program to help single teenage parents learn the rudiments of food preparation and child care.

I thought of the whole thing as the battle of the fittest. By the fittest I mean those groups who were the least controversial and the most traditional. IN Father's mind there was nothing wrong with serving the Opera Society or the Woman's Guild or the scouts. What harm would have been done by hosting the AA and Al Anon or a teenage single parenting program? Father D'Angellini must have had visions of drunks and drug addicts overwhelming his pristine world.

The parishioners took this all in stride. They had no desire to change their priest. The older women loved their parish priest and the feeling was mutual as far as Father D'Angellini was concerned. Most of the parishioners had no special interest in church activities and led their workaday lives outside the influence of the church. Christmas and Lent and Easter were times for church attendance and outside of christenings and weddings, first communions and baptisms, they all pretty much led their lives in their families and at work. They were not interested in social activism and were more than satisfied to let the church play its traditional role in the community. The rule for most of them was to attend church, but not to take it too seriously. Not until Father D'Angellini broke that long custom with his sudden conservative activism was there any interest; that turned out to be negative.

CHAPTER XIV

The housing project was a source of anxiety for the young priest when he took over the parish. He had a difficult time justifying the fact that he didn't aggressively seek parishioners among the poor. In his own mind, as much as he tried to deny it, he felt that many of the occupants of the project were unworthy. At the same time he saw the Salvation Army pursuing communicants to their affiliation and doing it successfully. He would rage inwardly when he saw the yellow Salvation Army bus taking people to services to the center on East St.. He felt they were beyond contempt. The Seventh Day Adventists were an even more serious problem because they sent cadres of true believers door to door and were much like the missionaries of the early Roman Catholic Church. Then there were the Evangelical groups who Father felt preyed on the poor and downtrodden. Their appeal was to the Portuguese and Spanish speaking immigrants who would normally attend a church like Saint Francis.

All the people that his church had traditionally appealed to were there for the asking and Father D'Angellini was unable to move in their direction. He prodded himself any number of times but something in his personality stifled him and left him inert. The project people gradually gravitated to his enemies and he could do nothing about it.

He was defeated, but in that defeat he suffered all the humiliation and turmoil of a loss in battle, a battle he couldn't wage with any conviction.

He would drive by the project, see the Salvation Army van filled with women and children driving to the Army Headquarters on East St. and his stomach would turn and he would inwardly agonize that he had lost more souls, but when he met those same women who led such lives of despair, he would turn away from them in dismay.

He had tried when he first joined the parish as an assistant. He was young and eager and it was his first assignment. He had tried going door to door, unannounced. At the first door he came to he was met by an older lady who was shaking from head to foot. Even without experience he suspected that she was suffering the D.T.s. She had a crazed look as if she were frightened and was experiencing the tremens. He moved into the room inside the door and the first thing he saw was a basket of dirty clothes on a table which had half spilled onto the floor. Beyond it he could see two little children lying on a couch watching television. They were covered in newspapers as if the papers would keep them warm. On the couch between them was a box of Cocoa Krispies with the little brown kernels of cereal spilling onto the couch and floor. She asked him to sit, but there wasn't a place where he could sit that wasn't covered with clothes, clean and dirty. From where he stood he could see the kitchen and the sink filled with dirty dishes and pans. He fled. He rushed out of the door and onto the sidewalk as if he was running for his life. Even dressed in black with his white collar, he had made no impression on the woman who had bellowed at the children, "Turn the damned TV down, you little bastards." Then she had turned to him and said, "What the Hell do you want? You want to talk to me, get me a drink."

He had stood mute looking at this emaciated, shaking wreck unable to move away; wanting to run and not able. He looked at the children who were watching a cartoon in a trance and he realized there was nothing he could do. In what he knew was a cowardly action he turned tail. It wasn't until fifteen minutes after he sat parked in the driveway of the rectory that he began to get his breath back and his breathing became normal. It took him days to get the vision of those little children with runny noses and dirty faces out of his mind

Things didn't get better when he made a visit to a newly widowed woman with one child who was a communicant of the church. Her husband had been killed on a construction job when a front end loader picked up a load of loam on a banking and then tipped over, burying him under the load of dirt and the wheels of the massive machine. He had been buried from the church and Father was making a call to commiserate with the family. The widow lived with her son in a building which was situated in the middle of the project. He parked his car and then made his way along a walkway trying to find the number of the house. The walk was littered with trash and he walked over cans and bottles and fast food cartons until he finally found the house he was looking for. There were four apartments in each house, two on each floor, and as it happened he was looking for Apartment A which he assumed would be on the first floor. He entered the vestibule and knocked on the door. The paint on the door was peeling and when he knocked he saw the dusty paint flying through the air. His knuckles were white where he had rapped and he immediately thought of his black suit which would most certainly be covered with the paint flakes he had knocked loose. No one answered, although he could hear movement in the house, so he knocked again. This time he heard a boy's voice asking "Who is it?"

"It's Father D'Angellini from the church. I've come to pay my respects to your mother," he said. "Please open the door."

He heard a shuffling inside, as if things were being moved, and after a few minutes had passed, the door edged open and he was able to push the door open completely and enter the room. He was shocked at what he saw. He saw what he thought of as a barricade of black plastic trash bags which were filled with God only knows what, piled one on top of another. Beyond the barricade he could see the widow. She was haggard and had the look of a crazed, demented soul as if she harbored some sort of evil creature inside her. Her eyes were wild and she stood in the kitchen doorway shouting, "Go away devil, go away, away, away, away, away."

She stood blessing herself over and over again and repeating, "Devil, go away, go away, go away." She repeated it in a singsong voice that was filled with anguish and pain.

He hadn't tried to enter the apartment and further. He knew that whatever was happening in that room was beyond his powers to help. He found himself turning to leave the vestibule, confused and disoriented. He found the office and asked for whomever was in charge. The secretary he talked to referred him to the social worker who was the only administrator on duty. He realized that was exactly who he wanted to see.

She came out of her office when the secretary buzzed her and invited the priest, standing in front of her, to come in and sit. She could see that he was upset and wasn't sure what she would be dealing with. She was new on the job and was feeling her way through every day.

When he sat and collected himself, he told her about what he had just seen and she tried to reassure him that she knew what was happening.

"Right now," she said, "she is suffering from paranoia. She saw her husband's death as the work of the devil and she feels that the devil is trying to invade her apartment. She is trying to keep him out. There isn't too much we can do because DSS doesn't think her condition is permanent. They think they will do a great deal more harm to her if they separate her from her son."

"That's ridiculous. The child is no more than ten years old and should not be living under those conditions under any circumstances," he said. "I have never heard anything more absurd in my life."

"That's not for us to say," she said. "We can only report what we see to the proper organization and hope they have a solution."

"It's as simple as that, is it? Is that what they taught you in school? Have you been in that house? Have you seen how they are living? Have you seen her?" he asked.

"Father, I would advise you to call the case worker at DSS and get your answers from her. I'll give you her name and telephone number," she said, dismissing him.

He called several times but was never able to get the case worker. He never did get in touch with her and finally he gave it up. He gave it up, but he was never able to erase the memory of that house from his mind.

The last time he visited the project was his most traumatic experience, and he determined never to go into it again. He was visiting one of the elderly parishioners at the request of her daughter. He was asked to give the woman the last rites and as much as he hated the project, he could not avoid his priestly obligation.

Housing for the elderly was adjacent to the western end of the project. A road divided the elderly apartments from the project itself. The elderly project stretched from one block to another and had about sixty units made up of one story apartments built in connecting fashion side by side. In the center of the elderly project was a community center containing facilities for washing and drying clothes, a visiting nurse's office and a maintenance and custodial staff as well as a meeting hall. A parking lot divided the unit in half. The whole project was a decent place for the elderly to live. Each apartment was large enough in living area and was maintained by the custodial staff. The elderly were well housed even though they were close to the problems that came out of the main project.

On that particular day Father had parked his car one block from the low income project on the western side of the elderly project. He did his duty to the dying woman and her family who were gathered around her in the one bedroom apartment and then left to return to the rectory. When he returned to his car there was a black woman leaning back against his car with her back to the driver's door. When she saw him she didn't move but crossed her arms on her voluminous breasts.

"Like some action, handsome?" she asked with a smile on her face.

"Goodness, ma'am, can't you see that I'm a priest?" Father asked in dismay.

"I can see that honey. But, you a man. In between your legs you got something that all men have and that needs lovin'," she said.

"Please move," he said. He was beginning to panic. He didn't know how he could get to his car. The woman was big and it was obvious that she was not going to move without a physical struggle.

She uncrossed her arms and pushed her breasts toward him.

"I let you suck on these if you want. All day. I love it. You give me 50 dollars and I'll do you half and half; half blow job and half fuck if you want," she said.

"Please," he said.

He was thinking that people would be leaving the apartment he had just left himself and see him talking to this woman. He was humiliated by this ugly woman standing in his way and using filthy language with him and yet was at a loss as to what to do.

"Sweetie," she said, "Fifty bucks gets rid of me one way or the other. Then, hon, I won't tell the project policeman that you were soliciting sex from me. I know you wouldn't like that. So, why not get rid of me now? No pain, no strain, no shit. Fifty bucks and I'm gone, sweetie."

"Please, go away," he said. He was actually frightened and he could feel the blood draining out of his face. He thought of going back into the old lady's apartment for help, but he was afraid she would make a scene. He stood in front of her, speechless and motionless.

She reached out and put a hand on his arm and said, "You know you want me hon, I'm a sweet thing. I'll make you happy. Mama will be good to you."

Her touch brought him out of his inertia. He was horrified.

"Don't touch me," he said pulling away.

He reached into his back pocket and took out his wallet. He opened it and then said, "I've got thirty-five dollars. Take it and leave me alone."

She reached out and took the money and moved away from the door.

"You piece of shit. Cheap bastard," she said and walked toward the elderly project along the walk he had used. He quickly moved behind the wheel of his car and drove right to the rectory where he sat in the driveway weeping and sobbing. The whole affair had not lasted more than twenty minutes, but for him it was the most humiliating twenty minutes of his lifetime.

CHAPTER XV

The phone rang at seven o'clock in the morning and when I answered it I heard, "Meet me at nine o'clock at the Newport Creamery at the top of President Avenue in Fall River, if you want information on the priest's murder. You can bring your mistress."

"Who is this?" I asked.

All I heard was the phone being hung up on the other end. I resented the word mistress. For a moment I wondered if I should go. But I knew I had no choice. Any information I could get from any source was worth it at this juncture in our investigation.

Marge and I drove to Fall River and parked in the Newport Creamery parking lot on the north side of the building. We entered the doors and were met just as we came in through the second set of doors by a huge figure of a man with a Santa Claus white beard and balding head. The mass of facial hair and the balding head struck me as laughable. It was almost as if the man was making up for the lack of hair on his head by letting his beard grow wild. The facial hair diverted attention from his obvious obesity. The size of his stomach alone was enough to make me shudder. His chest and breasts hung over his massive, protruding stomach so much so that I wondered how he could stand upright. He introduced himself as Marshall Jameson and ushered us to a booth to the right of the entrance. He walked with difficulty and I wondered how he was going to get into the booth that he had selected. After much heaving and groaning and by pushing the table so close to what was going to be our seat that we would hardly be able to slide in, he managed to get seated. Poor Marge slid into the booth with barely enough room to get in and I did the same, even though it was perilously tight for us.

"So you two are investigating this crime, are you not?" he asked with his eye out for the waitress.

"Not alone. But we are two of the people working on the case," I said. "Do you have any information for us?"

"In due time," he said.

The waitress arrived and he ordered two English muffins and coffee, while Marge and I settled for decaf. I took an immediate dislike to the man and I suppose I showed it.

"So, now," he said, "I was part of the Catholic body which represented the 'true church' on Sunday mornings at Saint Francis. I'm sure you have heard about us. We are the motivators for the rebirth of the Catholic Church in North America."

"We've heard about you attending mass at Saint Francis, but not much else," I said. "So, tell us about it."

"I don't know about telling much to a couple like you, living in sin," he said. "I understand you are not married and yet are living together."

Before I could answer, Marge said, "I don't think what we do or don't do is any of your business. It seems to me you have enough to concern yourself with, without worrying about us."

"And what should I be concerning myself with?" he asked.

"Just in the few minutes since we've met I would suggest the sins of pride and gluttony come to mind. I feel there is nothing you can say to us that would be worth sitting here listening to your arrogance. I certainly will not allow you to pass judgment on Noah and me," she said.

For the first time since I had known her, I saw an angry Marge. She began to move out of the booth and I had no choice but to slide out and let her squeeze her way out of the booth.

Mr. Jameson was speechless.

Marge got out of the booth, called the waitress and gave her a five dollar bill to cover our coffees, turned on her heels and left with me close behind her. She didn't say anything until we were well on our way back to the Point.

"I'm sorry about that Noah. I know we should have heard what he had to say, but I am afraid he made me lose my temper. He was so rude and so arrogant, he took me by surprise," she said.

"I certainly wouldn't worry about it. I just thought it was fun watching you lose your temper. I'm glad you don't lose your temper with me. I'm no match for you," I said.

We drove back to the Point then and I suggested a walk on the beach to get the whole thing out of her system.

About an hour after we finished our walk, we received a phone call from Mr. Jameson.

"I want to apologize for getting off on the wrong foot his morning," he said. "Please tell the lady that I am sorry."

"Apology accepted," I said in reply.

"Then could we possibly meet again? I have been given the responsibility of dealing with the police in this affair, but my time is limited. I am leaving for Ecuador and I will be gone for a month," he said. "Since this is my last day I would like to meet as soon as possible. Can we begin again, let's say in an hour at the MacDonalds in the same strip mall as the Newport Creamery?" he asked.

"One minute," I said.

I told Marge what had just transpired and she accepted his apology and okayed the meeting.

"Okay," I said, "We'll meet you there in three quarters of an hour."

We parked out car in the MacDonald's lot exactly at 12:30 and I knew most of the tables in the restaurant would be taken, not by young people, but by the elderly who used the restaurant for an inexpensive lunch and a meeting place. The time when the elderly men of the city met in places with names like the Italian Progressive Club or Sons of Italy or the

Acoreana Club was passing rapidly. The fast food restaurants made it possible for women to be part of the "hanging out" places. They no longer needed to stay at home or wait for their shopping trips to get them out of their houses. And from their point of view, their husbands were not out at all times of the day, drinking, under the pretext that they were playing cards, dominos or checkers.

We met Mr. Jameson who was seated at a corner table as far removed as possible from the group of seniors clustered about the middle of the dining area. He didn't make an effort to rise and I could understand why. Considering the amount of weight he was carrying and the area he was sitting in, it would have been a prodigious effort for very little. The empty wrappers and packages in front of him suggested that he had made the most of his wait. He obviously loved to eat, but unlike Jack, everything he ate turned to fat.

"As I said on the phone, I am leaving for Ecuador tomorrow for a month. It is part of our 'reformation.' We go to 'ora et labore' to pray and to work. The work we will do will be to build two new churches outside of Cuenca and to give medical treatment for many of the poor."

"I would think there are sufficient Catholic churches in Cuenca," I said.

"In the city itself, yes. We are building these two in the mountains so that the Indians can have a place to worship. It is not easy for them to come to the city. The churches will be small but will be greatly appreciated. They will not be elaborate structures, but will serve their purpose well. This is where the true Catholics are, not your cafeteria Catholics who pick and choose what they want to believe in. These people eke out a living from their surroundings and thank God through prayer for each day they live," he said. "Before we begin could you get me a number 3 please?" He placed a five dollar bill on the table and looked pleadingly at me. "With a coke if it isn't too much trouble," he said.

When I returned with his order, he ate a few French fries and began, "Father was a hero of sorts to us. We were attracted to him by his strong anti-abortion stance, first of all. He was not a man to shilly-shally when he felt something was wrong. He felt that abortion was a grievous sin."

"So, do you think that led to his murder?" Marge asked.

"No, I don't. I can't imagine it. The people who wrong-mindedly support a woman's right to kill her baby, don't feel as strongly as we do," he said.

He stopped talking then to unwrap his sandwich and then take a bite of it along with some French fries and a few sips of Coke.

"Gays are another matter," he said.

Marge asked, "In what way?"

"Gay men and women live by their own ethical code. They are the rejects of society and have learned to make up their own rules. Nothing is allowed to stand between themselves and their bestial desires," he said. "Including murder."

"This is absurd," I said. "I am not going to sit here and listen to this horrendously stupid talk. If you are here to accuse a gay society of killing Father D'Angellini on the basis of your prejudices, I cannot in good conscience be party to it."

"Your sensitivity to the gay community is misplaced. But, aside from that I have proof that they meant him harm," he said.

"Then let us see the proof," I said.

He then reached inside his jacket pocket and removed a sheet of paper which he unfolded very dramatically before handing it to me.

I held it where Marge could see it so that she could read it with me. It was a copy of an e-mail which read as follows:

My Friends:

On Sunday, July 7 we invite you, your relatives and friends, to attend the 10:30 mass at The Church of Saint Francis on Harold St., in Fall River. We ask everyone attending the mass to wear a white ribbon to indicate their commitment to our movement.

Let me make clear that this movement is purely religious in motive. We must send a message, loud and clear, to the hierarchy of the Fall River Diocese that we will not allow homophobia to go unnoticed in our presence. We will not be excluded from participation in the rites of Mother Church.

When communion is offered we will go to the altar as is our custom. If, as I suspect, we are refused the host, we will kneel in the aisle in which we are standing in silent protest. I emphasize "silent" because we will be in church and the mass is sacred.

We believe that Father D'Angellini is being used as a spearhead in an anti-homosexual crusade. We must stop this movement using any means possible.

Mark

"Did you make note of that last line?" he asked. "That should be proof enough that those creeps would stop at nothing."

"As far as I am concerned," Marge said, "I see no proof of a desire to kill Father D'Angellini here. You're grasping at straws."

"Are you blind woman?" He snatched the paper from my hand and read, "'We must stop this movement using any means possible.' I think that is a pretty clear statement if you ask me."

His anger was palpable. His voice had risen. His face turned crimson and even his massive jowls vibrated. He looked for all the world like a rabid English bulldog in his anger.

"It is a generalized statement meaning nothing specific. It is hardly proof of a desire to harm Father D'Angellini. I think you are stretching it a bit here," I said.

I looked at Marge and she nodded her agreement.

"Well, I can see where you are leaning," he said. "You can be sure the District Attorney will hear about this along with a demand that you be taken off this case immediately."

Marge said, "Before we leave, I have one question to ask you that bothers me."

"Go ahead, ask," he said as he prepared to get out of the booth where he was temporarily wedged against the table.

"I don't understand how you can profess to be part of the Catholic Church and yet be filled with so much hate and venom and so little love. It seems to me that what you espouse is the opposite of Christ's message."

"Who are you to judge me? It seems to me that you are the ones living in sin," he said.

"But I am not pretending to lead the 'reformation'. You are. And, aside from attacking me personally, you haven't answered me," Marge insisted. "I'll repeat it if you wish."

"I heard the question. The best way I can explain it is this. If you buy an old house and it is infested with rats, there is only one way to do anything about it and that is to exterminate them. You can't feed them cheese. You have to kill them and drive them out; there is no other way. From my point of view, abortionists and queers have infected the Holy Mother Church and I am asking the exterminators to come and kill them off," he said.

"So, the Church should be made up only of people who think like you. Exclude everyone else. And where do you draw the line? How about adulterers? Petty thieves? Prostitutes? Alcoholics? Druggies? Liars? Cursers?" she ran on.

"This is absurd," he said. He tried to rise from the table and only managed to push the table closer to us.

Then without warning one of the elderly men sitting closest to us said in a loud voice, "You haven't answered the lady's question because you can't you damned fool. You're nothing but a bigot. Damned fool should be excommunicated."

He pushed the table hard enough so I had to hold it away from us before he hurt Marge, but he was still wedged in.

Finally I rose and let Marge slide out of the booth, but he still remained in his seat.

The other elderly people who were not within earshot were curious to know what had been said, but the man who had spoken out only said, "The guy is an asshole. Not worth bothering with."

We left Marshall Jameson desperately trying to extricate himself from the booth.

CHAPTER XVI

Jack was excited when he told us about the meeting between Clarissa and Mrs. D'Angellini. They met her in her home, this time, with no attorney present.

"First off," Jack said, "the lady was shocked when she saw that Clarissa is black. I introduced Clarissa and, without giving her a chance to say a word, said that Clarissa had found a possible problem with the trust the way it was written.

"So, what is it?" she asked.

"I nodded at Clarissa and she took over and began, 'There is a provision here that says that if one or both children becomes mentally or physically incapacitated and unable to use or handle the money properly, the money reverts to the closest person to them as heir.'"

"So, what's wrong with that? If one of the kids gets sick, he shouldn't be handling the money," she said.

"Mrs. D'Angellini," Clarissa said, "Let's imagine that one of the kids get into a bad car accident and, God forbid, falls into a coma. Now, it is important that you follow me, even if what I say sounds crazy to you."

Jack said, "You should have seen Clarissa, she was in complete control."

"Follow me," Clarissa repeated, "A coma would make a child completely incapacitated, right?"

Mrs. D'Angellini nodded.

"Now suppose he begins using drugs or alcohol. The line is not so clear is it? I think you could come up with any number of scenarios that might be a basis for calling them or him unfit to handle a large sum of money. And suppose, too, that your daughter-in-law or son became desperate for money, is it conceivable that a good lawyer could make a case out of very little? Can you see what I am saying?" Clarissa asked.

"Yes, I do, but what can I do about it?" she asked.

"Now, that is going to take a good lawyer. You could probably start by declaring yourself administrator of the fund while you are still living and then consider who you would want as administrator when you die. Certainly tighten up the provisions under which the children could be called incapable of carrying out their duties. That the language that shows here is far too hazy is what I am trying to say. I don't consider myself savvy enough to solve the problem, but I am sure there are attorneys and financial people who can," Clarissa said.

Jack went on to explain how Mr. D'Angellini suddenly saw the light.

"The funny thing is," she said, "It would have been Marco who would find a way to get the money. He was greedy. I hate to say it, but he was. You wouldn't think a priest would be greedy, but he was the one who would have caused the most trouble, and he is the one who wanted that money. He thought it was his."

Clarissa reacted to Mrs. D'Angellini by saying, "Greed is with all of us. Jack says that most of the evil in this world comes from money and greed, but I haven't seen enough to say that, but I know it is everywhere."

"Where did you learn about money, young lady?" the older woman asked.

"I didn't actually. I work with numbers. I have nothing to do with money. Jack has taught me how to work with the financial markets, but it is still mostly numbers to me. Numbers were always part of my life and they still play a large part for me. Jack is the money man. I am his disciple," she said.

"My son was a disciple too. I think that is where things went wrong for him. They did go wrong you know. He got mixed up in his own head and people began to use him; push him where he shouldn't have been and he made enemies. I wish we could end this now before it goes too far," she said.

Jack said, "How do you mean that?"

"No, you don't. You won't get me started on that subject. I'm glad you helped me with this, though. I want this money to go to the kids to give them a good life. My husband didn't have much of a life and my two sons are not doing well, so I want the kids to enjoy life and not be worried about money. Maybe with a good education they can turn out like this lady here and be smart and lead a good life. I want them off Federal Hill. Our family has spent too many years here and it is time to move on. I'd like to see it before I die, but I don't think it's going to be. I think I am running out of gas. This death took a lot out of me," she said.

Jack described how they had sat quietly for a time without speaking. Mrs. D'Angellini suddenly seemed to have trouble breathing and Clarissa had taken it upon herself to get her a glass of water. She was gasping for breath and Jack became worried that something was going to happen. As it turned out, Mrs. D'Angellini slowly came back to normal and then told them that she would have to lie down for an hour or so to regain her composure, but before they left she wanted to know how they would follow through on what they had found for her.

Clarissa said, "I think that is up to you now. You have to find a good law firm that deals in this sort of thing and let them take care of it."

"How do I do that?" she asked.

"I can dig around for you," Jack said, "but the final decision has to be yours. Let me check things out and I'll get back to you with several names of law firms that specialize in this kind of thing. This will be old hat to them and I'm sure they'll tighten things up so there are no loopholes that someone can take advantage of."

Jack told us that Mrs. D'Angellini seemed restive and eager for them to leave, but she left them with her phone number and insisted that they call as soon as they had any information. So, they left her at that and Jack dropped Clarissa off at Brown on the east end of the city and came back to the Point to tell us about the meeting.

"I wonder what she meant by 'going too far'?" I asked.

"We'll know that fairly soon I think. The deeper we get into this the more we seem to unearth," Marge said, "and what we are finding is not too wholesome."

* * *

Father D'Angellini had great empathy for the sick and dying. The pain and revulsion that he felt dealing with the indigent and addicted, disappeared completely when he was in the company of the hopelessly ill. Visiting and comforting the sick was his special vocation and people loved him for it. Whereas his fellow priests hated those moments when they felt helpless and were stricken dumb before great suffering, Father felt spiritually whole with his special calling.

He felt that his unique gift was in guiding the dying into heaven. It was then that he loved his role in the priesthood. His was the gift of giving hope to the dying and making them feel that they were the chosen who would enter heaven; that they would leave the terrible pain of living on earth behind them and rejoice with their Father. He felt he had been chosen by God to fulfill this singular role. It was his raison d'etre. No matter what troubles he underwent, he would never consider leaving the priesthood because of what he considered his calling from God.

It had first come to him, when as a young man, he had accompanied Father Macri to a home on Broadway on Federal Hill in Providence where a young boy was in his death throes. The boy had been hit by a car while he was on his bicycle and had bounced off the hood of the car after smashing into the windshield. The priest had been called immediately and had arrived with Marco before the ambulance had arrived. The boy was in terrible pain and the family was gathered around him in what they knew would be his last moments. Marco, then a young boy, a little older than the dying child, had taken the boy's hand in his and had soothed him as none of the family had been able to do. When Father Macri gave the child his last rites, Marco had almost felt impelled to perform the rites himself had he been a priest. It was at that moment that Marco D'Angellini had decided that he would become Father D'Angellini.

When he became a priest, he had made it a habit to visit the parish sick in their homes every day when he was free of his parish duties. Word soon spread among the parishioners and neighbors of Saint Francis that a call to the rectory meant that they would be getting a call from Father. The women would prepare their favorite tea cookie or dessert for Father's arrival so that he could join them in a cup of tea and "a little something" after seeing their sick one. It became a ritual which he thoroughly enjoyed after the intense emotional stress brought about from serving the sick. The women, in turn, made the greatest effort to please this priest who honored them with his company. A big man, who gave the appearance of loving to eat, Father really didn't differentiate between the quality of what he was served except in the one area of sweets. He loved the Italian pastries that took him back to the times when his mother would bring home a pastry box filled with delicious canola's or meringues or any of the many desserts that were available to her on the Hill.

He began by making the rounds of his parishioners, visiting those who were stay-at-homes, the rare person who was terminally ill, the person who was recovering from an operation; they became his clientele. Then he had gradually made a point of visiting the two hospitals in Fall River almost daily to attend to the sick from his parish.. He would report to the main desk where the people in charge were so used to his arrival that they gave him the name and room numbers of anyone from Saint Francis. Gradually his free time was filled with calls to the sick. He never grew tired of it.

During his worse periods of self-doubt about his ability to remain in the priesthood, he never questioned wanting to remain a priest. His commitment to the sick was so engrained that he couldn't imagine life without the service he gave to those who were most needy of his comforting presence and for whom he did so much. There was little question that he was a shining beacon to the terminally ill. The nuns with whom he worked at the cancer home, saw him as a blessed figure and they literally worshipped him. The Church of Saint Francis and his special calling became the centers of the world he had built and he did not want to lose them. As the years went by, he became more and more determined to remain a priest and build on his strengths, rather than allow his weaknesses to deny him the personal satisfaction he took from his work.

CHAPTER XVII

It was Peter Madeiro who chased down Gino Alberto. He found that his credit card showed a plane trip to Fall River from San Francisco. There was no question that he had bought a round trip ticket from San Francisco to Boston. Whether he had taken the trip was another matter. Once we knew that the trip had been booked, there wasn't much question that it could be tracked down without too much trouble.

I personally contacted his mother by phone to verify that he had indeed visited. She hung up on me and refused to answer when I called again. I had no choice but to go to the house and knock on the door and, even then, she refused to open the door. Finally, I asked the District Attorney to have a trooper accompany me to the door and I suppose the man in the uniform frightened her enough so that she did come to the door. She didn't let me in immediately, even then. After much hemming and hawing she finally opened the door and admitted that her son had visited her. After that confession she was willing to give me his phone number in San Francisco. The dates when he had visited her, as per the ticket information, proved to be during the time that the priest had been murdered.

We had been active enough in the crime business to know that we couldn't jump to the conclusion that because Gino Alberto had been in the city at the time of the murder, it necessarily made him the murderer, although we also knew enough to make him highly suspect.

It was Patrick who called him. He admitted that he had been in town during the dates listed on the airline tickets although he claimed he had not seen Father D'Angellini and that he had not seen him for many years before. He claimed that he hadn't seen or spoken to Father for at least ten years. He agreed to an interview, but he would not consider returning to the city. Any personal contact would have to be made in San Francisco since he did not want to waste vacation time or personal days returning to the city. At any rate, he felt that we would be wasting our time interviewing him since he had so little to offer us in a criminal investigation.

Patrick thought otherwise and was willing to send one of his detectives to San Francisco for that express purpose. I thought it would be a great opportunity for Marge and me to get away and at the same time serve some purpose in the investigation. I thought it might be a tricky situation for Patrick to explain why he sent two elderly amateurs at taxpayer expense to San Francisco, so I volunteered to assume the costs involved at no expense to the taxpayers.

I jumped at the opportunity, in fact. It would give us a chance to explore Marge's newfound interest in art at the San Francisco Museum of Art and the San Francisco Modern Art Museum. We could possibly spend two says together exploring the city. I had never been, so we would be sharing a new experience for both of us. Fisherman's Wharf, the Golden Gate Bridge, the trolley cars, great restaurants; all of the silly images we carry with us, and then the delight of seeing all the things we haven't even considered. The richness and variety of the urban experience has always fascinated me and San Francisco was like a fairyland waiting for us. I could imagine the fragrances of exotic spices in Chinatown or the raw smell of fish on the wharves. But, most of all, it would be the sharing that would afford us the most fun and I knew it would be a special time for us, getting away alone for the first time since we had been together.

As it turned out we would be flying from Boston to Chicago and then on to San Francisco and that was even better as far as I was concerned. We could spend time in San Francisco and then come back to Chicago at least a full day in one of my favorite cities. I couldn't imagine a better time and I considered myself a very lucky man to have met such a delightful woman to enjoy it with, and to have the means to enjoy the time we were spending together without worry or anxiety.

At that point I called Gino Alberto myself to arrange for a meeting with him at his convenience. We set it up so that when Marge and I settled into our hotel we would give him a call and he would set a time to meet with us. He insisted that he knew nothing about the murder and that we were making the trip for nothing, but I would expect nothing less from a possible suspect. If anything, he certainly was not going to tell me that he should be a suspect if for no other reason than that his mother had lied to us to protect him. Why in the world would she feel that she had to protect her son unless she too thought he was a suspect or that we would think that he had had something to do with the murder?

The airplane trip to San Francisco was uneventful and as soon as we settled into our hotel I called Gino to set up an appointment so that we could get that part of the business out of the way. I certainly didn't want it hanging over our heads for too long. I felt that the sooner we put it behind us, the better off we were. He was very appreciative of our situation and we decided to meet for dinner in our hotel that evening. If nothing else, dinner would give the interview an informal air so that he would not think he was a prime suspect.

As planned, we met for dinner the next evening. Gino was not a handsome man, but he had the boy next door look with a shock of black hair and blue eyes. His eyes were stunning, a bright blue that was offset by his wavy black hair and heavy black eyebrows. Marge said afterward that he was a very attractive man although he wasn't what would be called handsome. On this evening he wore a light blue turtleneck under a darker shirt that set off his eyes. His slacks were dress slacks although of a light fabric and he wore loafers with socks. His look was of refined casual wear.

He made the clothes look good and they fit him to a tee.

He was most definitely effeminate in his actions and in the lilt of his voice. His hands were long and delicate and he used them to emphasize whatever he was saying. He made no attempt to hide his effeminate nature and we soon didn't pay much attention to it.

At one point at the beginning of dinner he said, "Right off, let's establish the fact that I am gay. Let me also disabuse you of thinking that Father D'Angellini somehow influenced me into becoming gay. My mother wants to think that, but that is far from the truth. I was gay from day one. If anything, all he did was to make me more aware of my sexuality at an earlier age than most kids. So, if we understand each other in that regard, I think we can go on from there and have a serious discussion about this whole mess."

"Well, since we are being frank, then I have to ask you if Father D'Angellini was gay," I said.

"Of course he was. You can't be very good detectives if you haven't found that out. He was cautious, but he most certainly was gay. I think I was the only boy with whom he had an affair up to the time I left the city. He was not promiscuous, but he had one or two adventures with fellow priests before me, unless I'm wrong, and I don't know about afterwards," he said.

"That makes things very simple and yet very complicated," Marge said. "You must know that he became associated with a group of homophobes and he went to great pains to act against homosexuals. He even refused them the Eucharist at an open mass. How can we justify the two, being a practicing homosexual himself and denying homosexuals the right to partake of the Eucharist?"

"I can't answer that. I can't even imagine it. I don't know why people didn't recognize him as a gay to begin with. It isn't as if he didn't give the outward signs of being gay. The priesthood, I guess, hides a lot because people make assumptions based on what people are supposed to be. And, he made efforts to hide his sexual orientation because he was a priest. Kind of sad really, to deny what you are because of other peoples' expectations. I know I have never been happier being what I know I am without reservations. Things weren't easy for me when I was in school, but since I came here, life has changed completely for me. For the first time in my whole life, I like what I see in the mirror. His problem was that he never did. He hated being gay, I think, but couldn't deny his sexual needs," he said. "I felt sorry for him when I realized what he was doing."

"One of the people we have spoken to feels that he was forced into it by the hierarchy. He took a strong stand on abortion and he began to get a conservative following, then they pushed him in the anti-gay marriage direction, the hierarchy that is. Would that make sense to you?" I asked.

"Who knows? I have no way of knowing. The side of him that he showed me was quite different from what other people saw, you know. He was my father, my big brother and my lover all rolled into one," he said.

"For how long, was he your lover?" Marge asked.

"Actually it started when I was in junior high school. I was with him all the time, you understand. I was his protégé. Everyone thought that I was going to be a priest so it was only natural that I be with him. He would say mass in the morning and I was his altar boy. Then he would take me to school and pick me up after school let out to visit sick parishioners at home or in the hospital. There was always something to do. Then gradually our relationship began to get more and more physical. It was a long time in coming. I would leave him and dream about him touching me and I would become aroused. I hope this doesn't upset you ma'am," he said.

"I'm an adult," Marge said.

"Well gradually our relationship did become physical. I was a young gay waiting for an experience and he gave that to me. Of course, I was a teen and confused, and like any teen the whole sexual experience was new and exciting and yet I was filled with guilt. I think he felt the same way. In many ways he was immature and filled with restrained passion. Everything he knew and had been taught fought against what he knew he was. His was not an easy time, and yet he loved me and that love became stronger as the years went by. It went on until I was eighteen or so and had to make a decision about college," he said.

"Was anyone aware of what was happening?" I asked.

"There may have been suspicions in the parish, but they never came to light. The priests on the Cape knew. We would go to the Cape whenever we could. A couple of the priests had summer homes and we would go there and be free to act without fear of discovery. Everything we did was undercover at home, was clandestine, and we were always afraid of being discovered. Father especially, was very cautious. It was very difficult and added a great deal of tension to our relationship. But, he was a different man on the Cape. It was there, in fact, that we had our big falling out," he said.

"And why was that?" I asked.

"I found him making love to one of the priests. He broke my heart. I was only a kid and I was completely devoted to him and he betrayed me. I almost had a nervous breakdown, but I pulled myself together and left the city. I did it quietly, but I did it. I think I broke my mother's heart," he said.

"So you didn't pursue entering the priesthood?" I asked.

"No, for me it would have been the ultimate in hypocrisy. I was openly gay; there was no question about it. Many of the younger priests that I met realized their sexual orientation over time and once they had committed themselves to the Church and a career, getting out wasn't easy. They were in it for the duration. The pressures are pretty great on priests if they don't fit the mold. Expectations are pretty high for them, more, I think, than in other areas of life. They carry the banner of a great many families. They become icons for them. When they fail, things are very hard. There is nothing more loving and adoring than the Catholic mother of a priest, and no one so scathing as the mother of a priest who fails in his vocation." he said. "Believe me I have seen enough priests caught in their vocations and their family's 'love' to know how difficult it is for them," he said. "For those who stay celibate there is no problem; they can survive."

Dinner came and we concentrated on eating. He was enjoying a special

152

dinner which he must have thought was payment for his information, so we didn't ask any more questions until dinner was finished. We talked about the parish and the people we knew.

"Oddly enough, there is an Italian parish here that I attended for a little while after I relocated here that is very much like Saint Francis. Hardly seems likely all the way across the country, but I think the motherland is more deeply ingrained in our people than I would have thought. You should visit it. You feel like you are back at Saint Francis. The accents are different but the people are so much the same that it would make you cry. The funny thing is that in a city filled with gays, the anti-gay feeling here is stronger in the church than back home. There is very little tolerance, so I stopped attending," he said.

Over dessert and coffee, I decided that I had better get a few of the questions I had in mind out on the table before he was gone and I sat stewing over the questions I hadn't asked him.

"Gino, the reason we are here, of course, is that you are a suspect in the murder of Father D'Angellini since you returned to the city and were there when he was killed," I said. "Did you see him at all when you went back?"

"I saw him once, but not to talk to. I dropped into the Dunkin Donuts on Quarry St. for a coffee and he was pulling out of the parking lot in his car as I entered. He didn't stop. I don't know if he saw me or not," he said.

"Would you have wanted to talk to him?" Marge asked.

"I got over him a long time ago, believe me. He hurt me terribly at the time, but like with most things, we tend to put them behind us. I put him behind me ages ago. Time moves on, you know," he said.

I wondered if what he said was as simple as he made it out to be, but I wanted to move on.

"Have you been back to Fall River, often?" I asked.

"Not often the first few years I came out here, but more and more now that Mom is getting old. I worry about her. She is alone and I can't get her to move into housing for the elderly. She could never be out here. My lifestyle would kill her and I can't go back to being sexually inactive or being alone for too long," he said. "So I visit when I can for a week or two, at least twice a year now, but that is about it. I try to get home for Christmas and sometimes Easter which are the two holidays most important to her."

"Why do you think your mother lied to us about you coming home? She inferred to us that you had never come back to the city once you left. Not only did she infer it, I think she out and out said it, if I am not mistaken," I said.

Marge said, "She did say it, Noah."

"Well, I think that is obvious, don't you?" he said. "She did not want me connected to Father's murder in any way. She knows I left the city because of Father and she does not want to think the worse. She probably thinks that I killed him. One of my problems with my mother is that she has never acknowledged that I am gay. She is in denial."

"That must make things difficult for you," Marge said.

He suddenly took on some color and his cheeks reddened.

"Yes, it is more than difficult," he said. "You have no idea what it is like to have to live in the denial of yourself. That's why I hate to go back to the city. I have to face her. Can you imagine what I feel like when she asks me if I have met a nice girl yet? You have no idea. She still pretends that nothing really went on between Father and me. She knows that isn't the truth, though, but she pretends. She is caught in a strange dilemma. On the one hand she wants to believe that Father seduced me and led me astray, that he ruined my life and deprived her of me and my company back home."

He stopped talking then and drank his remaining coffee, deliberately. His hand shook slightly as he lifted the cup to his mouth.

"On the other hand she wants to pretend that nothing happened; that whatever went on between us was platonic with Father assuming the role of a mentor leading me to a life in the priesthood. In this version I am not gay but merely confused and waiting for my life to sort things out," he said. "I'm sure she feels that now that Father is gone, I will come back to Fall River and live with her until the right girl comes along. You and I know that that is not going to happen. I suffered as a teen. I will not suffer now. I will continue to live my life as I am doing now, with no qualms about it."

"So before you leave, let's wrap this up. You say you went back to Fall River to visit your mother and you saw Father once but didn't talk to him. Was there any special reason for the trip since it wasn't Easter of Christmas?" I asked.

"I went back because my mother was having a series of tests done at Mass General and she was frightened to death and wanted me with her. As it turned out, she didn't have the tests done because she wasn't well and they had to be postponed. So, it was a wasted trip at a very inappropriate time. She wanted me to stay, but I couldn't. I had to get back here to work," he said. "But as I said, I can't go back to stay anyway. I am not giving up my life, even for my mother."

"So, you never heard from Father at all, then," Marge said.

"No. We wouldn't have anything to talk about. It was a long time ago and is all forgotten as far as I am concerned. There was really nothing we could say to each other. And, you tell me that he was in the middle of an anti-gay thing at the church, so he would have wanted to avoid any contact with me, I would think," he said. "That's the part I can't get over. How he could have been anti-gay I'll never know."

"Supposing he had become celibate again. Would it be possible that he would have taken his position as a result of a conversion of some sort?" Marge asked.

"Spoken like a true heterosexual. Celibacy has nothing to do with being gay. You are either gay or you are not gay. A celibate priest who is heterosexual is still heterosexual; he doesn't change his sexual preference because he is celibate. He might sublimate his desires, but he is still hetero. The same holds true for a gay priest. In this case, knowing Father Marco, there wasn't a chance that he could be anything but a gay and there wasn't any way that he could deny his sexual desires," he said. "Many of the gay priests are celibate, but Father Marco was never going to be one of those."

"Then the question becomes, how can we trace down some of the priests who were involved with him on his escapades on the Cape?" I asked.

"Wow, you don't hold back do you?" he said.

"We are not interested in an expose here. We want as much information as we can get to find out who killed him," I said.

"I'll give you one name and that is it. I'll give you the name of the priest I caught him with. Payback time. At the time, he was assigned to a church in Somerset. You'll have to track him down. His name is Father Harry LaChance. That's it from me. I'm out of here if you don't mind," he said. Then as he rose from his chair, he said. "Thanks for the meal. It was great. Nail him for me."

We spent two days in San Francisco and had a marvelous time caught up in the joys of the modern city. Our view of what San Francisco was supposed to look like came out of the movies. How many car chases have we seen in films? The cars racing down the hills, always flying down over the dips in the hills and seemingly bouncing into the air. And the views of the Golden Gate Bridge and Chinatown and, of course, the trolley cars. More than any other city outside of Paris, I had had the preconception of what I was expected to see. But the images projected by the cameras and the movies can't possibly catch the life of a huge modern city with all of its special noises and smells and people. That was what excited both of us. The living city was fun galore.

We visited the museums and the sights and enjoyed them. We took a boat tour of the harbor and found that exciting and even breathtaking as the sun was setting in the west. Both of us felt in many ways like it was our honeymoon and we enjoyed each other in this setting so far from our homes and our normal lives. The trip was an adventure that we would never forget. And not once did we think of the case at hand. After meeting with Gino Alberto we were able to put that aspect of San Francisco behind us and enjoy our brief time together exploring San Francisco which was new to both of us. We would deal with the case when we got back, but we had a vacation which would leave us refreshed and give us the energy to continue when we got back and that would be soon enough.

We flew to Chicago and spent a full day in the great city on Lake Michigan. We visited The Art Institute of Chicago over which Marge became quite emotional. The Impressionist collection was more than Marge had expected and I saw one of my favorite Picasso's, "The Old Guitar Player" along with the Chagall windows. We walked the lake front surrounded by bicyclers and joggers and walkers like ourselves and were amazed at the activity on the shore of Lake Michigan. All in all, it was a delightful three days and we were ready to return home and the quiet of our own house and our own surroundings.

We had the case to deal with, of course, but that had to be put on hold for at least a day after our return so that we could get our heads and bodies together.

CHAPTER XVIII

Jack was more than happy to see us back home. He claimed that he hadn't had a decent meal since we left. I doubted that, but I was willing to let him give us a back-handed compliment.

Patrick had been dealing with the Bishop's envoy during our absence. He had been objecting to us pursuing the homosexual angle with Father Marco. Word had reached the Bishop's Office that we had gone to San Francisco to interview Gino Alberto. The little officious priest claimed that since we had left they had received several complaints about homosexual activity by Father D'Angellini. Pedophilia was being put forward as a complaint against the dead priest. He claimed that the Bishop was becoming quite upset at the direction the investigation was taking.

Patrick held his ground and once again made it clear that his duty was to his constituency and that he would pursue any avenues that would possibly lead to the discovery of the murderer in the case.

His secretary told us that it had become hot and heavy before the little dapper priest stormed out of the office threatening Patrick with retribution at the polls in the next election.

Jack and Marge and I sat down with Patrick to fill him in on what we had found out about Father Marco from his former lover.

"So, he was an active homosexual. That settles that, unless you think this man was being untruthful," he said.

Marge said, "I have no doubt that the man was telling the truth. But when we get right down to it, I can't see what his sexual preference has to do with his murder. I have been thinking about it and I can't see where it is any more important than the other things we have discovered about the man."

"I have to agree with Marge," Jack said. "We can get side-tracked with this and waste a lot of time chasing after something that is only one part of the whole picture unless we find a decisive link to the murder."

"Well, I think we should follow up on the priest whose name Gino gave us. That could be important," I said. "The big question is whether or not Father had another liaison who may not have walked away as quietly as Gino Alberto."

Patrick said, "We'll have to check out the man's visit here as well. Find out if he was seen with Father D'Angellini; he may not be telling us the truth, you know."

Jack said, "I feel useless on this case. There isn't much of a chance that this whole thing revolves around money. And without money as the basis of the problem, where does that leave me?"

"Well, we've got our hands full," I said. "Marge and I will chase down this Father LaChance and see where that takes us. I'd like to revisit Mrs. Alberto too to see why she was lying to us about her son coming to Fall River."

Patrick said, "Jack why don't you check out the finances of Saint Francis? See if there is any connection between its finances and the shift to the extreme conservative position Father took."

"Okay, that should be interesting. Let's see if I can turn up anything of interest there," he said.

"Patrick," I said, "Have your secretary call the rectory of the church in Somerset where Father LaChance was located. Make it semi-official and if he isn't there, let's see if she can locate him for us. If she calls she will be doing it in your name and our chances should be better of getting through to somebody."

Patrick laughed and said, "You just want the little man here again, so you can watch the duel that goes on between us."

Marge and I went to see Mrs. Alberto hoping that in the meantime Patrick's secretary would have some success locating Father LaChance. Again we knocked on her door and although we heard movement inside, she would not answer the door. I knocked as loudly as I could with no results. I knew that she was avoiding us. I saw a slightly open window next to the door and I shouted into the house that unless she answered the door I would be forced to get the police. That seemed to do the trick and we heard the slip bolts on the door being moved and the door opened.

Mrs. Alberto turned as we entered and went to her rocking chair where she sat, resigned to listening to us ask embarrassing questions.

I wasted no time in getting to the heart of the matter. "First of all Mrs. Alberto, we have just come back from seeing your son in San Francisco. Did he tell you we had seen him?"

"You did?" she said, "He hasn't called me so I didn't know. How did he look?"

Marge said, "He looked fine to me. But, I haven't met him before so I have no idea what he looked like before."

"Good," she said. "Now what do you want with me?"

"First of all I think you owe us an explanation. He was here and you said you haven't seen him for years. He claims he comes home twice a year, and that he was here when Father D'Angellini was killed. He claims he didn't talk to him, but he was here. Why did you lie to us?"

"What did you expect? Did you think I was going to tell you that he was here when that priest was killed and get him in trouble? Are you crazy? I knew if you knew he was here you would blame him for the murder. Are you blaming him now?" she asked.

"To be honest we have no reason to charge him with murder. He is a suspect because of his prior connection to the priest but he is no more a suspect than anyone else," I said.

"What do you mean by a connection? What are you saying about my boy?" she asked.

"There is no question that he was close to Father D'Angellini. There is no sense in trying to deny that. He admits himself that he was close to the priest when he was young. So we get nowhere by denying that. What I need from you is to be honest with us, no more," I said.

"So what do you want to know?" she asked.

"First off, did Father try to contact him while he was here?" I asked.

"No, he didn't. He never came here to this house. I would have thrown him out," she said.

Marge asked, "Did he call him here?"

"No," she said but her face flushed and I could have sworn that she was lying.

"Are you telling us the truth now, Mrs. Alberto? It is important now. I'll repeat the question. Did Father call here or try to contact your son in any way during the time your son was here?" I asked.

She flushed again and again said no.

"Did your son ever visit Father while he was here in Fall River this time or on other visits?" I asked.

"No," she said curtly. "This upsets me. Anything else you want to know?"

"No, I guess not," I said. "Thank you for seeing us."

She practically leaped out of the chair at that point and moved toward the door to open it. It was obvious that she wanted us out of the house as quickly as possible. We were ushered out rather unceremoniously and found ourselves on the sidewalk outside of the house.

Aside from vinyl siding on most of the three tenement houses, the area hadn't changed much since I was a boy. Where the project was now, there had been a path going through the woods that separated the bottom of Arthur St. from the top. From Chestnut to East St. the area had changed very little. I could almost hearken back to my childhood as we walked from Mrs. Alberto's to the church. I felt it might be worthwhile for Marge to get a feel of the area which had been so crucial to me as a boy, growing up in the city. I could remember where some of my schoolmates and friends had lived and where we had played our games in the streets. As we turned into Henry St., I almost expected to see the older men playing bocci ball and hear the arguments that always seemed to accompany the game. We approached Magellan Park where I spent so many early evenings watching the softball games that drew such good crowds in the pre-television days. It had been converted to a little league field with a section beyond the little league fences in center field with a basketball court that always seemed to be busy.

We walked and talked, and it was Marge who said, "I think she was lying. She would never make a poker player, that's for sure."

"I agree. Why would she lie unless she was covering up for her son? I would bet money that he met with Father. The question then becomes how do we prove it?" I said. "Or at least, how can we find out?"

"There is obviously no love between that woman and Father D'Angellini. Gino gave us a hint of that when he said that his mother thinks that his problems stem from her son's relationship with the priest. He claims that the only effect Father had on him was to make him aware of his proclivity early. But, what does she think, is the important thing?" Marge said. "Things do get complicated."

"Complicated indeed and that is the fun of the whole thing. It's like doing the New York Times Sunday Crossword. There are a great many clues available but not until you get the theme of the puzzle do they all begin to make sense. The idea is to take all the separate clues and bring them together to come up with a solution. I suppose this is like a real version of the crossword puzzle. Here we are dealing with lots of information, some of it seemingly conflicting, some of it apparently useless, but when we find the theme, it will all fit together. In the meantime we plug along looking for that one thing that will give us the theme. Right now, I have no idea what will emerge," I said. "I wish we had Sherlock Holmes with us right now to figure the whole thing out."

We were walking aimlessly and I took Marge's arm in mine and turned to go back to the car. We were parked in front of Mrs. Alberto's house and we had walked several blocks from her house. We began walking back and we walked around the block on our way back. A group of boys were standing on the corner that we passed and I couldn't help but think that had it been some fifty-five years ago that I might have been one of them. We would have been talking about baseball then, comparing the merits of Ted Williams to Joe DiMaggio or the New York Yankees compared to the Red Sox. Now the boys were probably talking about the merits of different automobiles. Times changed, the subjects changed, but there they were "hanging" around the corner just as I once did many years ago. With Marge on my arm and on a beautiful day, I wouldn't have wanted to go back under any circumstances.

* * *

The battle Father D'Angellini waged with his demon went on for years. His personal demon was his sexual desire. He learned that early in his life. His time with Father Macri was the only time in his life when he felt free of guilt. The day he took his vows was the day that his real battle began.

His was not an attraction to women. His was an attraction to young boys. His vow of celibacy was one that he meant to take seriously, but one that he found impossible to keep.

He was faithful to his vows until he fell in love with Gino Alberto, although it was clear that Gino hadn't known that. He could never have explained why it happened or exactly when it happened. He was attracted to the child in his innocence. The boy was like an angel in his eyes. It began when Gino was about ten and was serving as an altar boy for the daily mass. It was his purity that attracted Father. Dressed in a white surplice the child looked like an angel from heaven. He was obedient and respondent to the priest and was obviously in awe of him. Father fought the attraction to the child, but found himself falling in love with the young boy. For two years he served as an altar boy and became Father's companion. He would be waiting in the church for Father to say the seven o'clock mass during the week and then be at the rectory as soon as he could make it back from school. For two years, aside from a touch here and there of a non-sexual nature, Father kept his distance, but he found himself dreaming about Gino. He knew he was in love with the young boy and found himself losing control. He had been a priest for twelve years and had never crossed the line between desire and actual fulfillment.

Then one day, caught in a rainstorm on his way back to the rectory from junior high school, the child arrived soaking wet. Father took him into the rectory and made the boy take off his shirt to dry. It began then, his uncontrollable urge to take the boy in his arms. And the boy responded in kind until they were hugging and Father found himself breathless with passion. It began then, innocently enough, and then continued over the ensuing months until they were touching each other and feeling their way through the love making that was sure to follow.

Then, began the agony of guilt for the priest. From then until his death, he carried on a battle with his nature. His was a matter of self-absorption. Never did he concern himself with the children he had molested and what harm he was doing to them. His concern was in overcoming his frailties, a process he always felt he could master and never could. Somehow he managed to make it his problem in terms of his vow of celibacy and his lack of will power to overcome those frailties. Even his confessor felt that the problem was his to master. Never did his confessor ask him how much harm he might be doing to the children whose lives he affected. Instead he advised him to turn to prayer to help him through his difficulties. Somehow, the higher ups in the hierarchy saw the problem in the same light. Not only was it the situation in the Church with the priesthood, but Noah had seen the same treatment in the schools. Teachers who were suspected of engaging in pedophilia were transferred from school to school as if transfers alone would solve the problem. It was a sign of the times.

But, until he died, Father D'Angellini lived in fear of exposure. His was the double agony of the losing battle he waged against his lack of will and the equally great fear of being exposed. He had nightmares about being discharged from the priesthood or being drummed out by an angry citizenry who would not tolerate sexual deviance from one of their priests. He lived his life waiting for the terrible day when his name would be splashed across the newspapers or he would be shown on television trying to escape the camera.

The one time he had been confronted by an angry parent had frightened him almost to death He had been beaten by that man and he felt he had been lucky to come out of the experience alive. He thought then that his worst nightmare had come true. He would be driven from the priesthood. Instead, he had managed to weather the storm. He had been called before the Bishop and had been harshly reprimanded, but he had been allowed to return to his parish with the understanding that it would never happen again and that he would seek help through prayer and repentance.

CHAPTER XIX

Patrick's secretary, after much calling, found Father LaChance. He was located in a small parish on Cape Cod in Sandwich. We had a decision to make in terms of calling ahead of time to make an appointment or showing up unannounced. We decided very quickly on making an appointment. Arriving unexpected had its merits but it was an hour's ride from the Point to Sandwich and I had no desire to lose time if he wasn't in at the time we visited. Marge pointed out that a phone call was the courteous thing to do. We had Patrick's secretary call, representing the District Attorney's Office. Father LaChance, as we anticipated, was hesitant to meet with anyone about Father D'Angellini's murder, but agreed to meet unofficially with whomever was representing the office.

Two days later Marge and I found ourselves driving to the Cape on I95E through New Bedford and the small towns along the way. The new highway made the trip to the Cape quick, but unfortunately, missed the little towns along old Rte. 6. The beautiful town of Marion was marked only by a highway sign and the town of Wareham got hardly a notice.

In less than an hour we were at the Bourne Bridge and fortunately found that the summer traffic was no longer with us. The bridges over the Cape Cod Canal, the Bourne and the Sagamore are a nightmare during the summer months when tourists come to spend their vacations on the

Cape. On this day we drove over the bridge and then around the rotary to the east to Rte. 6A, the beautiful coastal road along the north shore of the Cape. It wasn't far to Sandwich and as it turned out to the church which was located on the old road just outside of town.

We had an appointment for 11:00 and it was only 10:15 so I drove down one of the side roads off Rte. 6A which led to the beaches on the north shore. We drove along a narrow road through what looked like marshland to a point where the marshes gave way to sand before we saw the beach and the beautiful blue water beyond. We parked the car, kicked off our shoes and walked barefoot to the soft sand at the top of the beach some hundred feet from the water. It was a beautiful fall day. It was perfect New England weather with just a nip of coolness in the air. The tourists had gone to wherever they came from and we were left with the Cape to ourselves. There were a few people on the beach, a far cry from the hordes that fill every bit of space under normal conditions. We walked down to the water's edge and along the beach on the hard sand. From where we were I thought I could see Plymouth across the bay, but I wasn't sure. There were any number of sailboats on the water and seeing their white sails against the blue water made me wish that I had brought my camera. The half hour went very quickly and we had to actually rush back to the car to get back to 6A and our appointment at the church.

Father LaChance was waiting for us at the side entrance of what I assumed was the rectory. We introduced ourselves and then he surprisingly asked us to go somewhere else for the interview. He obviously did not want to be questioned by his superior, I assumed, about why we were there. I suggested that we go to the beach we had just been at, if it was okay with him, and he agreed. He was nervous. I actually felt sorry for him and I could see that Marge was uncomfortable herself at his discomfort.

I took the same road that I had taken a few minutes ago and in no time we found ourselves at the edge of the beach. He followed our lead by taking off his shoes and socks and he also removed his suit jacket and collar and we walked down to the water's edge once again.

"Now," he said, "Please tell me what this is all about."

"Well, first of all, it has to do with an investigation into the death of Father Marco D'Angellini. You've certainly heard of the murder," I said.

"Yes, of course, I have," he said. "Something as terrible as murder does not escape the eyes of priests in the diocese, especially the murder of one of our own."

"We are in the process of chasing down every lead, no matter how slim the connection to Father. We are not interested in sensationalism here. We are only interested in finding out who shot Father D'Angellini," I said.

"What does this have to do with me?" he asked.

"There is no sense beating around the bush here. We know that Father D'Angellini was gay. This is not easy to discuss, but I have to do it. We have been in contact with a man who claims to have been a former lover of his, a young boy at the time, who has now settled in San Francisco. He is a suspect in the murder of Father D'Angellini," I said.

We were walking on the beach away from the sun that was shining on our backs. It was warm but the breeze cooled things down and I felt comfortable even though I felt terribly uncomfortable discussing the subject with Father LaChance.

Without looking at me he snapped, "So, what has this got to do with me?"

"He claims you were one of a group of young priests at the time who had a number of places on the Cape where you would meet to escape the eyes of your parishioners," Marge said.

"So what?" the priest said.

"He also claims that you not only were out of sight of your parishioners but you were sexually active with each other. He attended with Father D'Angellini at the time," I said.

"I deny that unequivocally," he said.

"Before we go any further, let me explain something. Our interest in sexuality in this case stems from the fact that we want to make sure that any sexual entanglements he may have had, did not lead to his murder. If he was a pedophile there could be a motive connected to his death. Then there is the anti-gay stance that he actively promoted in his parish. So, we are not looking to tar and feather anyone, we are looking for facts that would lead us in the right direction. Is that understood?" I asked.

"I understand, but it has no connection to me," he said.

"Well, we have information that it does. Now whether you cooperate with us or not isn't that relevant right at the moment. So at this moment, unless someone is reading our minds or tapping our phones, no one knows that we are here and that we are talking to you. However, should it be deemed important that you testify we will issue a warrant for you to appear for a deposition and that will not remain secret," I said.

"Are you threatening me?" he asked.

"I'm not threatening you. I am trying to protect you from the embarrassment of being summoned to make a deposition. We are looking for information that will help us go in the right direction. Hopefully you can help us. But, what I will say is that you don't have to make up your mind this minute. Think about it. I'll give you our number and you can call us in a day or two with your decision," I said.

We turned then to walk back to the car. He didn't say a word as we strolled slowly along the beach. We were walking into the sun now and even with the breeze, it was warm, even early in the day. I suspected that we were in for an unseasonably warm day.

When we arrived at the car and we were fully dressed, he said, "I'll meet you in Fall River. Is there a place where we can meet that is not official and affords us some privacy? I can dress in civies. I served in Somerset, but I am not a familiar figure in the city."

"Since this isn't a formal meeting, I think we could meet at my house on Westport Point. No one would know you there, I'm sure, if that is okay with you. Marge and I live together, so that would make it convenient for us. How does that sound?" I asked.

"That would be fine," he said. "I agree, but there can be no taping. I have to have your word on that."

"Agreed," I said.

He set the day as two days from then at 11:00 in the morning and I gave him directions and my telephone number.

We dropped him off at the rectory and we asked for his recommendation for lunch and he suggested the Daniel Webster Inn in Sandwich. It was an old, attractive inn which had a lovely dining room with an eclectic menu, including the old standby comfort foods, but new age foods as well, which satisfied our concern over consuming foods rich in calories and fat.

Marge and I had a lovely lunch in a lovely setting and we both agreed that life was good for both of us. We were healthy, had the means to do what we chose to do, and were intellectually involved in interesting, but not exhausting work.

CHAPTER XX

The Fall River Police had had quite a few dealings with the project that Father D'Angellini hated so much. Drug trafficking was a continuous problem and they had sufficient records to fill us in on what the relationship was between the dealers and Father D'Angellini.

After a week of investigating the drug connection, our new friend Peter Madeiro, decided that there was very little going on between the priest and the major dealers. Actually, his only connection came from the fact that he had been very upset because one of the dealers had taken a house directly behind the church and made it into his central distribution point. According to the detective, the dealer had been under surveillance for months and was close to being brought in on drug charges.

"We should have a watertight case against him. The Fall River Police Department has this pretty much wrapped up and I don't think an arrest is far away. The problem came about because Father D'Angellini was hounding the Police Chief to get this hood out of the property and out of his back yard. The last thing the Chief needed was to raise the alert," he said.

Jack asked, "Do you think this had anything to do with Father's murder?"

"I can't imagine a connection. He wasn't exactly a confrontational type if you ask me. He had a few friends in politics and they were putting pressure on the Mayor to get the dealer out of his house, but that was as far as it went. I guess when the Mayor called the Chief, he was told to back off before he ruined everything. They couldn't very well come back to the priest and tell him what was going on, so the guy kept putting pressure on, but never directly. I doubt he ever even talked to the dealer," he said.

I said, "You sound like you knew Father personally."

"Oh, sure. He was a guy that everybody knew. He was always looking for things for nothing. My brother-in-law and sister were parishioners of his for a while before they moved out of town. Somehow he found out I was a detective and he got it into his head that I could help him with his church picnic. Believe it or not he wanted me to direct traffic and take care of the parking for him. I tried to tell him that I never had anything to do with traffic, but I'll tell you, he must have called me at least five times until I told him I couldn't do it. But he had a reputation for chiseling from different people all the time," he said.

Marge said, "In what way?"

"Well, I heard from a friend of mine who owned a dye factory that Father hounded him for yard goods that he could sell at his annual rummage sale. The guy said no matter how much he gave him, he never could give enough. The funny thing was that the guy is Jewish. He has nothing to do with the Catholic Church and had nothing to do with Father D'Angellini. He told me that he happened to meet the priest one time at a funeral of one of his workers and that was it. Next thing he knew he had a friend looking for leftover yard goods," he said. "You understand he was always having sales of some kind or another and he never paid for an item he sold. They all do it, but this guy pushed it all the way."

"It sounds to me like you didn't like him much," I said. "Did you ever have a personal problem with him?"

"Not me, personally. Aside from the fact that I am black, and he wasn't enamored of blacks. I had a friend who had problems with him. He was stationed in Texas and was being shipped to Nam. His girl friend was a parishioner of Saint Francis and they wanted to get married before he left. Father D'Angellini gave him a song and dance about not attending the three Pre-Cana sessions together before they could get married. He wouldn't marry them. They ended up getting married by a justice of the peace," he said.

"Isn't that awful," Marge said.

"But the worse part came when he came back. He served two years in Nam, was discharged and came back to live in his wife's folks' tenement. So then they have a baby and the priest wouldn't baptize the baby because her parents were not married in the church. The priest refused them baptism. They ended up going to a Portuguese church where the priest felt sorry for them and the baby. I would have told all of them to go straight to hell, but the girl wanted the baby baptized," he said.

"They must have been pretty upset about it," I said.

"My friend came back from Nam kind of messed up, so he had enough to worry about without worrying about some stupid jerk priest. His wife was upset, though. My friend is okay now, but it was a rough go for a while. But, you know he is okay and Father D'Angellini is dead. You think there is a moral in that? Can you imagine a priest turning down a baby? The guy wasn't too much to be honest, but nobody should die like he did," he said.

"So you don't think it might have been the drug people who killed him?" Marge asked.

"Like I said before, not a chance. They are as sleazy as they come, but they kill for a reason. There was no reason to kill this guy. He was no problem for them. He would never face up to them. He probably didn't even know what they looked like. They are more worried about competition than they are about what people think about them. They'd kill each other off without giving it a second thought, but they don't need murder just for the sake of murder. You better look somewhere else for your killers. I'd put money on that."

We thanked Peter and invited him out to dinner that night.

"Will Clarissa be there?" he asked.

"I hope so. We're going to Providence. Meet us at the house at six and we can drive to Providence together," I said.

We were in the District Attorney's Office so we dropped in to see Patrick to see if he had anything for us.

"What surprises me most in this whole case is that we have had no hue and cry about the murder from the public. It has been surprisingly quiet. I would have to guess that he wasn't the most popular priest around. Does that surprise you?" Patrick asked.

"Not really," Marge said. "What surprises me most is that he is seen in a different light by everyone we talk to. It is almost as if he appeared differently to different people. I had a girlfriend once, who seemed to change her appearance dramatically depending on what color she wore. It was almost as if she were transformed by what she wore. I see the same thing here. This man was seen differently by anyone who came into contact with him, except that unlike my girlfriend, he always wore black."

"I think that's right," I said. "It seems that not too many people were indifferent to him. Someone even hated him enough to kill him."

CHAPTER XXI

At dinner that night, Jack was able to tell us that The Church of Saint Francis would most likely be closed.

"The church is financially unsound. For the past five years it has been carried by the diocese and now that the priest has been killed it is unlikely that they will continue to take the losses," he said.

"That may explain why he went on his rampages against abortion and gays," Marge said. "He was probably being threatened with closure."

"Not probably, but definitely," Jack said. "The parish has been dead for years. The number of communicants has shrunk from year to year and Father D'Angellini was caught between trying to induce outsiders to come to his masses and going over the edge in supporting conservative movements."

"Where'd you learn all this?" I asked.

"One of my financial friends is big with the Church. He is a leading financial advisor to the Bishop and he is big in church finances. He is in the front line, so he pretty much knew what was going on with that particular church. He most definitely knew that that church was going under," he said.

"So the implication is that he was forced to take the road he did, or see the church closed, is that it?" I said.

"My man wouldn't go that far. He claims to know nothing other than that the church was in difficult financial straits and that it wasn't long for this world. There were other churches here that were closed, that were in much better shape than this one," Jack said. "The question I asked was 'Why did this particular one stay open?' And all he would say was that he had no idea."

"Nevertheless we know that it became the center of the anti-gay movement in the area. So, it would seem to me to be logical to assume that the Bishop was using this parish as a testing ground," I said.

"I don't think there is any question about that. They were using this guy and the poor dupe had no choice as far as he was concerned. He was trying to save his church, but he didn't know they were going to close him anyway. I sincerely hope that his murder isn't related to any of this."

"Why was the church in so much trouble?" Marge asked. "It has existed for years. Why now?"

"I suspect it is just numbers. According to Noah, it was always a small parish and as the years went by it relied more and more on outsiders who were coming in for the short mass. The people began moving to the suburbs in the fifties and that began the slow erosion in numbers. Then there were no new members to replace the old parishioners as they died off. It was slow but inevitable. Then, of late, it has become progressively worse and the young people have tended to drift away from the church in this area," Jack said.

"I don't think there is any question about that. I remember there used to be four masses on Sundays. Now I think there are two. There was a seven o'clock mass, followed by an 8:30, a 9:30 and a 10:30. Now they are down to two masses on a Sunday and I don't even know if they are full," I said. "Saturday afternoon we would wait in line to go to confession. Confession was at 4 o'clock and two priests would be in the confessionals to hear confessions and we felt lucky to get out of there by five."

Marge asked, "Do they still have confessionals or confession for that matter?"

I said, "I really don't know. I suppose they do in some form, but I am sure that it is nothing like it was."

"My source says that a great many of the problems with finances came about because young people have pretty much deserted the church. The whole business of pedophilia frightens mothers with young children. Young people have walked away. He claims that church attendance drops every year as more and more young women, especially, are searching for other churches. Family after family is finding that the older people still attend mass and are believers, while middle-aged and young people are rapidly drifting away," Jack said. "I have no history with the Church so it is hard for me to relate to any of this. But he is very despondent over it."

"There isn't much question but that he is right. At one time I think we can honestly say that the church was the center of people's lives here. Now I think it hardly plays a part. Something happened when fewer and fewer people entered the ministry. The number of nuns fell dramatically and the number of young people entering the priesthood suddenly declined. Why, I have no idea. There are so many factors that enter into it. Vocations were off. The whole business of pedophilia came into play and that has caused more problems. And then I think Pope Paul tightened the reins in his conservative thrust and that has alienated more and more of the flock so that what remains is highly regimented, disciplined and homogeneous and many of the liberals have been pushed out of the flock completely. It would take a wiser man than I am to figure it out," I said.

Marge said, "I see it among my friends. Most of them feel alienated within the Church although I would say that only about a quarter have dropped out completely. Their children are gone almost completely and they all feel sorry about that. They sent them to Catholic schools and gave them what they thought was a good Catholic education and very few of them even go to church. One of my best friends told me that she had eight children and not a single one of them goes to church."

"Well," Jack said, 'that probably explains it. For the most part the elderly have limited incomes and give money to the church in the fashion in which they always have. It would be anticipated that in today's society with salaries and incomes as they are, it would be the young who would be expected to open their purses. If they're not going to church, the church is receiving contributions at the pre-inflationary rate that doesn't reflect the new standards of living. The old lady who has given two dollars a week to the church for years doesn't necessarily take inflation into account when she goes to church. She still gives her two dollars a week and feels that she is doing her fair share even though her two dollars doesn't go very far. That may seem kind of far-fetched but I know if my Mom and Dad came back, they would be appalled at prices. I can't imagine my Dad being willing to pay twenty dollars for a puny steak in a restaurant. He would have an apoplectic fit."

"I remember my mother gave me five cents every week to put in the collection basket. You're right. That never changed. I was in high school and I still gave the five cents every week. Only you would think of that, Jack, but you're right," I said.

The rest of the evening was spent pleasantly at dinner. Peter and Clarissa, it seemed, paid very little attention to our discussion of the case. They were far more interested in each other and ended up discussing Clarissa's favorite novels and compiling a reading list for Peter.

CHAPTER XXII

We received a call from Father LaChance saying that he would be willing to meet us at my place on Westport Point or somewhere in an out of the way place where we wouldn't be seen or overheard by his parishioners or fellow priests. I suggested that he come to my house on the Point as a place where we would have no danger of being seen or heard. He agreed and I gave him directions and he set the time when we could meet later the same day.

He came at three o'clock that afternoon and we met him at the front door after he had parked his car in the driveway behind ours. We had warned Jack not to pop in because we did not want to spook the priest, who wasn't very comfortable to begin with. He was, not surprisingly, dressed in civilian clothes.

He was noticeably nervous and I could certainly understand that, considering his concern over any notoriety. I felt sorry for him, but we had our job to do and with that in mind, I thought we had best get the questions out of the way and let him go back to his business as soon as possible.

"To get right to it," I said, "we understand from a number of sources that Father D'Angellini was gay and active. Is that correct?"

"Yes," he said.

"Then why did he go on an anti-gay crusade?' I asked.

"He was forced into it in a way. He was never too happy about his sexual orientation. You have to understand that. He lived in guilt. The odd thing is that many of us don't really know what our orientation is because from the time we make up our minds to become priests, we tend to sublimate our sexual feelings. Marco was not like that. He knew even as a young man. He had been taken in hand by a priest who initiated him into all of the sexual proclivities of gay men," he said.

"Then why did he feel guilt?" I asked.

"Marco wanted above all else to be a successful priest. He wanted it with all his heart. He knew in his heart that what he was doing was wrong for him. He hated what he was, but at the same time he had to struggle with his natural desires and his vow of celibacy. You have to understand that being a priest is a very lonely life. We have too much time to ourselves. In this day and age our duties are more limited than they have ever been. A man who begins to drink finds himself fighting the demon with all kinds of free time. Parishes have become smaller and smaller and we are dealing with the true faithful who cling to us out of habit and faith, but they have become fewer and fewer in number," he said.

He seemed to be ready to get everything off his chest. He must have had a few sleepless nights since we had seen him, and I suppose he saw it as an opportunity to tell his side of the story and the story of countless numbers of his fellow priests.

"We find ourselves in decline. We are clinging to a past that may never exist again. We are divided among ourselves. Under Pope Paul the conservatives have pretty much come to the forefront and the rest of us have been pushed aside. So many of us sit waiting for change, which is hardly likely to come. I find myself being pushed out of the Church along with many of my peers. I don't have long before I make the move, but I want to go out on my own terms. I have been making plans for a year. I will probably leave in the next six months. I have prepared my family and they are reasonably in accord with my decision," he said. "But I don't need my sexual preferences exposed now. Do you understand that?"

"Yes we do," Marge said.

"Marco was caught in a different position. He was an active gay. No question about that. But as I said he wanted desperately to be a priest. He had wanted it his whole life. Never did he want to be a fireman or a ball player or a movie star; his lifelong dream was to be a priest," he said.

Marge asked, "Is that what you wanted too? Was that your dream too?"

"Yes, it was. But, now I can't live under the fear of exposure. That is my great fear. I am not a pedophile, but I am an active homosexual. You can't imagine what it is like living under that threat. The alcoholic priest lives under the same threat, but somehow alcoholism is accepted by the society and, believe it or not, so is heterosexual activity by a priest. But, the people still see homosexual activity as outside the range of acceptable behavior and we get no tolerance at all," he said. "The difference between me and Marco is that I have learned to live with what I am. He never could."

"To your knowledge, then, did he have many affairs with young boys? This could be significant in terms of his murder. There is always the possibility that an angry father or mother might have shot him, if that's the case," I said

"I don't know of any. After that one kid, I never saw him with another. I think I would have known. We weren't close, close friends, but Marco always seemed to spill his insides to me. I have no idea why, but he would talk to me for hours on end about his problems. I know he didn't do the same to our mutual friends, so I think had he taken up with another young person I would have known. You have to understand that he was following a pattern with that young boy. When he himself was just a boy, an altar boy, he had been taken under the wing of a priest in Providence. It was then that he was introduced to his sexuality. He told me many times how he had been in love with the priest and how they had been together for years, in fact until he went to the seminary. He was doing the same thing with, what's his name, Gino."

"If that was the case, why was he so upset about his homosexuality?" Marge asked.

"Well, I think it was because before he became a priest, he didn't see it as so very important to him. When he became a priest and continued his sexual activity he felt that he was breaking his vows. Think of it another way. How does a mother of four feel when she is having an affair with her husband's best friend? She knows that she is doing everything wrong. She stands a chance to lose her husband, destroy her family, hurt her children terribly, but somehow she goes on. How many times have I heard the same old story in the confessional? Sin is part of life, I'm afraid. I'm reminded of the old priest who chided his parishioners because they confessed so little after missing confession for a year. He said, 'If you tell me that you haven't been to confession for a year and your only sins are that you lied once and swore once, I am going to leap up and declare that the Virgin Mary has returned to earth.'"

He was feeling comfortable sitting in my kitchen looking out at the harbor below. It was one of those crisp New England days with a clear blue sky above, dotted with white puffy clouds. The birds were feeding at the feeders that Marge had set up and some chickadees were darting to and fro taking one sunflower seed at a time and then returning for another. Marge served coffee and some biscuits that I had baked fresh and he seemed to be enjoying them, although he ate only one with a cranberry jam that we had picked up on the Cape.

"I felt sorry for Marco, actually. He was in a terrible bind. He thought, that as time went by, he would be able to put his sexual activity behind him, but it didn't happen. I gave up on that idea a long time ago. That's why I am getting out," he said.

"Now do you think there is any possibility that one of his friends or lovers might have killed him?" I asked.

"As far as I know, he didn't have a lover. Nor was he indiscreet. He was not a man who searched out sexual encounters. You already know that we had a house on the Cape that we used as a meeting place. Understand that the house was a refuge where we sought to escape everyone's eyes. It was not a place where we conducted orgies or anything of the sort. If you have an image in your mind of some sort of wild, sexual encounters, then remove it. It was far from that. We were a tight circle of about six priests. Rarely did an outsider get invited. The time Marco brought that boy, he was met with a great deal of resistance. It was like we were being invaded. He never brought an outsider again," he said.

"You know he was in Fall River when Father D'Angellini was killed. Do you think that Gino Alberto would have done it?" I asked.

"I doubt it. I think when the man left for wherever he went, it was over. Marco mentioned him once or twice to me because he felt some guilt about hurting the boy. But outside of that I don't think they even had contact; at least, not that I know of. I would wonder if they ever talked to each other once he had left Fall River. But I can only go by what I feel in this instance. I have no knowledge about him one way or the other," he said.

"So as far as you are concerned Father's sexual orientation had nothing to do with his killing?" Marge asked.

"I can't say that definitively. You know I am in Sandwich and he was in Fall River. Except for the fact that he liked to unload his problems on me, it wasn't like I was nearby or in a position to see him very often. At most, I would see him once a month. I will say that, at least to my knowledge, he had no long term liaison. If he did I didn't know about it. Unlike me, he tried desperately to be celibate. So as far as I know he would go relatively long periods of time without sexual contact. That was the message he gave me, anyway," he said.

"Now, how about the anti-gay movement that he sponsored in his church? Why did he do that?" I asked.

"That's more difficult than you think," he said. "First off, there was a movement in the state legislature to get a ban on gay marriage in the Commonwealth. There was a lot of pressure put on the Bishop to join the anti-gay crusade. Of course, the Catholic newspaper, The Anchor, came out against gay marriage, but it wasn't enough for the activists. They wanted a full-fledged frontal attack. We had a local state representative who was a raving maniac on the subject and he was pushing hard. He managed to pull together a group that was willing to be active within the Church. And, that's where Marco came in. He didn't have many gifts, but he could speak, and he had been very effective with the Right to Life movement."

He had been very forthcoming and I thought Father LaChance was not holding anything back. He struck me as a bright man, probably too much so for the position he held as a curate in a small parish on Cape Cod. There was a great need for priests, and yet, here he was serving a small parish with an even smaller group of churchgoers in the winter months. In my mind, I felt that he had been shunted aside for a reason and the reason was quite obvious.

"There was something about Marco when he stood to deliver his sermon. I try to copy his delivery style, but I can't. He, first of all, had complete voice control. He instinctively knew when to raise and lower his voice. Marco made people like him in person, but when he spoke you almost felt he was speaking just to you. It was a gift. Let me give you a 'for instance'. You like that 'for instance', Mr. Amos? That comes right out of Fall River and my childhood. Well, one Sunday, Marco was giving one of his anti-abortion sermons and suddenly he stopped and came to the front of the altar railing. In a very low voice he said, 'Those women in the church who have had an abortion in the past should not be wracked with sin and guilt. God forgives. Put that sin behind you. God loves you.' You could practically hear people breathing. It was so still in that church. Then he walked back to his podium, stood quietly for a minute or so and resumed his sermon. I looked around the church and saw at least four women crying. He had spoken just to them. It was his gift," he said.

He stood up from the table at which he sat and then walked to the windows overlooking the harbor. The birds were twittering around the feeders and there were still a few pleasure boats in the harbor below standing out against the bright blue water.

He turned then and continued, "It was that gift that caused him his problems. The powers that be, thought it would be wise to test the waters on the anti-homosexual, anti-gay marriage issue and they thought that Marco, because of his style, was the perfect choice. Marco was a quiet speaker, not a ranting fool. He was not the kind of priest that forecasts doom and a fiery Hell. He spoke quietly and effectively. It was his effectiveness that drew the attention of the hierarchy. He had developed a following when he spoke, week after week, about what he called 'the sin of abortion.' I heard him once, and I have to say he moved his audience, not to marching in the streets, but to careful consideration of what he was saying. I could feel it in the pews and within the walls of that church."

"It sounds to me like you admired him," Marge said.

"I'm afraid that isn't true. I admired his speaking ability and his gift at moving the congregation he was speaking to, but can I say I admired him? No, I did not. He was a weak man; weak and vacillating. He was caught in the terrible bind of trying to please everyone. I always wondered whether he was trying to please people or seeking their approval by agreeing with whatever they said. I never quite figured it out. But, that's what the Bishop saw in him. He knew he could take advantage of his weakness to make him do his will. So, he sent his underlings out to persuade Marco that the only way he could keep his church open was to raise money by using the groups that were supporting the anti-gay movement so heavily. They used the poor guy. He was a dupe," he said.

"That sounds harsh," Marge said.

"I'm afraid it was. That is only my opinion, by the way. I'm sure the Bishop's office would deny any such intention on their part, but I have no question in my mind that he was pushed and nudged into the position he ended up taking. I never talked to him about it, but I was shocked when I heard what he was doing. At any rate, I think I have just about given you everything I have to give," he said. "I don't know what else I can say. Not surprisingly, those of us who are gay, deeply resented the position he took on gays. Some of his fellow priests were very upset at him; myself included. It was like a stab in the back. We have struggled internally with this for a long time and many of us have had to think this through and make up our minds where we would go with it. I decided to leave the priesthood and several of my friends will also leave. But, some are staying and they didn't need one of their fellows to betray them, even if only with words."

"But as far as you know, there was no basis for murder in all of this, right?" I asked.

"I can't imagine it. His fellow priests were hurt, but he wasn't a threat to them in any way. Then the anti-gay thing had its life span and then it began to die. He couldn't maintain it without revving up the rhetoric and as I have already said, that wasn't his style. It had a short life and it was over. He may have left a great deal of resentment in his wake but I doubt he was murdered over that issue. I would think you would have to venture farther afield to get a motive there," he said.

He rose again and walked over to the windows and stood quietly for a few minutes looking down the embankment that led to the inlet below and seemed fascinated by the view. Then he turned slowly and said, "I could imagine living out my life here. You are very fortunate to have this."

Marge said, "Father you are too young to be thinking about where you want to live out your life. You have many years ahead of you. If I have learned anything in life, it is that every time a door closes and we think we are shut out, another seems to open."

I smiled inwardly at what Marge said, because I knew that the door that had opened for her, included me.

We shook hands and we thanked him for his information and I assured him that none of the background he gave us would ever be attached to him in any way. I gave him my word that none of what he had told us was on tape and that he was in no danger of being exposed in any way by us.

When he had left Marge said, "Is it his gayness they resent or his failure to be celibate that is driving him out of the Church or do you think it is a combination of both?"

"If he were a hetero, do you think he would be having the same problem?" I asked.

"No," was all Marge said.

CHAPTER XXIII

Providence, like the Phoenix, has risen from the ashes. In the last twenty years we have seen a defeated, beaten city, come back to life. It is ironic, that its mayor, Vincent Cianci, was the architect of the revival of the city and also the man who ended up in jail for doing the very things that Providence mayors have done for years.

College Hill, rising surprisingly rapidly from the Providence River which cuts through the center of the city, causes many a pedestrian to stop to catch his or her breath. Going up the hill one comes first to Rhode Island School of Design, known locally as RISD. I have visited their museum many times and on this day, I decided to take Marge for a continuation of our visits to museums. Jack took the opportunity to roam around the hill searching out the many Federal buildings which are unique to Providence.

The RISD Museum is a small gem. There is one room which always catches my attention. It is no more than twenty by twenty, but contains a Manet of Berthe Morisot seated on a chaise lounge, a beautiful Monet depicting a boat scene, a Cezanne painting of a landscape, a lovely Renoir and a Pissarro. I have mentioned to the retired, part-time guards standing watch over the paintings that they find themselves in charge of fifty to a hundred million dollars worth of paintings in a tiny space, which always brings out a smile.

The museum was small enough so that Marge and I were able to see what we wanted to see without exhausting ourselves or becoming bored. Marge was particularly taken with the room containing the Renaissance paintings and statuaries, including a large cross with the figure of Christ beautifully represented.

"I remember visiting homes with my mother when I was a little girl and noticing that there weren't too many homes without a cross displayed in an important part of the house. It was as much a part of the house as a couch or dining room table. I didn't have one in my house and we don't have one in the house we live in now Noah," she said.

"I hadn't thought about that," I said, "But now that you mention it, I have to agree with you. My mother always had one hanging in the parlor and in the kitchen and definitely in her bedroom. My father even had a St. Christopher medal pinned to the visor of the car."

"We definitely date ourselves with those," Marge said laughing.

We met Jack and waited at one of the little restaurants on Thayer St. for Clarissa. Knowing we were going to be in the area of Brown, Jack had called to ask her to lunch with us. She arrived shortly after we did and we sat down to a quiet lunch before heading up to Federal Hill for our usual supply of Italian goodies.

Clarissa lived in a private apartment with another young woman who was earning her doctorate and she loved the area. It was indeed, a picturesque area of the city. In the course of its history the area close to Brown University has become more and more student-centered with Brown taking over many of the buildings in the adjacent area for dormitories and special purposes, especially office buildings. Just north of the immediate area around Brown was some of the nicest housing in the city which extended northerly for some distance. Where the smaller cities had seen a complete out-migration of the middle class, Providence had been able to keep its nicer areas intact and had been able to cling to its professional class in terms of its housing needs.

There was choice housing as well in the area south of the school and on the hill. This led to the Fox Point area where the Portuguese had settled, replacing the Irish who had been there before them. This area was limited in scope because it was located close to the bay which borders Providence on the south side.

As had happened in Fall River, the Portuguese immigrants had pretty much kept every other group out by buying up every available piece of property in an effort to keep their families together. So, even to this day, most of the people one meets on the side streets of Fox Point are of Portuguese origin.

We had a very enjoyable lunch and Jack was always delighted to see Clarissa. He saw her as his daughter, I think, and wanted the very best for her. She had come to the country from the Bahamas with not much hope of success and we had found her working as an assistant bookkeeper in one of the local stores. Jack had sensed something special in her and he had been right. He was hoping that she would get the education she had always wanted and that she would meet a man who was as bright as she was, so that she could live a full life in the United States. If not a husband, at least the opportunity to follow her chosen career without impediments thrown in her way.

When we had finished lunch we dropped Clarissa off at her apartment building and headed back down College Hill going west past the Brown campus and RISD and then through the downtown in the valley and then up the hill and under the pine cone to Atwell's Avenue and the other peak of the city on Federal Hill. We parked the car between Broadway and Atwell's Ave, in what was once the purely Italian section of Federal Hill. Not unlike Fall River, we came across the tenement buildings, but here they were mixed with what once had been two story houses which were meant to house two families. The houses were crammed side by side but even from the road we could see small gardens between the properties and an occasional grape vine growing in the back of the house.

Parking was limited since the day of the one car family was gone long ago and many of the houses didn't have driveways. Most of the families had to park in the streets, but since it was a working day and it was mid-afternoon, we were lucky to find a place almost immediately. Here the houses were well kept and Marge remarked that the occupants took pride in their properties in the same way we saw in the privately owned tenements in Fall River.

Jack wanted some spicy, freshly made Italian sausage and a large Italian flat bread and we picked that up in one stop at our favorite grocery store, while Marge ducked across the street for some of her chocolates. The chocolate shop could have been right out of Paris and it was a good place for me to avoid with my problem with diabetes.

With our shopping done, we decided to drive through the west end of the city which had been considered a slum or ghetto for years. There had been some attempts to spruce up the area but it had gone by the wayside. The area had been a haven for prostitutes and drug dealing, but on our short ride I saw no evidence of prostitution in the streets, so I had to assume that the Providence Police Department had done their job in that regard. Aside from groups of men standing on corners and around store fronts I have no idea if drug dealing was still taking place. I suspected it was, but had no way of knowing. The houses here were not as well kept as the ones on Federal Hill and there was a sense of untidiness here. Trash was everywhere. Barrels that had been put outside for trash collection were overflowing on the sidewalks and into the gutters. It was the yards that were so different. Many of them were overgrown with weeds and litter was everywhere. There was not a flower to be seen and even the trees seemed stunted. The sidewalks were cracked and the roadways had seen better times, with the macadam bulging in places and cracks showing as well as potholes to be avoided.

The area closest to the city was primarily populated by blacks but not too far along Broad St. we began seeing store after store that had Spanish language signs displayed and the visible population turned to Hispanics. From seeing black people walking the sidewalk, we were suddenly aware that almost everyone we saw was Hispanic. The change was almost imperceptible. But now there were Hispanic grocery stores, restaurants and used car lots. Storefront churches dotted the area and there were signs of a burgeoning economy with peddlers setting out their wares on the sidewalks. The activity was more intense than it had been in the equally poor area of the black housing on Broad St. I was more than surprised to see quite a few Portuguese language signs further down the road before we came to the nicer houses and a nicer area approaching Cranston.

In a short time we had seen a considerable part of the inner city. From east to west was probably no more than three miles. From the Fox Point area on the east side to Federal Hill was probably even less than three miles, but the diversity of life within that small distance was what made cities great. Each section of the city had its special features from the culture of RISD and Brown University to the simplicity of the Portuguese feasts in the church on Fox Point or St. Joseph's Day in the Italian section. There was a richness in the diversity of life that could not be overlooked and was to be enjoyed.

We drove back to Providence and found an area that had been completely rebuilt. It covered two city blocks and was made up of single family houses, which, although close together, gave the rundown section a completely different look. There were any number of Afro-Americans people on the streets around the development and I saw some black children playing in a small playground in among the houses, so I had to assume that the houses were populated by blacks and I couldn't help but think that it would be an amazing development if the whole area could somehow be rehabbed to provide decent housing for black families. I had no idea who had done the job here, but Jack said that he could find out if it was public or private investment that had gotten it going.

We drove through the section and came to I95 East which took us along the south side of the city. Before us we could see the buildings on the east side of the city where we had started our day and before we knew it we were racing toward Fall River and Westport Point and to the quiet of a small New England farm town. At one time Westport had been just that, a small New England farm community with the addition of a lovely coastline that attracted summer residents and hordes of beach lovers during the hot summer months. Things had changed when city dwellers discovered the advantages of living in the suburbs and Westport had not avoided the influx of city dwellers looking for serenity. I spoke to more than one native Westporter who had grown up on a farm and then discovered that the land he was tilling was far more productive as a housing development than as a farm. It didn't take much insight for families to see that the tremendous amount of labor they expended for small returns was not comparable to what they could make by selling off pieces of their farms. The closer to the water, either the ocean or the Westport River, the higher the price and the demand kept rising every year. There were those that clung to their heritage of farming but they were becoming fewer and fewer and it was obvious that they were living in the past.

So much of what we do, we do out of habit and without looking around us to see if what we are doing fits the present day situation. Farmers who work like fools for very little money could become millionaires overnight by selling off their land.

We hadn't done a thing on the case that day and it came as a disappointment when I got home to have a message on my answering machine. The voice belonged to someone who said that I had had him as a pupil in the junior high and that he had some valuable information for me if I was interested. He left his number and I called him back immediately. He didn't want to talk on the telephone and he said he would meet with no one but me, and that we should meet at the east gate of the Oak Grove Cemetery in an hour, if I wanted the information. Without giving it a second thought I said that I would meet him.

Jack and Marge did not like the idea but I thought, since it was still daylight and I would be meeting him during the busy part of the day in the cemetery, that I would be all right. I couldn't imagine why he would want to do me harm. We had ruffled a few feathers in our investigation but nothing enough to end in physical harm to me. I didn't feel threatened.

I took a quick shower and dressed in about twenty minutes. I had felt tired and dirty. The shower was just what I needed. I drove into the city and was at the gate with about ten minutes to spare. As soon as I parked my car I was met by a very tall, thin man in his mid to late thirties. I recognized him immediately but couldn't put a name to him. He must have been 6 foot 6 and I couldn't even guess his weight. Even with the change in size, though, I recognized his face, which surprised me.

He walked to me, put out his hand and said, "Sorry about the secrecy, but it has to be. I'm John Domingos. Do you remember the name?"

"Yes I do and it stands to reason that you are hardly the small boy I knew then," I said.

"Guess not. I shot up in high school."

"Do you want to walk?" I asked.

"That would be a good idea," he said.

We walked along the east side of the cemetery while I waited for him to tell me why he wanted to see me.

Finally, he said, "Father D'Angellini molested me."

I was taken aback by that statement. I had not expected to hear that, for some reason.

"This is very hard for me, but I think you should know what kind of a man you are dealing with here. He was not what he was cracked up to be, you know. I don't think I was the only one, either," he said.

"Have you ever talked about this to anyone else?" I asked.

"Not a soul and I am asking you not to talk about it either. Ever since I heard that you were going around asking questions, I haven't had a decent night's sleep, thinking that I should talk to you. I had to get it off my chest. I have three kids and a wife and I don't want them to know about this. You've got to give me your word that none of this leaks out," he said.

"You have it, then," I said. "How did it happen?"

"It was a nightmare. I was only about thirteen and I was just finishing up as an altar boy at the church. It was when I was in ninth grade. I was in your class then. I was so mixed up I didn't know what to do," he said.

We were walking slowly and the sun was directly overhead. We were in the new section of the cemetery where there were no trees overhead and I began to feel warm, so I suggested that we walk toward the old oaks and maples so that we could be shaded as we walked.

"It didn't happen all at once. It was slow coming on and I really had no idea what he was doing. I really can't relive the whole thing even now. The upshot of the whole thing was that he gave me oral sex. It only happened once. I was so scared I didn't know what to do. I never told anyone and I never talked to him again. I am sick just thinking about it now, but it is too late for that. Things happen that we can never take back," he said and he began to sob.

I found myself at a loss for words. We continued walking and I could see his body shaking with sobs. There was nothing I could do; nothing I could say. I felt helpless and useless as we continued to walk. The air was clear and in the shade it was not as heavy as it had been in the sun. We walked, with the silence only broken by his sobs, and then he seemed to draw himself up and the crying was suddenly past him.

"What difference did it make? One time was all. You would think that I would have forgotten it the minute it was over. But no, it has hung on my soul for close to thirty years. How could that be? Think about that Mr. Amos. It's crazy," he said. "The lousy bastard ruined my life."

We continued walking and I remained silent. I could not think of what I should say.

"You're the first person I ever told this to. I hope I get it out of my system by talking," he said.

"Maybe it will do you some good to get it out. You've been holding it in too long," I said.

"Maybe. But what I really wanted was for you to know that that was the kind of man he was. He was a priest, but he had the rottenness in him. He didn't care how much he hurt me and the reason I wanted to tell you is because there may be a lot like me. I bet I'm not the only one," he said. "Whoever killed the bastard did the world a favor. I wish it had been me. I thought of it lots of times you know, but I knew that was stupid. But how many other guys did he hurt besides me? Is there a long list of guys or just me? That's what I wanted to tell you. How long did his arms reach?"

"You were not alone, I can tell you that," I said. "We know of one other boy with whom he had a long-term affair. We've heard a report of one other, but we haven't identified him as yet. I am sorry that this happened to you John. I truly am, and I wish I could help you in some way, but I can't."

"It can't be helped and I keep thinking how silly it is that such a small thing should have such consequences. I am married with three good kids, I've got a good job and I make good money. I've been lucky. So this little thing of five minutes should be out of my mind forever. But I've read about some of the men who were involved in cases like mine when they were kids and it had the same effect on them. It's weird. I think as much as the physical thing, it was the idea of the betrayal of trust. I had complete trust in that bastard and then he did what he did and I couldn't stop him. I froze and there was nothing I could do about it. Now, I look back and I realize that if it had been a stranger, I'd have shaken it off. But, a priest, there is no shaking it off."

Some large rain clouds suddenly blocked the sun overhead and I felt a few drops of rain. Before we could go very far we were hit with a deluge. The rain came down in sheets and we ducked into the doorway of an above-ground tomb where we were at least protected momentarily. I could see flashes of lightning and hear the rumbling of thunder close by. In no time at all torrents of water were washing down the small inclines and I couldn't help but think what a difference a few minutes had made to us. The doorway we were standing in was deep enough so that we were hit with only a few splashes of water and I couldn't help but think how similar our situation was to what John had felt as an innocent boy so many years ago. One moment we were walking in the hot sun and then without warning we were protecting ourselves from the rain. I could just imagine what this poor sensitive boy had felt, the sense of betrayal and of shame. But we knew in our present situation that the clouds would move quickly and with them the rain and the sun would be shining once again. If we were lucky we might even see a rainbow. In John's case, for whatever reason, the clouds didn't go away and there was no sunshine and certainly no rainbow.

"Have you thought about getting help?" I asked. "Sometimes, just going through the whole thing with someone else can help a great deal."

"Believe it or not, just talking to you about it has been very helpful. I'll wait to see how I feel a few days from now when I think about it. I think I'll be fine to tell you the truth. I think I held it in too long," he said.

We walked back to our cars in the sunlight and away from the dripping trees. It became humid quickly as the hot sun evaporated the water that soaked the grass and the roadways, but I had no desire to walk under the trees which shed their newfound surplus of water with each breeze.

We didn't talk and I had the feeling that John was talked out. When we reached our cars we shook hands and then he said, "Mr. Amos I trust you to keep our secret a secret. I don't want my wife and kids to hear about this."

I said, "You can trust me. I will use this information, but no one will ever know where I got it from, believe me."

On the way back to Westport Point I couldn't help but consider that the event that had happened to John that was so devastating to him, had happened to him while he was my student. There he was sitting in my classroom acting like every other child in the room; listening to me, reading the text, doing homework, participating in class, answering questions, taking tests and all of the other everyday activities in my classroom, while at the same time he was being ripped apart by his dark secret, a secret so dark in his mind, that he did not feel free to speak to anyone about it.

How many other kids had been in the same situation? That's what bothered me most. How many were watching their families dissolve because of divorce and not saying a word? How many were living in abject poverty and were ashamed to talk about it? What kind of problems did the kids suffer from, without ever telling anyone? As a teacher, I saw my job as teaching those kids whatever I had to offer. Once in a great while a child confided in me, but that was a rare occurrence and aside from the obvious problems that most teenagers have, I wasn't really keyed into their personal lives.

Looking back, I remember a small number of teachers, who for one reason or another, were able to involve themselves in the children's lives. I could never fathom how they were able to do it. As for myself, I did have one or two students a year that I was closer to than the others, such as my benefactor who had problems with being overly effeminate in a setting that abhorred effeminacy. My student Harry was an outstanding student in a hostile environment and he needed help, but in his case it was obvious and I could not help but see it. It would have been another thing to probe into his private affairs to determine if he needed help. With all of the work I had to do to teach six classes a day, I doubt if I could have done it, even if I was capable of doing more than teach.

There is no way that a teacher can do it all. We have to do what we can do and live with our limitations or become so frustrated that we end up walking away from the job completely. I have seen many teachers do just that.

CHAPTER XXIV

Patrick called us to meet with him that afternoon since he had another meeting with Father Sousa from the Bishop's office.

"If I am alone in the office with him, I might be tempted to smash him one, so I think I need you guys to protect me," he said. "And, understand, I don't say that jokingly. He's hoping you can bring him up to date on what you have found."

It was after we had stopped on Quarry St. for Jack's nourishment that we drove to New Bedford to Patrick's office. Jack parked his car in the official parking slots at the Court House and we were stopped by a court policeman who was new to us. He looked at us dubiously when we produced our identification and he saw that we were part of the District Attorney's staff. We were tired of explaining what our relationship was, so we left him staring after us as we made our way into the building.

Jack was laughing as he said, "The only fit purpose for us Noah, as far as that man is concerned, is to be sitting in a nursing home somewhere singing 'Jeannie with the Light Brown Hair' in a dithering chorus."

Marge said, "Why 'Jeannie with the Light Brown Hair?'"

Jack laughed and said, "My father was always singing it along with 'She'll be Coming Round the Mountain'. It stuck in my mind as a song old people should sing."

We entered Patrick's outer office and his secretary pointed to his door and ran her finger across her throat to let us know that he had the visitor we were expecting. Even she could feel the tension in his presence. She called Patrick on his phone to let him know we were there and then told us to go right in.

Both men were sitting across from each other and we could feel the tension between them. Jack didn't hesitate but walked right up to the priest, held out his hand and said, "Nice meeting you again Father. You know Marge and Noah, of course."

That was enough to break the tension since Father Sousa had to respond, even if he did so curtly.

He said, "Can we get to this quickly, I have a busy schedule?"

From where I stood, I could see the side of his hair shining in the light and I was almost tempted to ask what he used on his hair to keep it so neatly in place, but I thought better of it.

Patrick said, "Father Sousa is interested in a summary of what you have discovered so far. Let's be frank and give him an honest appraisal of where we are."

"Honest, is the correct word," he said with a touch of sarcasm.

"Well, I have the least information," Jack said. "As of now and I suspect that won't change, I have found no financial tie-in with the murder. Father D'Angellini had very little money; enough for his needs, but certainly not enough to warrant a murder. His mother tied up all her assets in a trust fund for her two grandchildren, which would take any money out of the reach of Father D'Angellini. So, in a word, I don't think money was the motive for the killing."

"And you," Father Sousa said looking at me, "what do you have?"

His tone was nasty and for some reason it hit me the wrong way.

"Frankly, Father, Marge and I have been working too hard on this, to be talked to in that way. We are certainly not being paid and we are not young. So if you are not going to treat us with respect, I would suggest that you go about your duties and leave us alone," I said and I could feel the blood rising to my face.

Patrick was shocked and he said, "It's okay Noah, I don't think Father Sousa meant anything."

Father said, "I'm sorry. I don't think my comment deserved that kind of a reaction, but if it did, then, I repeat, I am sorry."

"Well, we have pulled together a great deal of information, some of which I am sure you are not going to like. I'm sure you know what we have found, but let's get it on the table," I said.

He looked at me and said, "Do that."

"First of all, Father D'Angellini was a sexually active homosexual," I said.

Father Sousa didn't react to that as I thought he would, so I continued on, "We haven't got a connection between his sexual activity and his murder, but one very well could be there. So, if that is the case, you should be ready for that."

"When you say sexual activity, what are you referring to?" he asked.

"Well we know of one affair with a young boy and another incident of a molestation of another. We also know of an ongoing relationship among a group of priests in a house on the Cape," I said.

"I suppose you find this titillating?" Father Sousa said.

"Quite the opposite, to be honest with you," Marge said. "I find it very depressing and sad. One thing keeps coming to my mind and I would like you to answer it for me. Your lack of reaction just now proves to me what I have known all along. You knew he was a sexually active gay man from the beginning. If we have discovered this in a few weeks, it could not have been hidden from you. I'm sure you can tell us the name of every priest who uses that house on Cape Cod. Am I right?"

"We are not being investigated here, ma'am, so I refuse to be interrogated," he said.

"Well, I have a piece of advice for you Father Sousa. Don't play poker. The truth shows all over your face. My point is that these men are going through terrible turmoil. They have devoted themselves to a career that denies them and they are getting no help from the people who should be helping them the most," she said.

"How do you presume to know what we are or are not doing? You are dripping with arrogance, ma'am," he said.

"I may be arrogant, but whatever I feel comes out of dismay. Was it part of your therapy or treatment to have Father D'Angellini be adopted by an anti-homosexual group and then to have him lead the charge against gay marriage in his own church? A gay priest who is refusing the Eucharist to his own is quite a twist on helping people out, I would say," Marge said.

She was extremely angry now and was ready to explode.

Thankfully, Jack stepped in and said, "Father Sousa is here as an envoy to Patrick from the Bishop and he is trying to find out what we have discovered about this murder. I don't think it's quite fair, Marge, to put him on the hot seat."

Marge stopped suddenly and sat back in her chair. She said, "I understand. Please accept my apology, Father."

"As of now, then, we have no motive for the murder," I said. "Father D'Angellini evoked a great many strong sentiments. If we have found out anything, it is that people were very strongly with him or against him. The odd thing about that, is that he was a man who wanted to please everyone. The last thing he would have wanted was to have enemies. He has been described to us as a man who changed personalities, a chameleon, to satisfy whoever he was talking to. This hardly sounds like a man who would seek out confrontation. But, he did have enemies."

"What does that lead you to?" he asked.

"Nothing, so far. But our job is not to be dramatic, but to pull together as many facts as possible until they lead us to the killer. Right now we are just scratching the surface. It would be nice if we had Miss Marple on our side, but unfortunately, we haven't. All we have is the hope that we turn up something that will give us what we need to solve this case," I said.

Patrick said, "If it makes you feel easier, you have to be aware that nothing has been said about this case. As Noah pointed out, we have two proven cases of pedophilia involving Father D'Angellini and they have not been made public. We have no desire to make them public unless they turn out to be the motive for the murder and we take the perpetrator to court. In that case we have no choice, but as we have said before, Father D'Angellini is dead and we have no interest in tarnishing his name."

"That certainly is our concern. And we certainly don't want to further tarnish the Diocese's name any more than it has been hurt recently," he said.

"We also have claims that gay activists may have perpetrated the crime, but aside from a generalized e-mail suggesting that Father must be stopped, there isn't anything definitive in that direction," I said. "There are a few things that bother me, but we'll just keep slogging along until we get some answers."

Jack said, "Unless we are mistaken, Mrs. D'Angellini is investigating the murder on her own using some private agency, I think. We have no idea what she has turned up, so it will be my job to pursue that avenue as soon as possible. She is not without resources. Has anyone contacted your office about his murder?"

"There are several requests on file for information which have been summarily dismissed," Father Sousa said.

"It might be important for us to know who they are," Jack said. "Could you send along the information to this office? Again, we will use discretion in following it up. I am due to meet with Mrs. D'Angellini this week and I would like any information I can get."

"We'll see," Father Sousa said.

I was getting the feeling that he was less suspicious of our motives and I thought he was even loosening up a bit in his relations with us. The edge had gone from his voice and he seemed to be more relaxed although it was evident that he was not a man who was ever off his guard. There was nothing to relax about in the Church in Massachusetts with all the scandal that had broken in the past few years. One of the worst and first cases had come out of the Fall River Diocese and the scandal was still a ripe topic in the parishes in all of Massachusetts as the case had opened the flood gates and any number of cases had followed. It was obvious that the little man sitting in front of us was not about to become familiar, but it would be much more comfortable for all of us and Patrick especially, if the threatening aspect of his personality could somehow be removed.

"From my point of view I have the feeling that this is a murder, not so much directed by issues, but by personality. Someone met with Father in the back of the church rather than in the rectory. Why there? Did he know something was going to happen so he clutched his rosary ring in his hand? Why would someone want to kill him in such a manner? Patrick's detectives have combed the area and not found one person who heard the shots. Someone hated that man enough to shoot him point blank. We'll find him Father Sousa, but we may not do it tomorrow. It will take all our patience and endurance, I suspect," I said, as much for the four of us as for Father Sousa. In any of these cases we are looking for miracles; someone to come forward to admit to the crime, or a sudden inspiration, a flash of insight. Even with my limited experience I knew that was not how it worked.

We finished the meeting and the priest rose to say goodbye. He hadn't taken any notes and I wondered if he had a recorder somewhere in his jacket. I realized that we hadn't said anything particularly revealing, so there was not much substance that he needed to record. There was something abut the man, though, that made me mistrust him.

We said our goodbyes and he was gone.

Patrick said, "That seemed to have gone a little better than our first meeting, but I wouldn't put much stock in that, because we didn't tell him very much."

Marge said, "I thought we did actually. He didn't react to the fact that we knew that Father D'Angellini was gay. That was surprising. I was expecting him to make a passionate denial. He said nothing, which, in itself, I thought, was very revealing."

Marge was deeply into this case. In the previous cases we had worked on together she had worked almost as a dispassionate observer. Now her cheeks were showing color and she was shifting in her chair and crossing and uncrossing her legs as if to get rid of some of her excess energy.

"Think about what the acceptance of that one issue means. It means that they knew perfectly well that Father D'Angellini was gay when they turned him loose on those poor people. They let him stir up hatred among people that were exactly as he was. Father Sousa, by not saying a word, has admitted that they did that, and that is despicable," she said. "This puts the Jesuits to shame."

Jack said, "One other thing upsets me. He doesn't care one iota about who killed Father D'Angellini. All he is concerned about is how it will affect the Church and its public relations. Think about that. This is one of theirs who was murdered and he obviously doesn't care who did it or why, only in so much as it causes or doesn't cause a scandal. I wouldn't want to be working for these guys."

We went through our tasks for the week. Jack and Clarissa were going to meet with Mrs. D'Angellini after meeting with her lawyers and I had set myself the task of trying to find out what happened to Father D'Angellini's breviary. The absence of the breviary had bothered me from the beginning and I thought it was important that I follow through on it, although I didn't know where to begin. Marge wanted to get back to Mrs. Alberto because she felt there was something below the surface there that we had not plummeted.

CHAPTER XXV

We went to see Dino Lagozza the next morning. I called him and he said that he would be in the church basement doing some work so I could meet him there. The breviary was on my mind and I thought Dino might be able to answer a couple of questions for me.

We found him in the basement of the church which served as a meeting hall and activity center when it was in use.

"Boy Scouts and Cub Scouts," he said. "They should give merit badges for cleaning up. They leave this place such a mess I'd like to get the leaders and make them stay afterward and clean, but I've been told more than once to be good to them."

The fact that he was griping didn't surprise me. For as long as I had known Dino, he had been a complainer. Sometimes I had even felt that he thought he ran the church and the priests were around only as symbols of authority.

We had stopped at Dunkin Donuts to get him a coffee and I offered it to him when we arrived.

"Hope you thought to get a decaf," he said. "I don't drink much regular coffee now."

"Sorry," I said. "But don't look a gift horse in the mouth, Dino."

He took the coffee then, put the broom he was using down and pulled up a chair for Marge at one of the tables that he had pushed aside to clear some space for sweeping and then sat down himself.

"What can I do for you?" he asked.

"If I'm not mistaken, Dino," I said, "I remember that Father D'Angellini always carried his breviary. Am I right?"

"Oh yeah, he did. We used to say that it was glued to his right hand. You know how some babies can't live without their little nipples in their mouths, we used to say the same about Father and his prayer book. My daughter called her baby's nipple a binky. The prayer book was Father's binky," he said laughing.

"Then where was it when the body was found?" I asked.

"I didn't think about that. I never saw it. Holy Jesus, I don't know," he said. He became quite contemplative. "Something to think about."

"I thought you were retired," I said.

"I am. Just killing time."

* * *

When the subject of the breviary came up with Patrick and Jack at one of our meetings, Jack didn't quite understand the significance of what I was trying to get across.

"First of all," he said, "what exactly is a breviary?"

"It's a little black book that priests use as a prayer book," I said.

Marge said, "It is a great deal more than that, I think. It seems to me that it is a brief presentation of a great deal of the different aspects of the Church. For instance I know that there are 150 psalms with a listing of precise ones to be said on each day of the week. For instance, there may be twenty-five psalms listed on a particular day and of those some are said at Vespers, and others are said at different times of the day. Then I know there is a section on Saint Days."

"I think I'd have to get one to know exactly what is in it, but I don't think that is too important. What is important is that Father's is missing.

What possible reason could there be for that? Somehow I think it ties in with this whole case. Maybe he had something written in it that his murderer did not want anyone to see. Who knows? The point is that it is missing; that's what I keep saying to myself. I think if we find out why, we go a long way toward solving this mystery," I said.

"Maybe you are putting too much stock in a hunch, Noah," Jack said. "Like my idea that it all comes down to money and greed. In this case I can't see my angle having much relevance."

"How did you do with Mrs. D'Angellini?" Patrick asked.

Jack laughed. He strode across the room to get a cup of water and then laughed again.

"She is one of a kind, that lady. She is determined to find out who killed her son, but she will do it in her own way. With Mrs. D'Angellini, the shortest distance between two points is as roundabout as you can get. Her mind does not move in straight lines. She sees life as a duplicitous puzzle that somehow she has to outwit. She sees shadows where other people see light. She won't admit to having private detectives working on the case, but I am sure they are about. Have we heard of any people asking questions on their own?" he asked.

"We haven't heard anything except from Father Sousa," I said. "I think we would have if someone were nosing around."

"Well. I know she has checked out San Francisco. What's his name out there, Alberto? She sees him as the killer, to be honest. She kept coming back to him in our talk. We were talking about money and she kept coming back to that guy. You talked to him, right?"

I said, "Yes, we did. He claimed not to have talked to Father D'Angellini when he was here. He says he saw him driving out of the parking lot of a donut shop and that was it. He claims he was visiting his mother and he does not deny that he was Father's lover as a young boy and teenager. He broke up with him when he found him in bed with a priest in a house on Cape Cod," I said. "It was then that he left town and went out to San Francisco."

"Well, for reasons that I can't fathom, Mrs. D'Angellini is convinced that he is the murderer. We run a thin line with that lady. On the one hand Clarissa and I both feel that she knows that her son was gay. On the other, she is in complete denial. She thinks that that Alberto man killed her son because of a lover's spat or whatever and then denies that her son was gay. Quite a set of antithetical beliefs going on here. But she is too much of a realist to really believe that he wasn't gay, so what does that leave us?" he said. "She has a mind that is unique. I find her fascinating."

Patrick said, "Is there any reason to believe that she is right? Should we follow up on this somehow?"

Marge said, "We are going to visit Gino's mother this afternoon. She lied to us about his coming here and I want to know why. Mostly I want to pursue the question of whether the two men communicated. Is there any way we can check her phone log to see if Gino Alberto called Father or the reverse using her phone?"

"Not really unless they were long distance calls. Local calls would be impossible to trace. Not much help there I'm afraid," Patrick said.

"By the way," I said, "She could very well be right. There is plenty of motive. A lover scorned to begin with. But, why so long after the fact? Gino seemed to be content with his lot, though. He was comfortable with his homosexuality, it seemed to me, and he didn't try to deny his connection with Father. He did mention that his mother blamed Father for pushing him into homosexuality, but he said that was untrue. He was gay from day one, according to him. He wasn't blaming Father and there didn't seem to be any animosity between them. He was more angry at Father LaChance. When he gave us his name, he was delighted to get him involved."

"We seem to have gotten Mrs. D'Angellini's trust fund straightened out or at least it is going in the right direction and believe it or not, she has taken a liking to Clarissa. I could see the shock in her face when they were first introduced, but she has forgotten her skin color, I think, and is dealing with the woman, and she likes her. She keeps winking at me when Clarissa says something that she thinks is well said or shows how bright the woman is," Jack said. "One other thing, by the way, Father had no money to speak of and what he had, he got from her. She kept him supplied with the extras he needed. His salary was enough for him to live on, but the extras, which weren't necessarily extravagant, came from mother. She is very proud of the fact that whatever she gave to her son, the priest, she gave equally to her other son. Everything was fair and square with her, not favoring one son over the other."

Marge said, "Why would she feel she had to do that?"

"Clarissa had the answer for that. Mrs. D'Angellini was in a strange situation. One son is a cheap crook. He lives off whatever illegal activity will give him a dollar, but he doesn't hide what he is. She expects to hear that he has been arrested and is going to jail. On the other hand, Father lived the lie. Here he was a priest and doing good as he saw it. He ran a parish successfully against great odds. But the idea that he was celibate was a lie and then she knew he was a pedophile. There were enough incidents to tell her what her son was dealing with. He didn't leave a long line of hurt children behind him, but he wasn't clean either. Her older son had always been Father's protector and the last thing she wanted was to have him jealous of his brother. So whatever she gives one, she gives the other," Jack said, in what was a long speech for him.

But from his body language, I could see that he wasn't finished. He had been thinking hard about the woman and he had been trying to figure her out. He knew she wasn't guilty of the crime against her own son, but he found her to be a fascinating person.

"Put yourself in her place. She is probably the daughter of rum runners and she marries a thief and then gives birth to two boys. One of whom takes after his father and like his father ends up doing jail time. The other, an aberration from the norm, is a decent, God fearing little boy who becomes a priest. But, from the beginning she sees problems with her quiet son. He is weak and needs protection. He is far too effeminate in a macho environment. Then he hooks on to the priest and is with him all the time and his mother is wise enough and watchful enough to wonder if there is anything wrong. She would not allow her son to be unwatched. This is not Mrs. Alberto. This is Mrs. D'Angellini who trusts no one. She has to know that all is not right with the priest and her son, but she has to consider her son and what it means to him. Does she want a scandal? Not on your life, so she lives with the priest and hopes it passes," he said.

I couldn't believe that Jack would make such a long speech, but I knew he wasn't finished yet. He sipped some water out of a paper cup. Strode across the room and back and then sat heavily in his chair. He leaned back and stretched his legs in front of him.

"Then he grows up and does the same thing that that priest did to him and now what does she do? She waits for the day when the hammer falls. I'm sure she talked to him, but it did no good. Life is pretty miserable for her, I think, waiting for the inevitable. There is one attempt to get some money out of them, but somehow she scares them off. Maybe there were others that we don't know about. But, as bad as things got, they got worse when he was killed. Someone took her son away from her. Even with all his faults, he was her son," he said. "She is determined to find out who it was."

Jack insisted that he wanted a pizza for lunch after all the talking he had done. We drove across the river to Magoni's where Marge and I could find something else to eat while he ate a pizza and had a bottle of beer. Jack ordered his pizza and I was surprised to see that he wanted only a cheese pizza with pepperoni. I expected him to want a mountain of toppings for his pizza but then I remembered that he had an aversion to vegetables of any kind. Marge and I made up for his hatred of vegetables by each having a salad. It was while we were there that we noticed two strangers sitting at a table not too far from us who seemed to be taking an interest in what we were saying as we chatted. Marge was the first to notice them and we wondered who they were.

They were dressed in business suits and ties and were a distinct contrast from Jack and me. We were dressed in our usual casual attire while Marge had learned that there was no sense in wearing anything very formal when she was with us. She was wearing slacks and a blouse and sweater with flat heels.

Our food came after about a twenty minute wait for Jack's pizza and our neighbors ordered their meal and were waiting patiently. I went to the men's room and took the opportunity to walk into the bar and to ask the waitress there if she knew who the men were. She went back to the kitchen where she was able to get a good look at the men and then she came back to tell me she had never seen them before.

I returned to the table and told Marge and Jack that they were strangers and Jack laughed and said, "Finally, we have the lady's detectives in our sights. Shall we invite them to join us?"

Jack rose from his chair and walked across to the two men and I heard him say, "Excuse me gentlemen, since we are all here, and unless I am wrong, you are representing Mrs. D'Angellini, why don't you come and join us at our table, so that we can introduce ourselves and maybe talk a bit. If I have made a mistake please accept my apologies."

The older of the two men rose from his chair and said, "Good idea."

We were sitting at a large round table that easily accommodated five and after calling the waitress to our table to inform her of the move, we settled down to introductions. When the men were standing, we realized that they were father and son. They were tall and slim, very well groomed and rather handsome men. The son had the look of his father without being a mirror image.

The older of the two spoke first, "We have just come into the area after being out on the West Coast with the Alberto man. We know you two have interviewed him and I suppose we have just followed up. We may have discovered a few things you didn't know."

"Can you be specific?" I asked.

The younger of the two men said, "He really didn't want to talk to us. I think he thought we were going to try to hurt him somehow. But we did our investigating on our own. He works for the Post Office Department but he is on sick leave. We haven't found out why, but he has been out for several months. We've got people working on that now. We followed him around for about a week and had him under surveillance but we didn't see anything that would explain why he is out of work. We've got a man working on that now."

211

"What do you think you're working with?" Jack asked.

"Well the first thing that comes to mind is AIDS, but we have no proof of that. The guy is gay and AIDS runs through San Francisco like it was the flu, but we don't know. Whatever it is, he doesn't look sick and he doesn't seem to act it. He walks normally and I have even talked to him without him knowing who I was and he sounds fine. When you met with him did you see anything odd or abnormal?" he asked.

Marge answered, "I didn't. We had dinner together and he seemed perfectly healthy to me."

Jack's pizza arrived and the waitress delivered the meals for the two men as well. Jack set to work on his pizza and a bottle of beer, while Marge and I poked at our salads. The two men had ordered a large antipasto which they shared.

The older man had a peculiar first name that was more Portuguese than Italian in my memory. His name was Idalino Saraiva. I knew of an Idalino whom we called Del, but I couldn't recall it as an Italian name. Neither of these men fit the Italian stereotype that has been publicized in the movies. The older Saraiva was obviously well educated and I was not surprised to learn that he had graduated from Bowdoin, along with his son, who graduated a generation later.

Mr. Saraiva spoke with a deep voice. He enunciated every word he spoke and he spoke slowly and gave the impression that words were important to him and were not to be used unwisely. His son was more casual and seemed far from being reserved. I wondered what kind of a business they were in and finally, I decided to ask the question.

"Are you private investigators?" I asked.

Mr. Saraiva answered immediately, "Yes, we are."

"Pardon my saying so, but you don't quite fit the common perception of private investigators," Jack said.

Mr. Saraiva, the elder, smiled and said, "And, what is that common perception?"

"Oh, tough guys, carrying gats under their jackets. Heavy drinkers and smokers ready for a fight at the drop of a hat. Wise cracking guys in a tough world. Does that sum it up?" Jack said.

"Well, I don't think we fit that perception, but that doesn't come from real life, it comes from Mickey Spillane and Dashiell Hammett. No, we fit a special role. The Hill and its environs was not a pleasant place and a great many times the residents needed someone to dig below the surface without causing a great many problems. As it turned out, I seemed to fit that need very well. One of my first experiences had to do with a young girl who eloped with an older man. The family wanted her back, but didn't want the scandal. My job was to bring her back in one piece and to pay off her 'lover'. It took two months, but the affair was settled without the newspapers catching it or even the neighbors for the most part. And, that's when my business began. I enjoy the excitement of it and my son has joined me," he said.

Reggie, his son, said, "Ours isn't the rough and tough variety of private detective agency as you can tell. Dad has set us up to handle affairs that need discretion, like this case. We can't compete with you because you know this parish and the people, that's why we would like to share information."

I was quite taken with the two of them. When we think of Federal Hill we tend to think of the stereotypes and that isn't quite fair. It isn't as if everyone on the Hill is a thief or a criminal going around smashing people's knees and bumping off enemies. Certainly these two men didn't fit the stereotype nor did most of the Italians I knew from the parish. My acquaintances were ordinary working men and women, who like the rest of us, struggled to keep their head above water.

"So," Jack said while he was eating his pizza, "What do you think happened here?"

Mr. Saraiva said, "We have only the connection between Gino Alberto and Father D'Angellini right now. I personally think we have to look no further, but we haven't a shred of evidence against him other than that he was here when the murder took place. We do know that the gun used was a thirty-eight revolver. Now we have to find a connection between the thirty-eight and Mr. Alberto if one, in fact, exists."

I said, "We don't have anything tying him to the murder either. We are meeting with his mother again this afternoon to push her a bit. She shows a great deal of anxiety and that's why we want to know what she knows about a possible meeting between Father and Gino while he was here. She lied about him being here, but that doesn't mean much in itself. She shows a level of anxiety that makes me wonder what she is hiding."

"We know you've met with the priest whose name he gave you. We have another name too. It seems that he had an affair, a platonic one, with a Father O'Hearn who is in a parish in Taunton. We are going to check that out to see where it leads. Other than that and a couple of local contacts, we are just getting started. Now we can make a pact. If you come up with anything let us know and we'll do the same," he said.

Marge said, "Will there be any violence if you find the killer?"

"I assure you, our only interest is to see the killer brought to justice. A court of law is all we are interested in. I want no part of a vendetta and I know Mrs. D'Angellini does not want that. She wants the killer of her son punished as any mother would. The last thing we need is to be mixed up in another murder," the elder Saraiva said. "You're thinking of the stereotype again. This isn't the movies. This is real life."

Marge said, "You're right. I apologize."

Reggie Saraiva said, "By the way. We checked you out. You've had quite a record. You are like all the famous detectives rolled into two and now three. How do you do it?"

Jack said, "We'd like to take some bows, but we don't feel we are that good. We just plod along waiting for some breaks, like in this case. Something seems to turn up sooner or later if we just keep plugging along."

We finished our meal, while Jack ordered dessert, Reggie joined him and we sat over coffee as if we were old acquaintances or even old friends. Somehow the subject changed to the Patriots and we all chipped in with our thoughts on Tom Brady and Adam Vinatieri.

Reggie said, "We may not fit the stereotype, but we do love our Italian sports heroes and Adam is pretty high up on the list. He has replaced Joe

DiMaggio as the greatest of the heroes in New England right now. In my dad's time it was Dimag and Phil Rizzuto; now we are talking the 'kicker'."

"I'm not sure Dad's time goes that far back," his father said. "Dimag finished his career in the fifties which puts me at about five years old. I don't mind being dated but you'll have me talking about Italian prizefighters like Rocky Marciano and Willie Pep before long."

"Let's not knock it," Jack said. "They were favorites of mine back then and I wasn't a baby. Especially Rocky, because he came from Brockton which is only twenty-five minutes or so from here."

We finished and exchanged telephone numbers, although I had the suspicion that they already had ours. I didn't pursue it, but managed to get the check and pay for all of us. They thanked us and left with us after I had paid the bill.

Marge was the first to comment when we were in the car and heading back to the city, "Well, they were interesting. Do you think they can be trusted to turn the killer over to the police? I wonder."

Jack said, "I have no idea. They present us with a quandary. It's a problem for Patrick, I think, and not a decision we should make without his input."

CHAPTER XXVI

Marge was anxious to see Mrs. Alberto again and after we left the restaurant and dropped Jack back at the office, we drove to Mrs. Alberto's house hoping she would let us in. By the time we were on our way it had begun to drizzle. For the last hour the clouds had begun moving in and the day turned gray before the rains came. The light, persistent rain was not enough to cause problems, but enough to keep the windshield wipers of my car moving at the lowest speed. There was no wind, so I felt like I was driving through a hazy mist that hung over the car and gave everything a gloomy cast. Somehow, it seemed appropriate that we were visiting Mrs. Alberto on such an uninviting day.

We knocked on the door as we normally did and it took some time for her to answer. I could hear movement in the house and Marge said she saw one of the Venetian blinds to our left move. She suspected that Mrs. Alberto was checking to see who it was before she answered. We waited patiently and then we heard the slip bolt sliding and the door opened very slowly.

Mrs. Alberto was not well. We could see that at a glance. She had large, dark bags under her eyes and she looked like she had been crying. Marge saw it immediately and asked me to wait a minute before going into the house. I found myself standing on the doorstep wondering what to do next. It was still drizzling, so I decided to sit in the car and wait for Marge to come out and call me in.

It was at least three quarters of an hour before Marge did come out of the house. She didn't come out to call me in, but rather to tell me what she had learned from Mrs. Alberto.

"Let me get my head together first, Noah and I'll fill you in," she said.

I thought it best to get away from the front of the house and I drove to the highway to take us back to Westport Point and home. Marge looked upset and I almost thought that she had been crying as well. It wasn't until we were on Rte. 88 on our final leg to the house, when she let out a deep sigh and said, "Her son has AIDS and is dying."

"My God, that's awful. No wonder she was crying. When did she learn this?" I asked.

"She's known for quite a while. She just fell apart before we came. She says she spends hours crying," Marge said.

"That explains the sick leave, to begin with. He didn't give us any signs that he was ill when we saw him. Unless I missed it. Did you feel that he was sick when we sat down with him?" I asked.

"I can't say that I saw anything, even in retrospect," Marge said. "But from what Mrs. Alberto told me there can be no question. The woman is close to a breakdown and I think she needs medical attention. How do we get it to her? The only thing I can think of is to contact her son and let him handle it, unless he is beyond helping. She is close to collapse if I'm not terribly wrong."

"Did she say anything that would help us understand more about this case?" I asked.

"That's the part I am not sure about. She was raving, but she kept coming back to Father and her son. She blames him for all her trouble. She feels his influence made her son gay, that he left the city because of him, that he has AIDS because of him, that he was taken from her. The list goes on. This all comes out not in any logical way, but in a hodgepodge of mixed up thinking and almost deranged babble. It is hard to decipher.

She was crying, obviously grieving, and sick at heart, and then she would wail and wring her hands all the while rolling her eyes as if she was out of control. That's why I didn't bring you in."

"So she doesn't feel, as her son does, that he was a homosexual and that Father D'Angellini had nothing to do with his sexual preference later in life," I said.

"It's hard to know what she is thinking. She is so distraught. My father used to say that his mind was like a can of worms in which he couldn't tell one worm from another because they were all woven together. That's what her talk was like. I couldn't follow it at times. But from time to time I could pick out Father's name and what he had done to her son. That was a repeated theme. It was like the subject was never very far from the surface. All I could think of was something floating on the waves; it may sink beneath the surface temporarily, but it resurfaces quickly and floats to the crest of the next wave," she said.

Marge was upset and confused by what she had seen. She was trying to make sense out of Mrs. Alberto. Had we been properly dressed I think I would have taken her for a walk on the beach just to clear her head. The beach would be deserted now, but I couldn't expect Marge to brave the winds without proper clothes. So, I drove to East Beach where we could sit in the car, open the windows and still look at the water rushing into the rocky beach. The waves were breaking heavily and the misty weather we had experienced in the city was intensified sitting near the water. We were fifty feet from the breaking waves hitting the rocks but they sent the sea spray high in the air. Sitting in the car with the windows only slightly ajar was like sitting in a cocoon protected from the outside world. It served the purpose for Marge. We sat without speaking for a half hour or so in the midst of the seemingly endless showers of drizzling water and I could see Marge palpably relaxing while she enjoyed the quiet. When we got back to the house we were surprised to see Jack sitting in our kitchen.

"The door was open so I figured I'd sit down and relax and wait for you and try to think this thing through. After sitting here for an hour, I'm no closer than I was when I walked in," Jack said.

I laughed and said, "Bet we are one pint of Ben & Jerry's less to show for it, though."

Marge told him about her session with Mrs. Alberto. He, like us, had no idea what to make of it.

"How is she physically?" Jack asked.

"She doesn't move very well at times. Then there are times when she is almost sprightly. When she is having trouble walking she seems to have hip or knee problems. She barely makes it to the door when she comes to answer it and she moves very slowly going to her chair. But other than that I wouldn't know what to look for," Marge said.

"So, what do we have now?" Jack asked.

Marge or I were expected to answer but I was in a quandary. Looking out of the back windows I could see nothing but a mist hanging over the water and light drizzle condensing on the windows and running down the panes.

"It's like this day. Looking out of these windows we know there is a sweep of lawn leading down to the water. We know the lawn is there and we know the water is there, but we can't see them until this fog and mist passes. When it does, and the sun comes up tomorrow morning, we will have an unimpeded view. Right now we see nothing, but, that doesn't mean things aren't there. We know they are. We somehow have to feel our way through this until the sun shines again," I said.

"That is as good a way of putting it as any, Noah. Now, to get that mist to clear do we have to go back to any of the people we have talked to so far? I've got absolutely nothing going on the money end. There is no sense in pursuing that. His brother would have no motive for the money involved because I have found out that Mom is willing to give him what he needs. She wants no harm to come to the kids. So, Mrs. D'Angellini gives him more per year than her other son had in all," he said.

Marge said, "So we can eliminate money as a motive. Let's run down the motives and see where that takes us."

Jack said, "Is this all about Father being gay, or have we made this the issue when it is really secondary?"

"I can't see how it can be a secondary issue," I said. "The fact that he was gay in itself is not the issue. I don't think anyone killed him on the basis of his being a gay priest. I think it is more a question of what his activity as a priest did. Did he hurt some young boy and then get himself killed in retribution? That would seem to be the obvious answer. On the other hand, did he instill so much anger in people by taking such a hard stand on homosexuals in his church that someone on the lunatic fringe got incited and decided to eradicate him? My friend Izzy is a case in point. Was he so hurt by the treatment of his grandson that he decided to punish Father? I like Izzy, but it is not beyond the realm of possibility. Did Gino come back from San Francisco, run into Father, and decide to kill him? And, I'm sure we can go on and on."

Jack said, "I think you're right. But where do we go from here?"

Marge said, "First thing is that we better contact Gino Alberto and let him know that we are concerned about his mother. He may have some relatives here who can look in on her or he may have to return himself. But, I will feel a whole lot better if I know he has been contacted and is aware of the situation."

We found the number and Marge made the call, but there was no one home and she left our number and some information on the machine and asked that he get back to us. Even with this limited outcome I could see that she felt a great deal better and that she was measurably relieved.

CHAPTER XXVII

Patrick's detectives had searched the neighborhood to see if anyone had seen Father entering the church on that fatal day. They had no luck finding anyone who had seen anything. They scoured the neighborhood, but came up empty.

We decided to try our hand at talking to some of the neighbors to see if we could learn anything about any odd comings and goings around the church and with that decision made, we started with those houses closest to the church. The closest building was the rectory and Marge, Jack and I started there.

We were lucky to find the housemaid in. Loretta greeted us as if she needed and wanted someone to talk to.

"Come in," she said. "Who is this guy?"

We introduced Jack and we wasted no time in asking the question that was on our mind.

"Nope," she answered. "Wasn't here that day. Went to visit my sister in Taunton. When I got back is when I heard about it. I couldn't make out what to think. He wasn't a bad guy you know. Not like the old priest who was a peach, but not a bad guy. Just a kid who thought he was more important than he was."

"Why do you say that?" Marge asked.

Loretta looked puzzled and Marge said, "That he thought he was more important than he was."

"Father used to tell him that all the time. The old guy used to tell him that he should walk in Christ's footprints and stop trying to be a big shot. That all the noise he was making made him look like a jerk. The young guy would really get mad and one day he said a swear and the old man laughed and that made him madder until he ran out the house," she said.

She was having a good time. It was obvious she didn't have much respect for the young priest and less love for him. We were standing in the rectory office and she motioned for us to sit while she sat in the chair behind the priest's desk. From her ease of sitting, I realized that she often sat in the chair where she was within reach of the telephone and I wondered how often she sat there fantasizing about being in charge of the parish instead of being its cleaning woman.

"So did any of your friends see anything strange or different that day?" Jack asked.

"A few of my friends are mad at you people cause you couldn't be bothered to see them, but nobody said nothin' about seeing stuff. Nobody told me anyways," she said.

"Who do you think killed Father?" Marge asked.

"I keep asking myself. I have no idea. The only thing I can say is that the guy was a little twisted. Somebody could have caught up with him." she said.

"What do you mean by twisted?" I asked.

"Don't fool with me, I ain't stupid. I know you know. Everybody knows. So don't play games with the people here. Smarten up," she said and we knew we were being dismissed.

The room had a look of gloom. It was the office used by the priests and except for a cross on the wall, it reminded me of one of the offices in the old schools that had been built at the turn of the last century. Dark wood was in favor and while the classrooms had huge windows letting light flood the rooms, the principal's office was tucked away in some windowless corner. This office had two windows on the north side of the room with heavy dark velvet drapes blocking out the little light there. The door we had entered faced the side of the church, but when it was closed the church was invisible from the room. Sitting in the chair she was now in, Loretta could not see the church and that made me think that that was probably why Father D'Angellini might want to use the sacristy to meet someone with whom he did not want to be seen.

We thanked Loretta and asked if there was anyone in particular that she thought we would do well seeing. She mentioned a Mrs. Dimartino who lived half way down the street that ran perpendicular to the church entrance. She gave us the address and I told her that we would be sure to visit her.

We left her sitting at the desk and went directly across the street from the church entrance to a small white house that had a hedge and chained link fence surrounding it. We knocked at the front door and were met by a small, almost diminutive, older man. I would have guessed that he was in his late eighties. His wife was sitting in front of the television set and she too was quite elderly. I introduced the three of us and told him why we were there.

He became angry immediately.

"Not good man, that priest. No respect for other poor people. He think I am not worth anything," he said. He said this as he invited us in and went to his chair. He turned off the TV and then sat back in his chair catching his breath. "He think he a big shot."

"Why do you say that?" I asked in English and then repeated the question in Portuguese.

"For masses I tell him, tell peoples don't park in my driveway. My wife she sick. I have to go hospital. I can't get out my car. He no care. I go Portuguese church, he no care. I tell him tell people no park there. Every missa, they there. Block my driveway. Me poor people. He no care," he said and then added under his breath. "Son bitch."

I asked in Portuguese and then in English, "Did you see anyone go into the church the day he was shot?"

"No. Maria in hospital and I with her all day. Come home tired. To sleep," he said.

All the while she said nothing. I couldn't tell if she heard what was being said because she looked steadfastly at the empty TV screen in front of her.

Marge asked, "How is your wife now?"

The old man just shook his head and made the sign of the cross before saying, "Very sick. Very, very sick. Be dead." He went to her and touched the back of her shoulder with his hand and turned to us and said, "Very sick."

We weren't uncovering very much but we decided to be persistent and went to the house next door. The minute the woman of the house opened the door, I recognized her as a girl who had attended elementary school with me at the old Dubuque School. She knew me, as well, and we shook hands. I introduced Marge and Jack and after a few minutes of chit chat got to the subject at hand which was whether she had seen anyone enter the church the day of the killing.

"Oh I felt so bad when I heard about it. He was such a good man, Noah," she said. "You know when my husband was dying he was here every day to pray for him and to help me get through the worse time of my life. I don't know how I could have made it without him," she said.

"We hear so many different things about Father, we don't know what to believe. Your neighbor next door did not like him at all," Marge said.

"Oh he was asking Father to do the impossible. When church was crowded on a Saturday or Sunday, people parked anywhere they could find a spot. What was Father supposed to do? The old crab next door wanted him to put a policeman on duty to keep people from parking in the wrong places," she said. "Imagine hiring a private cop for four masses on a weekend, it would have cost Father a fortune. The guy used to even set up barrels to stop people from parking in his driveway, until he got too old to lug them around. Nobody listened to his whining after a while."

"What we are here about is to see if you saw anyone enter the church on the day Father D'Angellini was killed. We haven't had any luck finding someone who saw anything that day," I said.

"The only time I really look out is when I hear Father pull into the driveway. He bumps when he comes in and I can never get used to the noise. I always think someone has had an accident. My life is spent in the back of the house cooking and stuff like that, and the kitchen is always warm. I have no one to cook for, but I still keep cooking. I just took an apple pie out of the oven and it's still warm if you guys want a piece," she said.

Jack's face lit up and my old friend knew that she had scored a bull's-eye. Without hesitation she invited us into the kitchen and asked us to sit at the kitchen table. I explained that I was a diabetic and could only have a very thin slice to taste and Marge asked for a thin slice as well. She looked at Jack to get an indication of what kind of a piece he wanted and he just smiled and said, "Whatever is left."

She cut him a good wedge and offered us a glass of cold milk as an accompaniment to the pie. Jack took her up on that.

"Reminds me of my mother's kitchen," he said. "There is nothing like pie and whole milk. When I was a kid I thought nothing of downing a quart of milk with pie or cookies. Mom always had something fresh ready and to tell you the truth this pie is as close to hers as I've ever had. It is absolutely delicious. Your husband was a lucky guy."

Mrs. Margetta's face lit up and she offered Jack another piece of pie. He couldn't refuse and we sat and reminisced about the Dubuque School and what it had been like for us as young children during World War II. Her most vivid memory was of collecting tin cans for the war effort and the mountain of old tin cans that we were able to amass in a few short weeks that seemed to fill the back of the school yard. We found the cans in empty lots, in wooden areas, in dumps, almost anywhere where trash remained undisturbed, and we thought we were helping win the war. I suppose we were.

We left Mrs. Margetta with no more information than we came with, but I for one, found her to be a pleasure to talk to and I know Jack loved the apple pie.

We decided to walk down the street and around the corner going south from the church entrance to see Mrs. Dimartino. She lived on the second floor of a tenement and she opened her door before we had climbed to her landing when she heard the three of us coming up the stairs.

"Been expecting you Mr. Amos," she said. "Knew you'd get here sooner or later."

"Loretta from the rectory sent us to see you," I said. "We're hoping you can help us find out what we need to know."

She invited us into the house and into the sitting area in the center of the flat.

"What do you want to know?" she asked.

Jack said, "We'd like to know if anybody was seen entering the church or with Father D'Angellini the day he was killed. Hopefully someone saw the killer coming or going. So far, we've drawn a blank."

"That should be pretty easy. I'll just get on the phone and let people know what you're looking for. Personally, I haven't heard anything yet. Nothing on our grapevine yet about someone being seen. It should be pretty easy to track down, but don't be surprised if we come up with nothing, if I haven't heard anything until now," she said. "Outside of morning mass, nothing much happens in the church during the daytime, so if anybody was around they would have been seen by somebody."

She was a big woman with an enormous bosom and broad shoulders. There was nothing dainty about this woman in gesture or size. I got the feeling that Mrs. Dimartino was not a woman one took liberties with.

"One thing I would tell you to do before you go much further and that is to see Nick Marzilli. He had a son who had some doings with Father D'Angellini. I'll leave the details to him, but I would definitely see him. You want me to call him, I will right now and maybe you can go see him. He isn't going anywhere. He just came home from the hospital with a broken leg," she said.

I nodded and that was the signal for her to pick up the phone and to call Nick Marzilli. She spoke to him for a moment or two and then said, "He's two houses down from here on the first floor. He'll be waiting for you."

Nick Mazilli was waiting for us when we arrived. When he heard us enter the side door he shouted "Come in. The door is open."

We entered the bottom floor door and found ourselves in the kitchen and dining area of the flat.

"In here," he said, "I'm here."

We walked into the inner room and found Mr. Mazilli sitting in an easy chair with his leg encased in a cast, resting on a footstool. If Mrs. Dimartino was impressively large, Mr. Mazilli was massive. He looked to be well over six foot tall and powerfully built. When I saw him I realized that I knew him by reputation. He was one of the success stories in our parish. He had had quite a career as a college football player with Boston College and then had played a few years with the New England Patriots before being injured and being forced to retire.

Seeing him sitting in his chair it was obvious that the muscle which had made him an outstanding lineman, had turned to fat. Like my friend Izzy he was a heart attack waiting to happen.

"So the busy lady sent you. Sit down. Make yourself at home. My wife just went to the bakery. She'll be back," he said. "There's nothing that lady don't know."

I made the introductions and we settled on the sofa and one of the wooden chairs in the room and I asked why Mrs. Dimartino had wanted us to see him.

"My son was one of the kids that that bastard assaulted," he said. "It's as simple as that."

"When did this happen?" Jack asked.

"It was over a two year period. John was an altar boy and the priest took a shine to him. We thought it was innocent. He would pick him up here with a few other kids in the car and he would take them for an ice cream cone or a malted at Newport Creamery. We thought he was treating the kids, giving them a good time," he said. "Instead he was just setting them up."

"How old was the boy?" Jack asked.

"It started when he was about 12. He was an altar boy for about two years before that. It didn't happen overnight. The guy knew what he was doing. My kid and the others didn't have a chance. He was in a position of trust. He stepped over a line that is hard to believe. I've thought about it lots of times. Don't think in terms of a priest. You guys think of a woman school teacher when you were in school. Or ma'am you think of a man teacher who is, let's say your math teacher. He tells you to stay after school one day and then reaches out to touch your breasts. Or men, your woman teacher reaches down to touch your privates. Can you imagine the shock? You wouldn't expect it from those people you trust, would you?" he asked.

He sat back in his chair and tried to move his leg on the stool. If he wasn't in pain, he certainly felt uncomfortable and was trying to increase circulation in his leg, I thought. He nodded at his can of Coke and looked toward the kitchen and then said, "In the fridge."

I went out to the kitchen, found the fridge and found a can of Coke which I brought to him. He flipped open the tab and was ready to continue.

"What I'm trying to say is that there are people in places of trust that we never question. Did you ever think that your fifth grade teacher was interested in you sexually? Of course not. Now if you were a young boy or girl, would you think that your priest would do anything sexually to you? Of course not. Now carry this a step further. Supposing a parent took the complaint to the school principal. What then? Do you think she would sweep it under the rug? I doubt it. He or she would take it to the next level. Let's say the superintendent of schools in Fall River. Would he push it under the rug? You know that would never happen. The teacher would most likely be suspended pending an investigation. When cases like my son's and a lot of others dealing with priests in the Diocese were brought to the attention of the authorities, they were swept under the rug. This guy was only a minor player, but we had priests who left a long trail behind them. What happened to them? Nothing, until they were exposed and it became a national disgrace," he said.

He was becoming heated as he spoke. His face turned red and he had difficulty breathing. He took a few sips of his Coke and then sat still for several minutes. The room had suddenly become heated and I found myself perspiring as we waited for him to continue.

Marge asked, "How did you find out that something was going on?"

"Well, my wife picked it up. I was working nights and I was doing some coaching for a private school in Providence. I was the line coach and it took up quite a bit of my time, so between work and sleep and coaching I was pretty much a walking zombie. She began to notice that he was acting strangely. He was very moody; not like him at all. He's a good kid. Never got in trouble or anything like that. Then suddenly he began to act like a different kid. At first we put it down to his age and puberty, but we began to feel that it was more than that. Then one day he made a crack about the priest, about Father D'Angellini and it was like he set off an alarm in my brain," he said.

He was in obvious discomfort with his leg and he tried moving it on the footstool again. This time Jack stood forward and asked him if he could help. He asked Jack to move it so that it was in the middle of the footstool and Jack bent to lift the cast and to place it where he wanted it. He was still red in the face and was perspiring but he seemed to be more at ease as he continued.

"I pushed him hard until he finally broke down and told us the whole rotten story. I was so mad I could have killed the son of a bitch. I went right to the church rectory and met the guy and he denied everything. I blew up I'm afraid and banged him around a bit," he said. "They didn't call the police in on it. They wanted it hushed up. At the time my wife was scared stiff I would get in trouble, but actually looking back on it now, I wish they had taken me to court. I could have exposed the whole thing then and there."

Jack said, "You mean you hit him."

"Yeah, I did a bit of a tune on him. He was lucky I didn't kill him. They had to send him away for a few days to recover. More like two weeks. The son of a bitch was no good. The Bishop managed to get a restraining order against me on the quiet. I don't know how he did it, but they got one without it being public. Good thing too, because he would have gotten more. And, believe it or not, they didn't move him. They kept him right where he was. When he came back, it was as if nothing had happened," he said.

"Did you ever deal with Mrs. D'Angellini?" I asked.

"No, I never met the woman. She's his mother, right?" he asked. "I hear she is a tough lady. She'd have to be, to have a son like that."

"Someone tried to put pressure on her to pay them off to keep quiet. Do you know who it was?" I asked.

"Yeah. It was Mario Dinucci. He's a jerk. He tried to get some money out of her and I heard she ate him up. Tough. It wouldn't be hard to eat him up, though. He's a little wimp with a big mouth. They tell me he got a settlement out of the Bishop's Office," he said. "You should go see him too."

Jack said, "Did you get a settlement?"

"No. They tried that stunt with me. Some wimpy little shit of a priest and a lawyer had me in the Bishop's Office treating me like I was some sort of little nobody. That priest was lucky I didn't knock him down. I wouldn't take their money for any reason. What I wanted was to see the priest thrown out of the priesthood and that's what I demanded. I didn't want their cash. Dirty stinking money from dirty stinking hands. No. No money crossed my palm. And the bastards didn't understand why I wouldn't take it. They treated me like a dumb slob. Forget seeing the Bishop. He was too important to see guys like me," he said.

Jack asked, "How much were they offering and for what?"

"The payoff was $50,000 and an agreement that we would shut our mouths. We had to sign papers saying that we would be quiet and never bring charges and stuff. Dinucci took it. My wife wanted to sign too, just to get rid of the whole thing because she knew it was eating away at me. She was afraid that I would end up hurting myself," he said.

"How?" Marge asked.

"Either I would kill him with my bare hands or I would get so consumed with hate that I would end up hurting myself. I didn't do either," he said. "I had enough passion to kill him to be honest, but I think I am too smart for that and as it turned out, somebody did it for me. I'm grateful to whoever did it and I hope you never catch them. The son of a bitch deserved whatever he got," he said.

"How is the boy?" I asked.

"Believe it or not, he is pretty good. Some kids really got knocked for a loop by these scumbags but my boy seemed to put it behind him. After the initial talks we had, he clammed up and won't talk about it, but he is leading a normal life and I don't think it intrudes too much in his daily life. He was lucky. The Dinucci kid has never been the same," he said.

It was then that we heard his wife enter the house. We heard the rustling of paper bags, followed a few minutes later by the clicking of her heels crossing the linoleum floor. Then she entered the room and was surprised to see us.

"These people are investigating the priest's murder," he said.

"My husband had nothing to do with it," she said. "He feels bad that he didn't, but there it is. He was in the hospital when it happened."

She was a little woman and I couldn't help but laugh inwardly at the thought of the two of them in bed. The image of this monster of a man with this petite wife lying next to him tickled my imagination.

"Were you in the hospital at the time?" I asked.

"Well the day of the murder I snuck out of the hospital by putting on a nurse's uniform, one of those cute little white starched ones and snuck out on the service elevator. I stopped at the house to pick up my trusty 45 and snuck over to the rectory, pulled the jerk out of his office and took him to the back of the church where I plugged him. It wasn't easy with the pin in my leg, but I did it," he said laughing.

"Stop it," his little wife said, "we've had enough of that evil man in this house. He has poisoned us with his evil."

"You're right. Now that he is dead, we have to bury not only his body but the thought of him. Anyway, I couldn't have done it. It's over with," he said.

"It really isn't over with, until we find out who killed him. That is our job. No matter how bad he was, we do have laws. People just can't go around killing people," Jack said.

"Yeah, but someone did and I hope they get away with it," the big man replied.

"I have one question that is really on my mind now. I can't shake. May I ask it?" I asked.

Nick said, "Fire away."

"Well, we keep hearing about the priest abusing the young boys. What exactly did he do?" I asked.

Nick said, "I won't answer that question in front of the ladies. If they go in the other room I can tell you what I know."

He looked at the women and Mrs. Mazilli led Marge out into the kitchen. Frankly, I thought Marge did not need protection from whatever he was going to say, but Mr. Mazilli obviously felt embarrassed in front of his wife and Marge.

When they had left he said, "Each case is different and a lot depends on how old the kid is. My son was young and the bastard had him play with him until he had an orgasm. It started slowly until he would put the kid's hand on him and the kid would manipulate him until he had an orgasm. He tried to get the kid to suck him off, but the boy wouldn't do it. Mario's kid did it. Gave the priest blow jobs. Shocks the shit out of you doesn't it?"

"It really does," I said.

"Imagine how it would feel if it was your kid. Then think about facing him, watching him cringe before your eyes and tell me you wouldn't want to smash his face in. The little twerp for the Bishop's Office was worse with his lawyer. They wanted to treat the whole thing like a business affair. But, it had nothing to do with business. It had to do with betrayal, betrayal by a grown man using a young kid. The priest is dead now, but there were others and the bastards who let it happen are still in power. The Cardinal is gone, thank God, but the stuff is still going on in the Church even though the hierarchy is supposed to be keeping an eye out. At least they're taking it seriously now and that's a plus, but they are going to have to clean house before they're finished. And right now guys, I'm hungry and I'd like to call it quits so I can get something to eat," he said.

"I need Mr. Dinucci's address. Does he live close by?" I asked.

"Ask my wife. I'm sure she knows it. He lives on Freeman St. somewhere, but I don't know the address."

Mrs. Mazilli gave us the address and the phone number of the Dinucci house and we thanked them and left. We had a lot of information to digest and we needed a break. Jack wasn't about to pass up his favorite sandwich which was a grinder from Marcucci's bakery, so we stopped while he ran in for his large grinder with hot peppers and extra sliced mortadella. The sandwich was big enough for two people but we knew he would make short work of it.

Back at the house on Westport Point, Jack talked about money between mouthfuls of his sandwich. Marge and I had a cup of tea and some biscuits we had left over from breakfast.

"That figure of $50,000 bothers me. I would have thought they would have offered ten or twenty thousand as a feeler. The Church isn't known for throwing money around. People like Mr. Mazilli and, I'm sure the Dinuccis, aren't in the big money category, so $10,000 would seem quite a bit of money to them. Now, if they offered Nick Mazilli $50,000, I'm sure they would have been willing to go higher. That's how serious this game they were playing was. They were worried about major law suits; that's why they were looking for payoffs. Isn't it funny how we get caught looking the wrong way?" he said.

Marge said, "I don't understand that Jack."

"Maybe, looking the wrong way is not the best way to put it. Let me think what I am trying to say," he said.

He took another bite of his sandwich which was fast disappearing while he considered how best to phrase what he wanted to say.

Finally, he said, "It's just that we think of the Church as a place of worship, of ethics and morality; of obedience to a creed. Do you think for one minute that the people who met with Nick were giving him money to make up for what had been done to his son? Or do you think they were buying his silence? I don't have any question in my mind what was happening. That's what I mean by looking in the wrong direction. We don't want to think that any church would allow its priest or ministers or rabbis to mistreat children in any way. We don't look to the churches for that. We look for the highest morality and sincerity; we expect the noble and the honest; never the tawdry. What could be more tawdry than the kind of thing we heard from Nick? How cheap and disgusting can it be?"

"I agree. It is enough to make you sick. And, you're right; it is not what you expect from the Church or from its representatives. I can't justify it in my mind and neither can many other people. It is an unacceptable aberration," I said.

"The indifference to the crime itself is beyond belief," Marge said. "The disregard of the terrible wrongs to these children is as great as the act itself as far as I am concerned. Any priest or nun who perpetrated such acts should have been dismissed from their calling without question and from what we can see they were shuffled from parish to parish. In this case we have a priest who was allowed to stay in his parish. I can't imagine the hierarchy allowing it or the parishioners putting up with it."

"Loretta called Father D'Angellini twisted. Didn't the parishioners know? They had to know. They couldn't have been blind to what he was. And if he was hurting children, they had to have known that too," Jack said. "How was he allowed to stay?"

"We have to find that out as well as who killed him," I said.

CHAPTER XXVIII

We let Patrick know about the Saraivas. He made it clear that whatever contacts we had with them had to be kept on an unofficial level. For instance, he made it clear that we were not to meet with them in the office, whether his in New Bedford, or the temporary office in Fall River. We had no certainty how they would act if they discovered who the killer was, and he was very wary of any association with them. He had no hesitation to share information with them if it could possibly lead to identifying the murderer, but at the same time he wanted them held at arms length.

We received a call from them asking us to meet with them after they had interviewed the priest in Taunton, so we set a luncheon date at Magoni's in Somerset where we had met before.

They were punctual, as I knew they would be, and we all settled down to talk and eat. It surprised me that we all ordered the same dishes and we had a laugh over the fact that we didn't vary one iota in our selections.

The elder Saraiva began by saying that they had had an interesting session with the priest they had interviewed.

"He claims to be a celibate homosexual and I have no reason to disbelieve him. If we can have celibate straight priests, I cannot see why we can't have celibate gay priests. His relationship with Father

D'Angellini was an odd one according to him. He was his advisor. He makes a distinction between being a confessor and being an advisor because he frankly admits that he was in love with Marco," he said.

He was interrupted several times by the waitress and when she appeared he sat silently waiting for her to come and go. He struck me as a very patient man unlike his son who had difficulty sitting still while his father had the floor. One had the feeling that he would like to have popped in with some comments but knew that he couldn't interrupt his father in the middle of a sentence.

"Theirs was not a sexual relationship. They would go out to eat once a week, or so, and enjoyed each other's company. According to him, Father D'Angellini fought a lifelong battle with his sexuality that he seemingly could not control. According to Father O'Hearn, his friend wanted to remain a priest but suffered from the weakness that he found uncontrollable. So, he was torn between giving up his vocation and striving to control his passions. Too often the latter lost out," he said.

His son had been waiting patiently and then he added, "But as a result of his indiscretions he had a long line of enemies, any of whom could have had a motive to kill him. Father O'Hearn said that the man lived under constant fear that his past would catch up with him. And, it seems it did," he said.

Jack said, "So, you think the motive was revenge of some sort?"

The elder Saraiva said, "Yes. It is hard to think of another motive. Have you come up with something?"

"I think we're leaning the same way you are. Jack has pretty much ruled out money. We talked to Nick Mazilli yesterday and he made it clear that he was close to killing him. In fact, he gave him a beating in the rectory and he made no bones about the fact that he was happy to see him dead. But, he was in the hospital when it happened, according to his wife. We'll have to check that out. But he is filled with hate for him and his wife worries about him being consumed with hatred. We are due to see another victim's father tomorrow. This one received a payoff to be quiet," I said

"How does Mrs. D'Angellini feel about this? There is no question he was a pedophile. Does she know that?" Jack asked.

The elder Saraiva said, "No question. The gayness she knew from the beginning. She was his mother and she accepted that with no difficulty; in fact, she defended him from his father and brother. It is the pedophilia she cannot accept, although she knew about it. She tried to get him to leave the priesthood any number of times. She even offered to support him if need be or at least until he could find fulltime employment and even then she was willing to give him a generous allowance. He wouldn't do it because he felt that control was always right around the corner. He would be able to handle it."

"I can imagine he put her in quite a position," Marge said.

The younger man said, "She had quite a time of it. You know, recently we had a very tragic case in Providence. A young man in his early twenties came home and told his mother and father that he was gay. They made a terrible scene. It became so bad in the house that he fell into despair and then he committed suicide. Father D'Angellini didn't commit suicide but according to Father O'Hearn he had a very difficult time of it. His mother supported him all the way, though, not like this other family. No question. Whatever pressure he felt came from inside himself, not from the family."

Then Mr. Saraiva said, "Do you think your man Nick could have done it? Or could his wife have pulled the trigger?"

"I think that if Nick's alibi holds up it pretty much rules him out. That doesn't mean his wife couldn't have done it. There is a lot of anger in that house and we haven't met the son. We lack an eyewitness to anything. We spent the morning talking to Loretta who is the cleaning lady in the rectory and we visited the houses around or near the church and we came up blank. No one saw anything. I, for one, don't know how to get at it. It just seems to me that someone had to have seen someone entering or leaving that church," I said. "The killer was not invisible."

"Well, we just keep plugging away," Jack said. "We seem to be in agreement that the person who shot Father D'Angellini did so for revenge. So, with that as a basis, let's look at the people he hurt and start there. That seems to be as good a starting place as any. So far we have Gino Alberto and his mother. He was here at the time and I suppose he has as good a motive as any. But why wait so long to get revenge? Izzy and his family and grandson who were refused the Eucharist may have taken umbrage and one of them might have thought he had reason to kill the priest. Then there is Noah's former student who suffered for years because of the shame he felt and has just now opened his heart to someone. Then there is Nick whose son was involved with Father and who shows nothing but rage toward the dead priest still. If it wasn't him could it have been his wife? And we have the Dinucci boy who was paid a goodly amount by the diocese to be quiet. There may be more that we haven't uncovered yet. We'll try to get to the Dinucci family tomorrow and try to get a feel for where they stand. I would say that takes care of the children hurt by that man."

"I agree that that about sums it up. Can anyone think of anybody else?" I asked.

There was no reply.

"Then the way I see it," the elder Saraiva said, "we should split up our duties. Let us chase down the gun as best we can and you go after checking out the molested children's stories. You guys try to interview them along with their parents and see if there are any holes there. Does that sound reasonable?"

Jack said, "Sounds good to me. Marge and Noah, how do you feel?"

We nodded our agreement and finished our meal talking about things in general. Actually they were pleasant conversationalists and we had a good meal followed by coffee for all and dessert for Jack.

* * *

For some reason, Jack decided that he wanted to go to the docks in New Bedford to see the fishing boats and to talk to some of the fishermen. During his high school and college years when he summered on the Point or with his grandparents on Martha's Vineyard, he had worked the fishing boats. He felt a special connection to the boats and the men who fished in them. Just as Ishmael had gone to New Bedford to the whalers, Jack returned to New Bedford to the wharves when he needed to connect to his past or when something was upsetting him.

We pulled into the wharf area and Jack walked immediately to the old beat up fishing boats lining the pier. The four shining new Norwegian boats docked at the end of the pier had no appeal to him. He walked along until he came to one fisherman sitting on the deck of his boat filleting a good-sized cod fish which he cut into large slabs and wrapped in old-fashioned butcher paper. Jack asked if he was filleting the fish for a special customer.

"Ain't doing it for my health, damned sure," the fisherman said.

"I used to work the boats here when I was a kid," Jack said. "Used to work for Captain Popeye Afonso. Long dead now."

Jack stepped down on the boat and sat on a coil of thick rope that was two feet high.

"Never knew him. When he was here, I was still up in Gloucester, but I heard he was a good shit. Hard worker. Like the rest of us, he killed himself working for peanuts," he said.

"I worked for him, let's see, 1947 to '53 when I was in school. Hard work for a kid. Some of the greatest days of my life. I worked the big sail boats too out of the Vineyard, but I liked the fishing boats best. Learned a lot here, let me tell you," Jack said.

We could see that he was settling in for a long talk so we strode along the wharf to the very end where we came close to the Norwegian vessels that made the old fishing boats look diminutive in comparison. These were sleek looking black hulks that showed no signs of wear and tear. The old fishing boats that were locally owned were piled high with rusty machinery, twined ropes and empty barrels. They were like night and day and one look at the vessels side by side spoke volumes about the problems that the old New Bedford fishermen were facing in trying to survive.

The breeze began to pick up as we approached the harbor at the end of the wharf and I could see Marge begin to shiver. Across the harbor was the Fairhaven shore and I could see the marinas filled with pleasure boats getting ready to be stored for the winter. The weather was beginning to turn and winter wasn't far away. There was already a chill in the air and I got Marge back to the car before she began to get too cold.

The warmth of the car with the windows closed was just enough to make me drowsy as we waited for Jack to finish talking to his new friend. I couldn't see him from where I sat, but Marge said she could just see the top of his head as he sat listening to the fisherman. Out of courtesy to Marge I fought nodding off and then finally resorted to opening the window a crack to let some cool air into the car.

When Jack returned he thanked us and remarked on how refreshed he felt just getting everything off his mind.

"These guys are having it tough, though. Even on the best of days they can't get a full haul and the cost of fuel is skyrocketing. And then the competition is fierce. This guy feels there won't be many fishing boats left in very long. I feel sorry. It will be the end of an era and a history of fishing here in New Bedford. Moby Dick and the Pequod will be a lost memory when these wharves are barren," Jack said. "I think it was here that I learned what it was to become a man. My mother worried that I would learn some bad lessons from the men on these boats. She thought they were uncouth; they swore and drank and did all the other things she associated with fishermen. Actually they spent so much time working as hard as they could, that they couldn't do the things that people thought they did. They were basically family men who spent most of their time yearning to be with their families and wanting to be home; great people that I will never forget."

I decided to drive through the city rather than hop right on the highway. In southeastern Massachusetts it seemed that we never drove through cities but used the fast Federal highways that made access to the Cape easy and fast. I hadn't driven through New Bedford, except to go to the courthouse where Patrick had his office, in years, and I suddenly wanted to see if there had been any major changes in the last twenty years or so. I drove up from the river on the short rise to the crest of the hill leading to the old part of the city where the Captain's houses still remained. These were large colonial houses with wraparound porches and widow's walks that sat above the city and overlooked the harbor that had seen so many ships come and go. The ships that had gone to the Far East bringing back exotic wares and had delivered the sugar and molasses from the Caribbean that was turned into rum and had made New Bedford a thriving port.

But like the city of Fall River, it was obvious to me that the city of New Bedford had gotten poorer and poorer with the passing of the years. The industry that had formed the base of the economy had gone. The textile mills were a thing of the past and the large industries like Revere Copper & Brass which had kept so many men and women working, had long since left. Even the sewing shops that had given many of the women employment had finally been defeated by the competition with Taiwan and China and the poor countries of the Far East. The biggest industry in the seaport city had become the drug trade. The seacoast city that had been famous for whaling, and then smuggling, and even later the smuggling of illegal hootch during Prohibition, now became a prime player in the illegal importation of drugs. Prostitution in the infamous Weld Square area was a major industry among the pathetic young women caught in the terrible vice of drug addiction. A series of murders had taken place in the area and the murderer of at least nine women had gone free. The Big Dan Trial had made the national news and had captivated a television audience for several weeks and then become the subject of a movie. Rape on a pool table was the kind of news that the American people loved. The Big Dan Trial gave them everything they wanted to see and hear.

Signs of poverty were everywhere in the city as I drove through the old areas going west through the narrow streets. Groups of older men huddled in doorways talking and passing the time away and trying to escape the cold breezes which had begun to pop up. The younger men were on street corners talking and harassing each other in their typical, but peculiar way. The older men had a stooped haggard look, while the younger men were active even while "hanging on the corner."

The streets were littered with the remains of wrappers and the gutters were lined with debris. Trash cans were overflowing and black trash bags looked like they had been ripped open by animals searching for scraps of food. Empty soda bottles and beer cans were to be seen everywhere along with losing scratch tickets scattered haphazardly along the sidewalks. We could see the same thing block after block along the streets while many of the yards and houses showed the wear and tear of years of abuse without upkeep and repair. Any number of windows were boarded up with plywood and we had no idea whether the houses were occupied or not. It was not a pretty sight.

We drove by one project that looked liked it needed razing. The buildings that had been originally painted white were peeling badly and many of the windows were covered with plywood and several that we could see had broken panes. A few of the outside doors were cracked and there was litter everywhere. Many of the automobiles in the parking spaces reserved for the project looked like they had seen better times and a number of them were lifted on blocks and without tires. There were children everywhere and they were amusing themselves as best they could in the streets in between the rows of houses. What had once been lawns in front of the houses was now packed brown dirt with a tuft of grass or weeds growing here or there. It was certainly not an ideal environment for a young child. These were the poorest of the poor and it was almost a certainty that most of the households were single parent homes and that the single parent was a woman depending on welfare money to survive.

Marge said, "Oh those poor children. Look at them. Playing in the street, barely clothed and dirty as can be. Some of them are not even school age. How can they possibly survive in these surroundings?"

"It's been my experience that they do somehow. If they don't fall prey to drugs and alcoholism, they can make it. The hardest thing for me to figure out is not so much what makes them fail because I think that is self-evident. Rather I would like to figure out what makes them succeed; the few who do, that is. And the odd thing is that some of them do succeed.

Look at those kids we just saw. There were maybe twenty of them playing in the street. Now, we can understand how they cannot overcome their environment and their poverty. The poverty includes many things we don't think of off-hand. Just think about their health. Not many of them are getting decent health care. They suffer from all sorts of diseases that go untended and untreated by anyone. I'm sure most of the kids have bad teeth that go uncared for. How many of those twenty kids are going to make it? The odds are definitely against any of them getting out of this environment without the scars that go with them for life," I said.

"When I see that, I can't help but feel lucky to have gotten away without having to face the problems these kids face," Marge said.

Jack just shook his head and said, "Amen."

CHAPTER XXIX

The Dinucci household did not show an infusion of money. Whatever the $50,000 was used for, it was not used to improve the household. When we entered the first floor apartment we were all struck by the shabbiness we saw confronting us. It was apparent immediately that the house was not in good repair and was poorly maintained. With our first step into the house we felt the linoleum give under us where it was cracked and when I looked down I realized that a piece of it was missing. A chair on the side of a breakfast table had a cushion that was torn and directly above it I saw a piece of wallpaper that had come loose and was peeling away from the wall. I noticed these things, not because I was looking for them, but because they jumped out at me. I'm sure I could have found a great deal more with a closer inspection, but that was not why I was there.

Mr. Dinucci was a small, mousy man who was extremely uncomfortable in our presence. He flitted around Marge as he escorted her into the sitting area in the room next to the kitchen dining area. It was the middle room of three and was obviously where the family settled in, in the evening, to watch television. The little man led Marge to what he must have considered the most comfortable chair and Jack and I sat on straight backed chairs that were most likely never used by the family, while Mr. Dinucci turned his arm chair rocker to face us.

"My wife won't be here. The boy will be in, in about a half hour," he said. "My wife is too embarrassed to meet with strangers. The boy is very sensitive, so be careful what you say to him."

"Well then, before he arrives, suppose you fill us in on the details of what happened," I said.

"Details? What do you mean by details?" he asked.

"When did this happen, for starters?" Jack asked.

He continued to be uneasy. He had the habit of running the fingers of his right hand through the hair that protruded slightly over his forehead as if he was brushing it away from his eyes. I couldn't think of how we were going to settle him down. That was usually Jack's role but I could see that Jack had decided to press the little man with questions rather than try to soothe him.

He sat thinking and then he said, "Six years ago. Doesn't seem that long."

Jack continued, "What happened? Can you tell us?"

"Well you already know that he was molested by Father D'Angellini. What else is there to know?"

"How did he take it? Have there been any lasting problems for the boy?" Jack asked.

"Well, it hasn't been easy for him. For the first few months after it all came out, he couldn't sleep nights and he would wander the house. If you ask me he has been a nervous wreck since the whole thing happened," he said.

"Did he hate the priest when it was over?" Jack asked.

"You mean enough to kill him? No way. You trying to pin this on my kid? You're out of your mind. You won't get away with this. You guys aren't even cops," he shouted. He was shaking now and I wondered if he was going to be able to pull himself back together.

Jack leaned forward and said, "Relax. I'm not accusing anybody. What are you getting so excited about?"

"Sounds like you're trying to pin that murder on us. That's what I'm excited about," he said.

I waited for Jack to respond, but he didn't and then I said, "It's okay Mr. Dinucci, we're all getting tired. We're getting worn down and short-tempered. Jack is just showing the signs of strain. We really don't suspect you."

"Good," he said, "Because we really didn't kill him. Somebody did us a favor, but we didn't do it."

"I know, I know," I said trying to soothe him. "Why do you think he was killed?"

"I bet Nick did it or had somebody do it for him while he was in the hospital. The perfect alibi, right? Think about it. He's in the hospital, right? He gets somebody to bump off the priest and he has the perfect alibi. He's the one who really hated him. Did you know that?"

"We know he disliked him," Marge said.

"You've got to be kidding. Disliked him? He beat him up so bad, he had to go away for a month. The guy was black and blue. Nick was lucky he didn't kill him then and end up in jail for manslaughter," he said.

Now that the pressure was off him, he began to feel more at ease. He stopped moving from side to side in his chair and crossing and recrossing his legs. His eyes began making contact with ours even if only very quickly. Somehow he reminded me of a hummingbird moving quickly from flower to flower. Nick had described him as a "little twerp". He was tiny in stature but more catching than his small size, was his seeming lack of muscle tone. That impressed me. He wore a long sleeved sweater that hung off his shoulders. The shoulder sockets hung a quarter of the way down his arms and the sweater was sunken into his chest as if he had no pectoral muscles.

"So, you didn't know that?" he asked.

"We've heard something about it, but we were told it wasn't serious," Jack said.

"Well it was. He was a football player, you know. Big deal too. If you saw him you know he's a buster. So he wanted to blame us, huh? Baloney.

I say he paid to have it done. There are a couple of guys here who break legs for money. So, why not kill for money?" he said. "And, Nick knows those guys."

"Do you have any proof of what you're suggesting?" Jack asked.

"That's your job, not mine," he said.

It was then that the young man arrived. His appearance was startling. He was no taller than his father. At most he was five foot four or so. But there the similarity stopped because he was a weight lifter. He had an enormous barrel chest which strained under his short sleeved T-shirt. His biceps and forearms were enormous in comparison to his stature. He had on a pair of jeans and I could see the muscles in his thighs outlined through the straining cloth. His head was shaved bald and I could see the beginnings of a tattoo on the back of his neck which I felt quite sure ran down over his shoulder blades. He hardly gave the appearance of a sensitive young man.

We went through the formalities and introduced ourselves and we learned that his name was Rudy.

"So let's get this over with. What do you want to know? But before we start, I didn't kill that lousy scum," he said. "If I would of killed him I would of used my bare hands to squeeze every drop of blood out of him."

"Who do you think killed him?" Jack asked.

"I got no idea. Pop here, thinks it was Nick. I don't know, but I'm glad he got it," he said.

Marge asked, "How exactly did you get involved with Father D'Angellini? Can you tell us that? We've heard a great deal, but nothing specific. It's hard for me to understand exactly what happened."

"What do you mean involved?" he asked.

"I mean whatever happened came about because you were an altar boy. Is that correct?" she asked.

"Yes it is. I started serving when I was about ten years old. He was always taking the other altar boys places and I was kind of jealous of them. They would go to the ice cream parlor for a treat and he bought them sundaes and stuff. I wanted to go too, but the other boys said I was too young," he said.

"How many were there?" she continued.

"Two older kids, then me and two little kids. The two older kids were special. He used to do all kinds of things with them. He'd take them to Pawtucket to the Red Sox games or some times the hockey games. Once I remember he took them to a Celtics game in Providence; one of those preseason games. He used to get free tickets all the time for nothing."

"And you were jealous of them?" Marge asked.

"Oh yeah. I didn't get to go anywhere. Then they left being altar boys when they went to high school and I was the big man. I got to go places then, but we were alone," he said.

"And you think being alone led to the problems?" she asked.

He seemed to be responding well to Marge and there really was no reason for us to become involved. He didn't seem to be the least bit reticent and he spoke freely without too much pressure being applied on our end. She was leading him, but he didn't mind.

"Well yes. It was all right at first. For the first year I think. Maybe, even longer. Then little things started happening. He started giving me presents and telling me how nice I looked. He would pat me on the head all the time. I didn't think anything of it. He didn't rush it. He was like flirting all the time without going too far. And always there were gifts. He was always giving me something. Not expensive stuff, but something all the time; lots of things, and, I felt pretty special," Rudy said.

Then without excusing himself by word or gesture he left the room and we heard him open the refrigerator door. In a few minutes he was back in the room holding a bottle of beer in one hand and a bowl of popcorn in the other. He put the bowl on top of the television set and sipped beer and ate popcorn while he talked.

"I should of known something was happening, but I didn't see it. I was just a kid. The presents came and all of the attention. We would go for ice cream, even places to eat like in Providence when he went to see his mother. I was with him all the time," he said.

"And then what happened?" Marge asked.

"The trouble started. I ain't going to tell you more than that. I just wasn't ready to handle it. Let's just say he let me know that if I didn't do certain things , he wouldn't bother with me any more because I would be showin' him that I didn't love him. It started real slow with little things and then it got worse and worse, until I couldn't stand it no more and I told my Mom. I didn't know what to do," he said.

"Is that where you came in Mr. Dinucci?" Jack asked.

"Yep. First we had to make sure the kid was all right. He didn't look then like he does now. If a priest tried anything with him now, he'd squash him like a bug. Then he was a skinny little kid," he said.

Rudy said, "That's all screwed up. It had nothing to do with strength. He was smart, that guy, and he sucked me in."

"Well, anyways, we made sure he was okay and then we decided to make the bastards pay for what he did, what that priest did. We heard about the mother, so we went after her first. That didn't work out," he said.

Jack asked, "Why not?"

"It's a long story but it just didn't work out," he said.

"She scared the shit out of him, is what happened. She told him if he opened his mouth her friends in the Mafia would wipe him out. He came back here shaking like a leaf. Real chicken. I could have handled it better myself," he said.

"You're playing this up to make your father look like a weakling. How do we know you aren't just saying that to make us believe that he wouldn't kill Father D'Angellini? We heard the same thing from Nick. I think you're just setting us up," Jack said.

The attack mode was not Jack's normal style. I wondered what there was about these people that made him take that approach.

"Think what you want," the boy said.

"Then what did you do?" Marge asked.

The elder Dinucci said, "We went to the Bishop. We never really met him, but we did meet with Monsignor Sousa and a lawyer. At first they tried to talk us out of any complaint, but when they knew we meant business, that was it."

"And, they offered you a settlement, I assume," Jack said.

"Well, we met a few times. Then they made us the offer and we took it. It was a good one and we couldn't pass it up," he said.

Jack said, "For how much?"

Mr. Dinucci said, "Fifty thousand."

Jack said, "That's a lot of money."

"It don't pay for how I felt for so long," Rudy said. "I had some rough times. Now that I have been lifting I feel pretty good knowing that I can't be pushed around any more. It would never have happened today because I got a life. That's what the whole thing gave me. Now I know that if I have a life no one can hurt me. The money is just like he gave me before. Another gift to make me shut up and do what they want. He used to give me little gifts, this is a big gift but it's the same thing. Just another way of buying me. The old man needs the money, so I don't care if he takes it, but I don't want it. As long as my Mom gets some of it, I don't care, but I won't touch any of it."

CHAPTER XXX

Patrick called us the next morning for a meeting in his Fall River Office. We were to meet again with Father Sousa to bring him up to date on where we were in the investigation. The weather had suddenly turned cold and the news was full of the possibility of frost for the region. Marge had already begun stocking the bird feeders and a few of our feathered friends were making their frenzied feeding forays already. Once they were filled, the feeders had to be maintained and I knew that winter was not far off.

It took a few minutes for the car to heat up, but before we knew it we were driving on Rte. 88 to the city. It was only twenty minutes to the office, but we managed to get there a bit late.

Father Sousa was present in Patrick's office when we arrived. It was apparent that they had been having a heated discussion before we entered and the little man was still red in the face.

Patrick said, "Let's get right to it. I have an appointment in New Bedford when I finish here and I don't want to be late. Father is hoping you can give him an update on where you are in this."

I began by saying, "Well, we have eliminated all of the motives except with the single exception of one of the boys who were molested or their families. We think the murderer lies in that group."

"Group?" the priest said.

"Yes, unfortunately. You know of two of those; the Dinucci boy and the Mazilli boy. Then of course there was the original case which was Gino Alberto. I also met with a former student of mine who confessed to me that he had been molested by Father as well. There may be more," I said.

Marge suddenly said, "You knew about at least three of these, Father. Why in the world didn't you do something about it? You didn't even move him from parish to parish as you did in so many cases. You just left him there. How was that possible?"

"I am not under investigation here, nor is the Church," he said testily.

Marge said, "Oh yes you are. You are as guilty as if you had pulled the trigger."

Father Sousa reddened immediately and said, "I won't tolerate that kind of talk under any circumstances. This is intolerable."

Patrick was not hesitant in saying, "You don't seem to realize your position here. We are under some pressure now to show some progress in this case and I am sure you are aware that we have not issued one statement to the press. Not a word has been uttered by anyone in this room. We have shown the height of discretion. But most importantly, what we discover is not for you to pass judgment on. With that said, maybe Noah can begin to try to wrap up our findings so far."

I had the floor so I said, "As I said, we have just about eliminated every motive except those attached to the molestation charges. We do not have a suspect as of yet, but we are definitely changing direction in this case. We are honing in on one motive behind the killing which makes our job far more limited and enables us to focus our attention on a limited sphere. If we are wrong, we will be set back accordingly, but I don't think we are wrong."

Jack said, "Our biggest problem is that we have no eye witnesses. It's almost as if the person who committed this crime was invisible. The crime was committed during daylight hours and yet no one saw anyone entering or leaving the building that we can identify. We have talked to the neighbors and we are now going to ask Patrick to assign some men to do door to door questioning in the neighborhood to try to find someone who saw anybody at the church that day."

"It's strange. Here we are in a highly populated area with lots of pedestrian traffic and no one saw anything," Marge said.

"The scene of the crime offers us nothing. It has been scoured for prints and any clues to tell us who was there and nothing shows up," Jack said. "So now we are going to concentrate all our energies on the molestation events and see where that takes us. That means checking every alibi and motive until we get a break or make a break."

"So, what you're really saying is that you have made no progress at all after all this time. What makes you think you'll do any better in the next few weeks?" the priest asked.

"We have no idea as of right now. But, from past experience we've found that if we keep after this, something will break," I said. "As of now, I don't think we are too far away from getting to the truth of the matter. In the meantime we'll just keep at it."

"Well, speaking for the Bishop, I think we are very unhappy with the conduct of this whole affair. Turning this over to amateurs is highly questionable on your part Mr. District Attorney and I think the Attorney General should have some say in all of this," Monsignor Sousa said.

"So, what you'd rather have is some ambitious professional prosecutor making headlines by announcing that the murder was probably committed because the priest was gay and he was molesting little altar boys. I think it would make good reading and certainly be entertaining on the evening television news. It would give the prosecutor all the advertising he'd need for his career, wouldn't you say? Let's not be ridiculous. You've got the best of all worlds here. You've got three people who have a proven record and who have no interest in the spotlight, in fact, who do everything to avoid it," Patrick said. "So, now you want to threaten us with going over my head to remove them from the case, is that what you are hinting at here? Well, if that's the case I am sure the Bishop's Office could pull it off. But, is that in your best interests?" Patrick said.

"I'll think about it," the little man said.

He rose then and turned to Marge and said, "I expect an apology from you for those remarks earlier."

Marge put her hand on his arm and looked him straight in the eyes and said, "You will have a long wait if that is what you expect. I meant what I said. It is not for publication because I have an obligation to the District Attorney, but the damage you have done and allowed to happen is reprehensible and I will go to my grave despising you and the Bishop and all your cronies."

He turned then and strode briskly out of the door. We could hear his heels clicking on the floor as he got further and further away.

Marge turned to Patrick and said, "I'm sorry, but that has been welling up in me for days. I should have had more self-control. He just gets under my skin."

"No harm done. He has to understand that he is not the judge of what we do or don't do," Patrick said.

Marge insisted that she had to go back to visit Mrs. Alberto to check on her condition. She had been very concerned when they last met and felt that we should not leave her unattended for too long without a visit. In the interim, she had called the woman's son and he planned to visit her as soon as he could get away. In the meantime, she felt that we should keep in touch with Mrs. Alberto.

We arrived early the next day and had the same problem getting into the house that we had experienced before. Standing at the front door, I could hear movement in the house but there was no response to our knocking. Finally I saw the window blind moving and I knew she was preparing to open the door after seeing who we were.

She looked dreadful. The widow's weeds that she wore added to the look of gloom about her. She was dressed from head to foot in black, even to the shawl that covered her thinning gray hair. She was tiny to begin with and the black outfit seemed to diminish her further in size.

She looked at me questioningly and Marge caught the look and said,

"I'd like Noah to stay if you don't mind. We won't keep you long. I just wanted to see how you were doing."

Mrs. Alberto said nothing while she made her way to her rocker. She moved with difficulty, shuffling slowly along until she turned, and grasping the arms, lowered herself into her seat.

"So, what do you want?" she said.

"We want to see if you are feeling okay," Marge said.

"You want more than that. Why should you care how an old lady feels? I'm here all day by myself. Nobody calls and nobody comes to see me. Now you come and I want to know why. You want something. I haven't got any money you know. I know you probably want to take my money, but I don't have any," she said.

"We don't want your money," I said. "Marge just wanted to make sure you were all right."

"Sure. I bet. But no matter what you do to me, you're not getting it. That's it. So get out now and don't come back. My son is coming and he'll take care of you."

She was obviously suffering from paranoia, but she seemed completely under control. She was exhibiting no signs of fear. If anything, she was angry at us for trying to steal her money. Before my father died I had seen him in a state of paranoia, but his had been a matter of sheer fear. He had been frightened by shadows on the wall in his bedroom and the fear he exhibited was even frightening to me. That fear made him appear almost crazed; his eyes would have a wild look and he would cower in his terrible agony. There was none of that here. What she showed was more anger at us for trying to steal her money from her. She saw us as hoodlums about to steal her pocketbook or uncover her secret cache of savings.

I saw that there was no point in questioning her, but Marge said, "When is your son coming home?"

"Never, never, never. That man stole my boy from me. He is a bad man. My boy went away and never comes back," she said. She started to work herself up into a frenzy in a matter of moments. "He no good. Took my boy away."

She began to mutter unintelligibly and I saw what Marge had been so upset by; the sense that she was so out of control and that she would hurt herself. From time to time, as she spluttered and muttered her words I caught a word like "Gino" or "Bad" but I couldn't tie them together to make any sense.

Marge went into the bathroom and returned with a wet towel that she used to wipe the poor woman's forehead. The coldness of the wet towel seemed to bring her slowly around and we waited patiently for her to come back to normal.

"He was a good boy until that man got him. Now, he is sick," she said.

"How is he sick?" Marge asked.

"I don't want to talk about it," she said. "You shut up in front of that guy. I don't trust him. He will try to get my money. Get him out of here. He's not good here."

Before she worked herself out of control again, I left the house just as Marge pulled a chair up to her and began to try to settle her down again. I waited in the car for at least another half hour before Marge came out. She was visibly upset.

"I wonder, Noah, if she could have killed that priest. I really am beginning to wonder. I wish we could have a psychologist or someone of that ilk talk to her and listen to her. It seems to me she is trying to suppress something that is just below the surface. It may very well be that her son killed the priest and she knows it and the thought that he could be caught is really disturbing her. Whatever it is, she is almost going mad, I think," she said.

"We had better get in touch with him again. He has to be informed of the seriousness of her condition. If nothing else, she should be on some sort of sedative, I would think," I said.

Marge said, "I'll call him again today. Let me see if he will agree to having a doctor come in to see her."

* * *

At dinner that night Jack finally let out his frustrations about the case.

"I feel I've been worthless throughout this whole affair. It's a different world to me. To begin with it has nothing to do with one of the few things I know something about, money," he said.

Marge said, "It's frustrating for all of us Jack."

"Yeah, but at least Noah is playing on his home field. I am playing in a strange ball park. This whole church thing is foreign to me. The Catholic Church has always been a mystery to me and it is more so now. At any rate, I have contributed nothing here and I am ready to fold up my tent and go home," he said.

He had just eaten a steak and he was relaxing over a cup of hot tea and some fresh cookies that Marge had baked just for him. He was showing his appreciation by eating one after another, but very slowly and with the utmost enjoyment. Freshly baked cookies took him back to his mother's kitchen where he had had many such treats growing up.

Sitting at our table now he was nothing if not the handsomest man I had ever seen for his age. He was slim and yet well built, and there was a sparkle in his eyes that signaled intelligence. His hair always had the uncombed look that came from his constantly running his fingers through it. He had been blond and there were still traces of the light hair mixed with gray. He had a full head of hair which he said was a genetic throwback to his father as were his teeth which he took care of diligently, but which held up under all the bad food that he managed to eat.

Normally he was upbeat, but on this night he was having a downer.

"I haven't contributed anything here. I don't even have a clue what is going on or what happened. Marge, this seems to be your case. You're invested in it. Tell me what you think," he said.

"I think Gino Alberto shot and killed Father D'Angellini. I think he came back home to visit his mother, saw Father in the driveway of the doughnut shop and that stirred up a lot of old feelings. He called Father later in the day and asked to meet him. He met him in the sacristy to avoid busy eyes in the rectory and then shot him. Somehow he got in and out of the church unseen, but did it, nonetheless. His mother found out about it and is going through the torment of being afraid that he will discovered. That's what I really think, but I have no way of proving any of it," Marge said.

"Well, it makes sense to me. It is a matter of elimination. I'm sure the Dinucci father didn't do it and the son seems to have overcompensated with his weight lifting," Jack said. "Does that sound reasonable?"

"I agree about the father. I can't imagine him having the courage to confront Father face to face. I'm not ready to eliminate the son. The kid gave us the clue, though. He wouldn't have wanted to shoot him; he would have wanted to use his strength to kill him. I can imagine him showing off his muscles then, strangling the priest to death. Somehow his weapon of choice would not seem to be a revolver," I said. "Somehow I can't see the boy doing it."

"How about Nick's son? We haven't even seen him. I think he is worth a look. Assuming Nick was in the hospital and his wife didn't do it, we are left with his son. I think we should get back to that family and get to talk with the boy. I don't even know his name. There is the possibility that the father built up so much hate that the boy couldn't handle it and took the big step," Marge said.

"How about your former student?" Jack asked.

"I doubt that very much. He seemed to be venting finally and had he been the killer I can't imagine him coming forward to talk to me of his own accord. I have to rule him out," I said.

"So," Marge said, "Unless we are dead wrong we seem to come down to five possibilities. First, the Dinuccis, mother or son. I haven't ruled out the mother. Then the Mazillis, mother and son. And finally Gino Alberto. Does that do it?"

"Pretty much I would think," Jack said. "If the Saraiva's have any luck tracing the thirty-eight revolver it would certainly help. Actually if I have learned anything tonight it is that you guys are as lost as I am in this. I don't know why it should make me feel better, but it does."

I knew he was feeling better when he rose, opened the freezer and took out a pint of Ben & Jerry's ice cream. It was half gone so he didn't bother to put it in a dish, but ate directly out of the pint. Neither Marge nor I ever ate it, so he knew we would not be offended if he ate it directly out of the box. He ate the ice cream along with the cookies and I think the only thing he missed at that point was a quart of whole milk.

In between spoonfuls and bites he managed to say, "Noah, imagine what it would have been like for you if you had been approached by that man. What would you have done or thought? The thought keeps coming back to me. I try to picture what he actually would do. That's the hard part for me to visualize. How did he begin? What exactly did he do? Did he try to talk seductively? Do you get what I am trying to get at?"

"I think I do. It gives me the creeps. It is one thing to talk about in general, but quite another to be specific. to think in terms of what was actually said and done. I would imagine I would have been frightened not knowing what to expect or what to do. The priest is such an authoritative figure and these children were prepubescent so they would have been totally unprepared. At ten years old, I would have known nothing about sex. I suppose I would have been confused at any sexual approach," I said. "The whole thing is unthinkable."

Marge said, "But it did happen. And we know it happened to at least four boys right here in this one parish. And, they weren't all pre-pubescent. What is unthinkable is that nothing was done about it."

"But, Marge, something was done about it. Father D'Angellini was shot and killed. We can't escape that. The man was murdered," Jack said. "Maybe nothing was done by the people who should have done something, but something was done nevertheless; something that led to death."

CHAPTER XXXI

The first snow of the season came the next morning. It was light and had no chance to cover the ground for any period of time. It fell in swirling currents and was blowing in swooping circles. The slate colored juncos appeared as if from nowhere. They came to feed off the ground; to eat the seed thrown out of the feeders by the more aggressive birds. I never understood where they were hidden until the snow came. Without snow on the ground I rarely saw them, but with the white snow serving as a background for their slate colored backs and gray breasts, they stood out.

Marge had set up the feeders with sunflower seed in two feeders and the chickadees, house wrens, nuthatches and titmice were regular visitors. The sparrows and grackles made a beeline for the mixed bird feed while the jays feasted on whatever was available.

The first snow meant that Thanksgiving was not far away and then Christmas would be upon us along with winter. On the Point, winter was a time for hunkering down and hibernating until the weather broke in the spring. We didn't run south for the warm weather but enjoyed the New England winter along the coast. We needed to put this case behind us. Jack may have been frustrated by what he thought of as his lack of participation in anything leading to a solution, but I think we were all getting tired. We all needed a good, long break. I had visions of going to Milan for a week to enjoy the Italian climate, the food, the people and most of all, the opera. I was in the mood for enjoying something that would stimulate my senses and give me a spark. After years of pinching pennies and concern about making ends meet, I finally had the means to enjoy myself and now I found I had less and less time.

At seventy-four years of age, time became more and more of a factor in my thinking. There was so much to see and do that I began to fear that time was passing me by. I knew that Jack had some of the same feelings and although Marge was younger than we were, I caught glimpses of the same thing in her. There were times when fatigue began to show its ugly face, but those were rare, and I knew I could keep going. The case hung over our heads, though, and I was determined to put it behind us.

The first step was to retrace our interviews. I wanted to meet with the Mazilli boy and to see what he was like. Fortunately, when I called Nick, he said that his son was home and would be in for several hours before going to work and that if we got to his house within the hour we could meet with him.

We made a beeline to the tenement next to Magellan Park where the Mazillis lived. John Mazilli opened the door for us and we were shown into the room where Nick was sitting with his leg on the footstool. I wondered if he ever got up to move around the apartment or to go to the bathroom. I knew he did, but he looked odd sitting in the same place as we had seen him last time.

John was a huge man. He was a duplicate of his father in bulk and stature, but one look showed that he was soft and flabby and hardly had the makings of a football player. He was at least six foot six in height and must have weighed close to three hundred pounds. His face was a younger Nick and aside from age, the two men could have been twins. There was a hardness, though, in Nick, aside from his physical hardness, that was not to be seen in his son. The young man was mild spoken and had none of the stridency of his father. It was obvious that he had neither the toughness nor the self-assurance of the older man.

"Let's get to this. Dad says I should talk about it, but I'm not very comfortable going back over it. So, let's get this out of the way. I have to get ready for work," he said.

"Then," Jack said. "Let's do just that. Did you shoot Father D'Angellini while your dad was in the hospital?"

"No, I didn't," he said. "Not a chance."

"How did you feel when you heard that he had been murdered?" Jack continued.

"I didn't care. I have put it as far behind me as I can. The whole thing is a bad memory and I have forced it out of my head. It works. I found out that it was making me crazy. I knew he didn't care about what he had done and I was the one getting myself sick. So what I did was push it away before it hurt me. Now, it's gone and things are going good for me. I'm not breaking any records but I'm making a good life for myself," he said.

Nick said, "He got his, though, thank God."

The young man turned to his father and said, "Makes no difference Dad. He doesn't count for anything, dead or alive. Forget him."

We could see that the young man was trying to protect his father who was obviously consumed with hate for the priest.

I asked the question directly, "John it sounds to me like you are trying to sell your father a bill of goods. Are you really telling us the truth about your feelings about Father D'Angellini?"

"Yes. Did you ever hear of ALATEEN?" he asked.

"Can't say as I have," Jack said.

"Well, it's mostly for kids who have druggies or alkies for parents. They come together to talk about their problems. So even though I don't have those problems, I started going to meetings to deal with my problem. What I learned was that there is enough shit to go around and mine was only part of it. The kids I met with had a lot worse problems than I did, because they had them every day. Mine happened, but was over and only in my head, so I figured that I could forget it and I would be good. Compared to the other kids I had it made. One kid was getting beat up every day by his old man. Another kid, a girl, had her stepfather trying to get into her pants every minute she was home. So, hell, mine was easy," he said.

He was calm as he explained why he had put the whole business of Father D'Angellini behind him and he was certainly believable. There was no anxiety in his attitude and his body language signaled complete control and a lack of nervousness on his part.

"Dad needs to go to ALANON but I can't get him to make the move. He's one of those guys who thinks it's weak to look for help; has to solve his own problems in his own way. Well, anyway, I didn't kill the priest and my Mom and Dad didn't either, so you'll have to find your killer somewhere else," he said.

He was convincing enough but I asked the question, "While your father was in the hospital what were you up to?"

"If you're looking for an alibi, I don't even remember when it happened. I got no alibi. When Dad was laid up, Mom spent most of her time with him and I was working or home here alone during the day. One thing you can do is check my work schedule to see if I was working the day it happened," he said.

"We will," I said.

Marge said, "Mr. Dinucci is convinced that you hired someone to kill Father. He figures you could use your stay in the hospital for an alibi while your hired killer did the job for you. How do you respond to that?"

"I can't," the big man said. "How can I prove that I didn't? All I can say is I didn't do any such thing. The little twerp is trying to put it on me." He began laughing and said, "He is something that little runt."

"Do you think he could have done it then?" Jack asked

"No way. The guy is incapable of doing anything but whimper. His son might be another thing, though, but I don't think he would do it either. The strong one in the family is the mother. Now, she could do it. She is hard as a rock. Nothing soft about that lady. I could see her standing face to face with that man and making him beg for his life and shooting him down in cold blood. No doubt in my mind," he said.

"If that's the case, why did she allow her husband to accept a fifty thousand dollar settlement? That doesn't seem to make sense to me. The Church would have settled for a lot more unless I am badly mistaken," Jack said.

"I have no idea," Nick said. "She is no dummy, I can tell you that. But at the same time $50,000 would seem like an awful lot to them. She might have figured to take it and run."

"Maybe so," Jack said.

The three of us had a good feel for what we were interested in finding out. John Mazilli was not a killer. He seemed to us to be an intelligent young man who had overcome a problem which had been thrust on him. He had learned what his father had not learned. Hate eats away at the hater and does not affect the person who is hated. He was trying desperately to show his father that hate would end up hurting him while Father D'Angellini was beyond hate. To me he showed a great deal of wisdom in a relatively young head.

Jack had an idea that he thought was worth testing. He told us to wait in the car while he took a walk. He walked up the street to the church and walked up the side stairs to the side entry. It was closed and he descended the stairs and walked up the front stairs to the door. Again he tried it, and it was closed. He walked down the stairs and went to the basement door on the southeast side of the building and entered the basement. He was in the building for no more than five minutes and then he came out of the church and stood on the sidewalk. Loretta came out of the rectory and we could see her talking to Jack. He looked up and waved at someone across the street and then came back to the car.

"Two people saw me that I know of," he said when he got into the car. "In the ten minutes I was there, two people saw me. Yet we had a killer go in and out of the building and not one person has come forward to say they saw anything. That is hard to believe."

Marge said, "Unless the person who went into the building was invisible."

Jack and I both laughed and Jack said, "Marge, how invisible?"

"Let's say that you stood out," she said. "You are the visible presence because you are totally unexpected. Loretta looks out and sees you and wonders what you are doing there. You're not supposed to be there. The same thing happens with whoever saw you from across the street. They look out and your presence jumps out at them."

"I see your point," I said.

"Now the sexton, Dino, would be invisible. He would be such a common presence that no one would even notice his coming and going. He could walk in and out of the church and he would be invisible. How about Mrs. Sousa, the woman who teaches the young children to prepare them for First Communion. I can envision her visiting the church often, in one capacity or another. Her whole life seems to center on the church. Would she be invisible? Could she walk in and out of the church and not be seen or noticed?" Marge asked. "I think so."

Jack said, "Maybe you've hit on it Marge. Whoever killed Father D'Angellini was so familiar that no one noticed him."

"Or her," Marge said.

"This needs some thought," I said. "I think we should go to the office and see if we can plot this out."

"No," Marge said. "Let's go back to the house and sit in the kitchen where we do our best thinking. We can have a cup of tea, watch the birds, the water and the sky and relax in the comfort of our usual surroundings. I never feel quite at home in the office."

"Good idea," Jack said, "Let's stop to pick up a few doughnuts before we go back. I'm hungry."

The weather had suddenly turned mild after the snow of the day before. Thus goes New England and anywhere along the shore. As we drove along the highway back to the Point, I was struck by the sky which was a bright blue with puffy white clouds floating across it. The whiteness of the clouds and the bright blue of the sky couldn't have formed a more beautiful contrast.

It wasn't long before we were sitting in my kitchen looking through the broad expanse of windows at the rolling lawn sweeping down to the water's edge. The water, with the sun reflecting off it was like the blue of a Fra Angelico painting. The birds were fluttering around the feeders, squawking and fighting for position on the feeder bars.

Marge put on the tea kettle and Jack spread his cache of donuts and sweets on the table before him, using the empty Dunkin Donut bag as a tray, waiting patiently for the tea to be poured.

Marge said, "Let's think about what we have learned today in terms of the suspects we have in this case and I think we will come to the one person who could have done this murder. None of the boys would fit the 'invisible person' as far as I am concerned. Do we agree on that?"

We both nodded in agreement on that. The tea kettle whistled and Marge poured the hot water into a tea pot that contained the tea leaves and she brought the pot to the table where she let it sit to brew.

"Then, who does?" she asked. "Who does fit the invisible person?"

Marge knew where she was going and was spinning out her logic in such a way as to keep us guessing. She was not playing a game, though, but was showing us how her logic was working.

"I have no idea," Jack said.

"We can eliminate both the sexton and the teacher since they apparently had no motive. But supposing a woman dressed just as Mrs. Souza dresses, all in black, in widow's weeds with a black kerchief over her head were to enter the side door to the basement. Would she be invisible?"

"Oh my God," I said.

"Yes. Mrs. Alberto. I'm convinced that she did it. Look at her uncontrollable anxiety. I have never seen anyone, so fearful in my life, of being discovered. She is going through agonies of self-torture. Jack hasn't seen her, but we have Noah. She is out of control. There is no question in my mind that she is the killer," Marge said.

I was surprised. I would never have thought that that little woman would have been capable of killing anyone, but at the same time I could see Marge's point. I had seen how she acted under no duress from us. She was on the point of collapse. There was no question about that.

"The question becomes one of trying to prove it, if she is, in fact, the killer. There is the matter of the failure to turn up a gun, no witnesses putting her at the scene of the crime, and really no evidence of any kind linking her to the killing. Patrick will look at us as if we are deluded if we come in with this story," I said.

"But, Marge, may have it. We have nothing else, so I suggest we put all our energies and resources to work on this angle and see where it leads us. Let's sit down with Patrick and see what he says," Jack said. "I'll call him now and see if he can meet with us late this afternoon. I feel like you've opened the door for us here Marge, let's not let it close before we satisfy ourselves one way or the other."

Jack set up a meeting at four o'clock that afternoon, so by 3:30 we found ourselves on the road to New Bedford. We had to allow at least ten minutes for our usual confrontation with the guard in the parking lot who refused to believe that two old men were representatives of the District Attorney. He was a retired fireman who worked part-time as a parking lot attendant and who took his duties very seriously. He was not about to let trespassers take up the limited number of parking spaces available to the District Attorney. We would show him our identification and he would look us over from head to foot. Two things that bothered him were that we were much too old and that we were so poorly dressed. He wanted young men dressed in suits and ties and looking the part of professionals. I'm sure he couldn't believe that a woman in her sixties belonged in the D.A.'s office, so Marge was certainly seen as an interloper.

We finally made it past the parking lot attendant and found Patrick waiting for us in his office. He was his usual professional looking self and I am sure he had been wondering why we wanted to talk to him.

Since we felt it was Marge's case now in many ways, we asked her to explain how she felt about the case.

She went through every bit of her logic bit by bit and when she was finished Patrick sat quietly ruminating over what she had said. He was silent for quite a while and then rose to walk to the water cooler for a cup of cold water.

When he returned he rested his arms on his desk in front of him and sat absolutely still and said, "Okay. I buy what you're saying. Obviously we have to prove it. I have no case, of course, as it stands now. Now, what's next? First I would suggest that we find out if she had a gun in the household or one available to her. How do we do that? Maybe that's where your Saraiva people come into play. It sounds like their kind of thing. I'm sure they have the kind of connections that will allow them to trace a gun, if there was one. Check that out as soon as possible. Then, I'll put some men on scouring the neighborhood to double check if anyone was seen near the building, even invisible people. Next I would definitely begin putting pressure on her, Marge, with your presence. Just show up constantly and talk to her. See if you can win her confidence."

He had given a long speech for him. Patrick was not a man to waste words. I felt from what he had said that he understood fully what Marge was leading toward. Her logic was simple and direct and he understood it and its ramifications.

"Then," I said, "Jack and I will stay with Gino when he arrives. We'll try to learn as much as we can from him."

"There are still some questions that I have. The biggest one is how did she lure Father D'Angellini into the sacristy. Noah says that he wasn't preparing for mass. What was he doing there? How did she know that he would be there?" Jack asked.

"Maybe we'll get some of these answers and others by concentrating on one person instead of spreading ourselves out. Noah and Jack, we could be going on a wild goose chase here you know. If we take this path and it comes up empty, we're nowhere at all," Marge said.

Jack said, "I'm nowhere as it is Marge. I personally can't do worse than I've done."

CHAPTER XXXII

We met with the Saraivas the next day for lunch at Magoni's in Somerset. They had had no luck tracing the gun to anyone. The new system of registering guns had been difficult because they couldn't attach a name to a purchaser. The first dealer they had gone to had shown them the registration log but it meant nothing to them without a name to attach to it.

We explained that we now had a name and that we were zeroing in on that name. The name was Alberto and we hoped it would give them a chance to find a buyer with that name if the gun was bought in the past few years. Otherwise the chances were pretty slim. Prior to that, records were more a matter of bookkeeping and included all materials, not just guns or weapons. Pawn brokers sold them and there was no record there and even gun shops did not require them to be licensed.

Marge repeated her description of her feelings vis a vis the killer. The elder Saraiva was rather skeptical when he heard the whole story. We had finished lunch and were settling in over a cup of coffee while Jack ate dessert.

"You're really going on your feelings, aren't you?" he asked. "You really have no proof of anything. Our problem is that we are on retainer to Mrs. D'Angellini and we have to justify what we do."

Jack laughed and said, "What have you done to justify your salary so far? I'm not saying that in a mean way, but I think you can see my point. So far, we've gotten nowhere except to narrow this down a bit. I say we spend a few days on it and see where it takes us."

"Okay," he answered, "You've made your point. Maybe you're right. Let's go with it then. We'll see what we can find out about the gun. It's not easy, but, maybe, knowing who we are looking for, will make it easier. We still think the prime culprit is Gino Alberto. Maybe he got into the building without being seen which is very possible and had a rendezvous with the priest. Who knows? But let's follow this up."

I could sense the tension around the table. Jack was busy eating his dessert which he did in tiny spoonfuls as if to make it last longer. He ate it in such a way that with each spoonful he managed a dab of whipped cream and part of the substance of the dessert which looked to me like tapioca pudding. I couldn't remember when I had had that dessert last. Aside from Jack at that very moment concentrating on his dessert, we were all anxious to end the case. I personally had had enough of it, but I could sense that the others felt the same way.

We outlined our plan to go after Gino Alberto as soon as he arrived and the fact that Marge would be a companion to Mrs. Alberto if she could win over her confidence.

"Are you going to wear a wire?" the younger of the two Saraivas asked.

"I'm not sure," Marge said. "If I do, it could never be used in a court of law as far as I know, but we would have the information we need. I think a clever technician can translate the mumbo jumbo she uses and have it make sense. You see, Mr. Saraiva, she loses control and starts to talk crazily. I can't decipher what she is saying so that it fits a pattern of language but I bet a technician could take the tape apart and make sense out of it."

"What do you mean by mumbo jumbo?" Mr. Saraiva asked.

"It's hard to explain. It is almost as if she is speaking in tongues. I get a word here and there, but mostly it is a hodgepodge of language that is meaningless. It doesn't make sense and she utters it as if it is coming from her mouth with no control on her part; like someone possessed. Now, I don't mean to imply that she is possessed, but it does remind me of that kind of thing; that somehow has taken over her body and mind," Marge said. "Noah has heard it."

"I know no more than Marge does. It is a strange phenomenon. It would take a far wiser person than I am, or at least one far more knowledgeable, to explain what I heard. It is like she is utterly confused and the words come pouring out of her," I said.

"Well, then I would think you would definitely need to wear a tape if you meet with her," the elder Saraiva said. "Even if it can't be used in a court of law, we will know if she did it or not."

"I leave that decision to Patrick. If the District Attorney feels it is worthwhile, then I will do what he says," Marge said.

* * *

Gino Alberto arrived in town three days later. We had asked that he contact Marge so she could give him a rundown on his mother's condition. He called the day after his arrival. We met him at the New York Bagel on President Ave. in Fall River. We introduced Jack to him and we quickly got down to business.

Marge said, "How do you find your mother?"

"You were right. She seems to be on the verge of a nervous breakdown. I'm taking her to the doctor tomorrow to see if maybe he can give her something to settle her down," he said.

"When we met, why didn't you tell us that you had AIDS?" I asked rather bluntly.

"It's not really something you bruit about in restaurants. I may be sick, but the world doesn't have to share in my sickness," he said.

"What is the prognosis for you, then?" Marge asked.

"As good as can be expected. I am under treatment and although it is unlikely that I will see a cure. I may have a few years left to me," he said.

Marge said, "Your mother knows and is upset, not at AIDS, but that you are ill."

"She knows it's AIDS, though, and thinks the very worse. The press has made such a big thing of AIDS that people like my mother have no idea what it really is, but think of it like the black plague," he said.

"You said you saw Father D'Angellini one day coming into the parking lot of a coffee shop just as you were leaving. Is that right?" I asked.

"Yes. I think he recognized me. In fact, I'm sure he did. Of course, we were in our automobiles, so we didn't talk," he said.

Jack asked, "Would you have felt comfortable talking to him?"

"Oh, sure. You have to understand that what happened to me as a teenager is long past. I didn't suffer the trauma other kids suffered, you know. I was gay then and I am now. So my time with him was my introduction to my sexuality, but it never left the terrible scars it leaves on straight kids. So, if I met him face to face or talked to him, it was no big deal. I didn't meet him, but it would have made no difference," he said.

"When was it that you saw him?" Marge asked.

"On a Saturday morning two days before he got killed. I couldn't believe it when I heard about it. I felt sorry for him. He was a very mixed up guy, you know," he said.

"In what way?" Jack asked.

"Well that requires a complicated answer. But here goes. Sex and the priesthood don't go together. Any kind of sex. Priests are supposed to be celibate. So any sexual feelings they have inside them have to be sublimated and pushed away; straight or gay. So if a guy is straight and can't control it, he seeks substitutes or the real thing. Substitutes can be masturbation, porn, you name it. Whatever he chooses is wrong and in his mind, sinful. If the substitute happens to be young girls, then not only is he sinful, but his activities are criminal. No different for the gay priest. He pushes it down or he does the real thing or he substitutes. Again if he has a penchant for little boys he is illegal," he said.

Gino stopped for a moment as if to retrace where he was in his telling. He had a captive audience and he seemed to be making the most of it.

"Now if a priest is sexually active, he faces the ethical and moral problem of staying in or getting out of the clergy. Most get out if they find that they can't handle it. Now, Father was a special case. He wanted to be a priest so badly, nothing was more important to him. And yet as hard as he fought it, he couldn't shake the need for sex. Gay sex was his preference and he found himself attracted to young boys. I know all of this because as cautious as he was, I know how he felt about me as a kid and the gay priests he associated with on the Cape. Leaving the priesthood would have destroyed him, but staying on took him apart. That's why he was so mixed up," he said. "I knew that, even as a kid. I haven't talked to him for years, but I bet he didn't change one bit. He couldn't handle it then and I bet he couldn't handle it right to the end."

He stopped then and looked at us. He had said what he wanted to say about Father D'Angellini and he sat back in his chair and relaxed waiting for us to ask more questions.

Jack said, "It seems inconceivable to me that you would know so much about the man based on something you learned so many years ago. How long ago was it?"

"It has to be thirty-five years. It's hard to believe that it is, but it certainly is," he said. "But it was an important part of my life and I remember it as if it was yesterday. Father D'Angellini was my first lover, you see. He may not have been my best, I admit, but he was my first, and as such he has lived in my memory. I'm sorry if that offends you ma'am," he said.

"I'm a woman who has seen and heard more than I like to admit, so your sexual adventures don't impress me one way or the other. But I would be curious to know how it affected your mother and father. Did they have any idea what was going on with you and Father?" Marge asked.

"What is the point to that question?" he asked.

"I'm just curious. Did they know why you left the city? Did your mother and father know what had been going on between you?" Marge asked.

"That is none of your business," he said curtly.

"Unfortunately, it is our business. We are trying to find out who killed your former lover and we are seeking every bit of information we can get. Everything is our business. Now I would appreciate an answer to my question, no matter how irrelevant you might consider it," Marge said.

Marge was determined and her tone was surprising to all of us. Even more surprising was Gino's answer.

"They were very upset. My father wouldn't talk to me. He was ashamed and his shame broke my heart. He tried to hide it, but I could see it in every look he gave me. I admit, looking back now after so many years, that I could have taken my own life then. Even when he died, I couldn't face him. I didn't come home for his funeral. It was terrible," he said.

He sat quietly looking at Marge. We said nothing. Whatever was happening to him in the present was nothing compared to the pain he had suffered from his father's feeling of shame in him. It took some time before he was able to go on.

"My mother shifted all the blame to Father D'Angellini. She couldn't accept the fact that I was gay. She tried to spread the blame around, but I think she knew right along. She still blames him for the fact that I am gay, I think, but that isn't true. I've told you before I was gay from day one. No doubt about that. Nobody influenced me one way or the other," he said.

"Well, as I told you Mr. Angelo, your mother is very upset. Do you think it is because of your sickness?" Marge asked.

"You mean AIDS? Of course she is. Wouldn't you feel the same way if it was your son?" he said.

"I agree. I would be pretty upset. Especially since she is alone and has no one to talk to. Has she any close friends?" Marge asked.

"I really don't know. You would probably know that better than I do. Right now, as you suggested, I've got to get her into a hospital to have her looked at. I think she needs some kind of sedative to settle her down. Maybe a change of atmosphere will do her some good, even if it is a hospital," he said. "I've made an appointment with her doctor and he will get her a bed for a few days to keep her under observation."

We left it at that for the day. Marge had established herself well enough without going any further. Jack and I had stood by without saying very much and had left it up to Marge to carry the ball. It was obvious to the two of us that it was her case and that she had to be the driving force in solving it.

Gino was anxious to get back to his mother and we let him get to it. I don't think we had learned much except that I felt sorry for him because of what he had told us about his father and their relationship. I remember how proud my father and mother had been of me when I graduated from college and had my degree in my hand and how important that had been to me. I couldn't imagine my father being ashamed of me and I sympathized with Gino over his disappointment.

We heard from Gino the next day that his mother was in the hospital under observation. Marge had herself wired for sound by a technician in Patrick's office and even though she had qualms about it, she decided to go through with it.

The plan was for her to visit Mrs. Alberto in the hospital and to talk to her and hopefully to get her talking. It was recognized that nothing she was able to get out of Mrs. Alberto was admissible in court. As Patrick pointed out, whatever information Marge could get out of the woman would be questioned because she was under a doctor's care and under medication. So whatever she picked up was for our information only.

Marge wasn't fully convinced that she was doing the right thing. She felt like a traitor using the woman's weakness to determine her innocence or guilt in the murder of the parish priest. But, at the same time, she felt that if as she really thought it possible that she had committed the crime, she should be punished for what she had done.

Marge visited her for three straight days in the hospital and was no wiser after that time than when she first walked through the door of Mrs. Alberto's private room. Under whatever medication her doctors had prescribed, she was quiet and in control of herself. Her mind didn't wander and she held a reasonable conversation. She looked a great deal younger without her widow's weeds and with her hair combed and tucked neatly into a bun. Marge realized for the first time, that she couldn't be much over sixty-five, even though she had looked much older to her sitting in her own home.

Mrs. Alberto returned to her own home after three days in the hospital. It seemed most likely that she had suffered a stroke which had hampered her walking and her speech. The doctors found that the left side of her body had been damaged and that she spoke with a slight, almost imperceptible slur. The feeling was that she had not lost her mental powers and that under medication to control her cholesterol levels and blood pressure that she would slowly recover, it not totally, at least partially. Gino was greatly relieved and decided to stay with her for several weeks before returning home to San Francisco.

The Saraivas came up with nothing specific, although they did find out that Mr. Alberto had once told his friends that he was a buying a gun to protect his wife against the "hoods" who were moving into the area when the project was built between Chestnut and Elm Sts. Like many of the residents of the area, he felt that the project would bring undesirables who would be a threat to the safety of the people living in the neighborhood. His home was only a half block from the project and he made no bones about trying to stop the project from being built. When that failed, he, like many of his neighbors, was fearful for his family. That was in the early fifties. If he did buy a gun then, the Saraivas felt that it could not be traced and it was hardly likely to be usable after so many years.

They too came up with nobody who had seen anyone near the church on the day of the killing. They had spent their time in the grinder and pizza shops and in one of the local restaurants trying to flesh out anyone who had seen anything related to the killing. They had been totally unsuccessful. Just as Marge had said, the killer was invisible.

Patrick's men combed the neighborhood and came up empty as well. They went from tenement to tenement and from house to house but were unable to come across one person who had seen anyone entering the church. Oddly enough, there was not a person who had seen Father D'Angellini entering the church either. That was such a normal event that it would come as no surprise that his comings and goings would pass unnoticed. He could very easily have left the rectory door, walked the few feet to the stairs, and then walked up the stairs and been in the building in a matter of some thirty seconds or so. The stairs were located between the church and the rectory and to be seen someone would have to be standing in what would amount to the alley between the buildings.

All in all, nothing came out of Patrick's men. They were professionals and if there was any information available to anyone, it would have been apparent to them. It was not there and there was nothing we could do about it. If there was a characteristic about this case that made it unusual it was that there seemed to be no hard evidence to work with. We were dealing in ifs and maybes and had no real direction to follow except for Marge's suppositions. Hardly the kind of thing Sherlock Holmes would have enjoyed.

CHAPTER XXXIII

Winter was approaching and there was definitely a nip in the air. We had had the first frost and the annuals that had carried the gardens in early September and through most of October and part of November, showed the burning that came from the freezing temperatures. The maples had turned and most of their leaves had fallen to the ground. Acorns were everywhere underfoot, but the oaks had retained their leaves and were just beginning to show color. The beach was empty now except for the gulls and terns being blown about by the breezes off the water. It was time for the state crews to begin putting up the snow fences to protect against the erosion of the seashore.

It was also time for us to solve the mystery with which we had been obsessed for weeks now. Jack had given up and I was close behind him. We needed a break in the case, but none seemed to be forthcoming.

Marge was visiting Mrs. Alberto daily and was giving Gino a break. She was staying with her while Gino did his errands or whatever business he could think of that would get him out of the house and away from the deadening atmosphere of the old home.

It was after one of those sitting sessions that Marge became excited and asked for a meeting with Patrick, Jack and me. She was, in fact, so excited that she couldn't contain herself. We were driving to New Bedford after we had contacted Patrick and it was then that she said, "I know where the breviary is."

Jack said, "I don't understand."

"Remember Noah said that Father D'Angellini carried his breviary everywhere? The prayer book was his symbol of the priesthood and he never parted with it? Well, I'll put my last dollar on the fact that she told me where it was today," Marge said.

"She told you?" I asked.

"Not told me, no, but the next best thing. We were sitting where we always do and Gino had set up a little electric heater near us. It got very warm and she had a throw on her lap. I got up and took it off her lap and placed it on the sewing cabinet next to her chair," Marge said.

Jack asked, 'What do you mean by a sewing cabinet?"

"It's a cabinet that opens at the top with an inner tray that is used for holding things like needles and thread and the things that are used in sewing and knitting. Then below that is a deep area where women would keep their wool for knitting or socks for darning or small items to be mended. I suppose you wouldn't call it a cabinet, but that's what my mother called hers and I still call it that."

"So, what happened?" I asked.

"She reacted to my touching the cabinet and I thought that was odd," Marge said. "Then without thinking and without any idea why I did it, I asked, 'Where is Father's prayer book?' Guess what? Her eyes flicked for just a second to the sewing cabinet. It was only a fraction of a second, but I saw her take a quick glance. I swear the black breviary is in that cabinet. Now the question becomes, how do we get to it? I think that is Patrick's field."

We were in no mood to play our usual game over a parking space and when the guard came forward Jack immediately set aside his objections and said that it was mandatory that we see the District Attorney immediately. The guard saw Jack's aggressiveness and stepped aside to allow us to park our car and enter the building.

Patrick was waiting for us and when Marge told her story, he immediately set about getting a search warrant for Mrs. Alberto's home.

"On the basis of your suspicions in the past and what you've told me now, as flimsy as it might appear to you, I think we can obtain a warrant. Let me begin the procedure," he said. "Let's hope this is it. If you're right Marge, you'll get a medal for this one."

We waited anxiously for two days for the warrant to be issued. When Patrick had it in his hand he took several of his men with him and the three of us. He thought it best that we approach the house quietly and enter as quickly and with as little noise as possible. With that in mind Marge, Jack and I entered the front door behind Patrick while his men waited for him to let them in through the kitchen door in the back of the house. Gino met us at the door and before he let us in, he checked the warrant carefully. He had no idea why we were there and expressed surprise that we seemed to be accusing him of the murder.

We asked him to take his mother into the bedroom while we began our search. He went to her immediately and helped her out of her chair and led her away. She must have sensed what was happening since she reached for her sewing cabinet as she was taken in the opposite direction.

We all knew then what Patrick would find when he took the top tray out of the cabinet and then took out a sweater and a bag of what looked like loose yarn. He brought out the breviary and much to his surprise, a pistol, which we all knew would turn out to be the pistol that shot Father D'Angellini.

At that point there was no need to call in Patrick's men and he went to the back door and asked them to wait out front until he needed them. The only question that remained was who had put the items there, Mrs. Alberto or her son Gino. One look at Gino answered that question for us. He was as surprised as we were.

We brought Mrs. Alberto back into the room and she sat in her chair. Patrick read the woman her rights and then turned to Marge to let her ask the questions that needed asking.

Marge began by asking if she had shot Father D'Angellini. She didn't answer but sat rocking in her chair without uttering a sound. Then she asked her where she had gotten the gun and again she was met by silence. The questioning continued for another ten minutes or so and each question was met with the same response; nothing.

Patrick felt he had no choice but to arrest her and book her on suspicion of murder. He called his men in and they followed his orders and arrested her even though they couldn't believe their eyes or ears. Gino was allowed to accompany her. Before we knew it they were gone and we were left standing on the sidewalk outside of the house.

Patrick had to follow the prisoner and get her booked and to follow all the procedures including having the gun entered along with the breviary as evidence. We were left to make our exits and to return home for lunch and some peace and quiet at last.

Marge was exhausted and yet excited. She knew that she had solved our mystery and that she had done it by instinct. I was happy for her. Before she met me she would never have been exposed to anything like the experience she had just gone through and it made me happy for her. Her woman's instinct had come into play and whatever it was that had worked for her, had worked to its fullest, and she had been able to bring her work to a satisfactory conclusion.

Jack was elated.

"I never thought I would ever be so happy to see anything end," he said. "This has been brutal. The only good thing that seems to have come out of this case is that maybe Clarissa and Peter may become a couple. Do you think we'll ever know what made her do it, Marge?"

"I think we know already. She felt that Father D'Angellini had made her son leave her. He was the most precious thing she had and then he was gone. He didn't want to come back because he couldn't face his father, so he was, in essence, taken from her. Then when her husband died he would visit from time to time and that gave her some happiness," Marge said. "She was a lonely woman."

Marge sat at the kitchen table and I could see her looking at the birds fluttering around the feeders. The sky had turned gray and I felt there was a chance of snow. I looked at the ground for the slate colored juncos, but none had appeared as yet.

"Then I suspect on the day when Gino saw Father D'Angellini, that Father must have gone back to the rectory and called Gino. He might have left a message for him asking him to be at the church at a certain time. That, I'm sure was intercepted by Mrs. Alberto. It would have been then that Mrs. Alberto made her decision. She knew that her son was dying of AIDS which she probably attributed to Father D'Angellini in some twisted way, and she wanted her revenge. We may never know all this. I think she is a sick woman and the pressure of being under arrest and in jail, even if only overnight, may be too much for her physically and mentally," Marge said.

Jack said, "But, thank God it's over."

* * *

We met with the Saraivas the next day. They were eager to get out of the case as well.

The elder Saraiva said, "This has been our worse nightmare. We couldn't have done more poorly. I don't know how, in good conscience, we can accept money for what we have done here."

"I will have no problem," his son said, "I have a mortgage payment to meet."

Marge again explained the whole thing. We felt it was her case and she deserved the credit for solving it. When she told how she had asked Mrs. Alberto what she had done with the prayer book and saw the old woman's glance at the sewing cabinet, both men laughed at how simple it had turned out to be.

"So, you were right about the invisible person. The little old lady dressed in black would not be seen by anyone unless she stopped to talk. I can imagine her going in by the basement door, taking the elevator up to the church level and then walking to the back of the church. She probably got there before he did, so that she was waiting for him," Jack said. "He must have been surprised to see her, for sure, and he must have known immediately what was waiting for him."

"Especially when he saw the gun," the young Saraiva said.

"So, now I suppose you can tell Mrs. D'Angellini that it is finally over. Do you think this will satisfy her?" I asked.

Mr. Saraiva said, "It has to. She has no choice. She certainly isn't going to go charging into the courtroom and shoot down Mrs. Alberto in cold blood. She legitimately wanted to find out who the killer was, and now she knows. I think it will end there, as far as she is concerned."

"All she seems to talk about is this Clarissa girl. She's a protégé of yours, right Mr. Crawford?" the younger Saraiva asked.

"Well, I would have to say she is the closest thing to a daughter that I have and I can understand why Mrs. D'Angellini has taken to her," Jack said.

"She wants to hire her as a lady's companion, but the poor kid is too busy with her studies to get into that. She has agreed to visit her one day a week and to take her for a walk around the city. The old lady would like that, although she is getting weak now. She has to be in her late eighties, I would think," Mr. Saraiva said.

We said our goodbyes at that point, although we were sure to meet again in court when Mrs. Alberto was brought to trial.

* * *

It wasn't long before Patrick had a visit from Monsignor Sousa and rather than having to face him alone, Marge, Jack and I were brought into the office to clear up what was left of the case.

The little priest began with a question for Patrick, "Will there be a trial?"

"I doubt it very much. I suspect that her attorney will enter a guilty plea and she will be sentenced without much fanfare. She is in no condition to hold press conferences or anything of the sort, so you have no fear that she will talk about her motives in killing Father D'Angellini. Rumors will circulate because there are enough people who know why she killed him, but you need not worry about widespread circulation of the story in the media," Patrick said.

The priest then looked at us as if to ask what we would be saying about the case.

Jack said, "Nothing will come from us if that is what you're worried about. We leave all the talking to the District Attorney, just as you leave major pronouncements to the Bishop. I expect you won't have any pronouncements from the Bishop's Office on this and neither will we."

"That's as it should be. But, that leaves us with the District Attorney. Sir, will you be holding a press conference?" he asked.

"That goes without saying. If not a formal press conference at least some questions and answers from the press when the trial ends. There is no way to escape that. I can only guarantee you that I will not exploit the situation politically, nor will I cover up for you. That's the best that I can offer you," Patrick said.

"Well, that may not be good enough, Mr. District Attorney," the little man said.

Then Marge said in a sharp voice, "Or would you rather I told the whole story from the mother's point of view? Because, that is quite a story. It is the story of a boy who lost his father because his father was ashamed of him and then the mother who lost her son because he went away. The newspapers and television would love that. And, Father, that is the true story here. I am so ashamed of what you have done and allowed to happen, that I don't think I could tell that story, but considering the circumstances, I think you have very little to complain about."

He bridled under that verbal assault from Marge and said, "Lady, you overstep your bounds."

I could be quiet no longer and said, "Monsignor I object to that statement. From the deep hurt she feels as a loyal Catholic, I think she is showing a great deal of restraint. She is keeping quiet about something which we all see as a disgrace. We know of four young boys who suffered at the hands of that man, and you allowed it to happen, knowingly. From my point of view you and your superiors should be stripped of your titles and be forced to leave the Church, but that is neither here nor there. Whatever bad public relations might come out of this mess, you deserve, so spare us the upper hand and supercilious attitude, please."

He rose abruptly from his chair, stood at his full height, and turned to walk out of the office. He looked quickly back at Patrick and said, "You haven't heard the last of this."

Patrick gave a sigh of relief and said, "Hypocrisy reigns supreme."

"And, arrogance is not far behind," Jack said.

"What happens now, Patrick?" Marge asked.

"Well, I think Mrs. Alberto will be arraigned, allowed out on bail to return back home and I would suspect that we will have a guilty plea entered along with a signed confession. Then, with a doctor's concurrence, she will be quartered in a state facility, in or out of the state, for as long as she lives. The chances are that she will never see the inside of a prison cell after she leaves here. That will be determined by the judge in this case. Having had a stroke already, I think it would be inhumane to put her in prison, and I can't imagine it. I certainly won't recommend it," Patrick said.

"So, you really don't think there will be a trial," Marge said.

"I doubt it. This should be fairly cut and dry. None of us like this, but murder is murder and the killer has to be brought to justice. In this case, she is guilty without a doubt," Patrick said.

* * *

As Patrick predicted, there was no trial. Mrs. Alberto pleaded guilty to murder and she was sentenced to life imprisonment by the judge. She was kept as a patient-prisoner in a state facility where she could be given adequate doctor's care. As it turned out she was in confinement for only four months when she had a massive heart attack which took her life at the age of 67. Gino attended his mother's funeral and then returned to San Francisco after putting the family house up for sale. We never heard from him again.

Mrs. D'Angellini summoned us to her home along with Clarissa to thank us for the part we had played in putting her mind at rest and bringing closure to her. She also thanked Clarissa and Jack for the part they had played in tightening up her trust and putting things on a solid footing. She was mourning the loss of her son, but felt relieved to have the thought of his killer behind her. She was gracious and thanked us for the work we had done and we could see that she was quite fatigued, so we cut our leave short after Clarissa took her to her room to lie down and get some rest.

* * *

It had been a long run and we were all tired. I felt badly for Mrs. Alberto. She had not understood what had happened to her son and had killed a man for revenge where no revenge was in order. The three other boys the priest had defiled had reason to seek revenge, but Gino had been a willing and even eager participant in what most of us would have called a sexual aberration between an adult and a child. Mrs. Angelo understood none of that. She had no idea that her son would have left home under any circumstances because he needed the freedom to live his life as he saw fit. He had moved to San Francisco and built a life for himself as he had wanted to live it. Father D'Angellini had nothing to do with the choice that Gino made.

It was inevitable that The Church of Saint Francis was closed along with any number of other parishes in the city and in the diocese. The closing was in the cards because of the small number of parishioners at Saint Francis and a shortage of priests. Some of the larger parishes were down to two masses a weekend, so a little parish like Saint Francis had little hope of surviving. The powers that be knew that and also knew that Father D'Angellini's attempt to save the parish was in vain.

Marge had always been a churchgoer, but now chose to visit the Methodist Church up the road from us as an alternative to going to the Catholic Church in Westport, and I wondered how many Catholics were doing the same thing.